What if Jake had wanted to make love to her last night? What would she have done?

Hot quivers flashed through Kelly at the very thought of it. But Jake *hadn't* tried to make love to her—and even if he *had* tried, she wouldn't have let it happen.

She hadn't asked for this—not any of it. Not the plane crash. Not being stranded alone with the most compellingly attractive man she'd ever met. Not the emotional tug-of-war that even now was threatening to tear her apart.

But she would get through this. She would carry on with her head held high, and finish with her dignity—and her heart—intact.

This was a matter of personal survival. If she let Jake Drummond destroy her, Kelly knew she would never have the courage to face life again.

Dear Reader,

Welcome to Silhouette **Special Edition**...welcome to romance. Our New Year's resolution is to continue bringing you romantic, emotional stories you'll be sure to love!

And this month we're sure fulfilling that promise as Marie Ferrarella returns with our THAT SPECIAL WOMAN! title for January, *Husband: Some Assembly Required*. Dr. Shawna Saunders has trouble resisting the irresistible charms of Murphy Pendleton!

THIS TIME, FOREVER, a wonderful new series by Andrea Edwards, begins this month with *A Ring and a Promise*. Jake O'Neill and Kate O'Malley don't believe in destiny, until a legend of ancestral passion pledged with a ring and an unfulfilled promise show them the way.

Also in January, Susan Mallery introduces the first of her two HOMETOWN HEARTBREAKERS. Was sexy Sheriff Travis Haynes the town lady-killer—or a knight in shining armor? Elizabeth Abbott finds out in *The Best Bride*. Diana Whitney brings you *The Adventurer*—the first book in THE BLACKTHORN BROTHERHOOD. Don't miss Devon Monroe's story—and his secret.

The wonders of love in 1995 continue as opposites attract in Elizabeth Lane's *Wild Wings, Wild Heart*, and Beth Henderson's *New Year's Eve* keeps the holiday spirit going.

Hope this New Year shapes up to be the best ever! Enjoy this book and all the books to come!

Sincerely,

Tara Gavin
Senior Editor

Please address questions and book requests to:
Silhouette Reader Service
U.S.: 3010 Walden Ave., P.O. Box 1325, Buffalo, NY 14269
Canadian: P.O. Box 609, Fort Erie, Ont. L2A 5X3

ELIZABETH LANE

WILD WINGS, WILD HEART

Published by Silhouette Books
America's Publisher of Contemporary Romance

For Clair

 SILHOUETTE BOOKS

ISBN 0-373-09936-3

WILD WINGS, WILD HEART

Copyright © 1995 by Elizabeth Lane

This edition published by arrangement with Harlequin Enterprises B.V.

® and TM are trademarks of Harlequin Enterprises B.V., used under
license. Trademarks indicated with ® are registered in the United States
Patent and Trademark Office, the Canadian Trade Marks Office and in
other countries.

Printed in U.S.A.

ELIZABETH LANE

has traveled extensively in Latin America, Europe and China, and enjoys bringing these exotic locales to life on the printed page, but she also finds her home state of Utah and other areas of the American West to be fascinating sources for romance. Elizabeth loves such diverse activities as hiking and playing the piano, not to mention her latest hobby, belly dancing. This is her first contemporary novel for Silhouette.

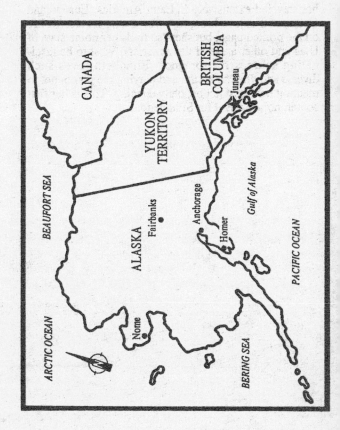

Chapter One

Jake Drummond would remember later that the sky was as gray as a shearwater's wing, and that the sheen of the long inlet was like the dark mother-of-pearl that lines an abalone shell. Later, when everything had changed, he would remember the feathered black spires of hemlock and Sitka spruce, the bite of salt water on the wind and the varicolored gleam of pebbles where the waves lapped the beach.

Later he would remember it all. At the time, however, Jake was paying no attention to such unimportant details. His mind was occupied with more urgent matters.

The DeHavilland Beaver droned like an oversized wasp as it eased away from the landing. The vintage fuselage quivered as the floats left the water and the little plane sailed skyward, just grazing the treetops. Jake loosened his grip on the edge of the worn passenger seat and tried to look nonchalant. He'd survived the takeoff, at least. Now all he had to do was make it to Juneau by two-fifteen. The pilot flashed him a swift glance. She was dark-haired and pretty— too pretty to be flying a rattletrap plane in the Alaskan bush, Jake thought. Worse, she scarcely looked old enough to drive, let alone hold a pilot's license. Jake exhaled slowly as the Beaver lurched skyward. If he lived through this flight, he swore, it was the last time he'd ever go up in anything smaller than a DC-10.

Gaining altitude, the plane banked into a sharp turn. Below him, Jake could see a dizzying mosaic of blue water and rugged islands, velvety with forest. Jagged mountains, crested with ice, crowned the eastern horizon.

It was beautiful country, he admitted. But letting Shamus and Roger talk him into this southeast Alaskan fishing trip had been a mistake. They'd insisted some time off would be good for him. But work had been his only means of survival in the nineteen months since Ann's death. Removed from that refuge, isolated, with time on his hands, Jake had tumbled into the pit of his own despair. The floatplane, arriving to fly him to Juneau for the SEA-MAR negotiations, had been welcomed as the angel of his deliverance.

And speaking of angels ... He stole another glance at the pilot. Her snub-nosed profile was turned away from him now, her whole attention focused on her job. She handled the controls as if she'd been flying since World War II.

Jake studied her smooth, sure movements, her easy balance on the foot pedals, her intent expression. Yes, he conceded, willing his taut muscles to relax, he was in capable hands.

She wasn't the regular pilot on this run. Grizzle-faced Charlie Barnes, who'd flown Jake and his two partners to the fishing camp, would be back at the end of the week to pick up Shamus and Roger. Jake, however, had needed to leave early because of the upcoming SEA-MAR conference. This flight was an extra, and he was the only passenger in the tiny four-seater.

A sudden gust of wind buffeted the wings. The girl—the pilot—shot him a knowing frown, her thick, dark eyebrows almost meeting above the bridge of her lightly freckled nose. Jake remembered that she'd wanted to delay the flight to the capital. "There's a squall blowing in," she'd said, squinting at the sky. "We'd better wait till it passes."

"Waiting's out of the question," Jake had insisted brusquely. "My company will lose a major contract if I don't make it to the SEA-MAR board meeting this afternoon."

She'd hesitated, glancing from the sky to the plane.

"Look," Jake had argued. "There are millions of dollars riding on the outcome of that meeting. I *have* to be there."

"All right, then. Fasten your seat belt and hang on." She had swung into the cockpit without another word, leaving Jake to climb up with his gear. Three minutes later they were airborne.

The Beaver was already bucking wind. Jake could sense the strain in its lumbering forward motion. He could feel the claws of the wind tearing against the thin metal wings. He exhaled, forcing his tense body to relax. Everything was fine, he told himself. In no time at all, he'd be in Juneau, changing into a business suit and laughing at his own queasiness.

The girl at the controls was as cool as a daiquiri. Her small, tapered fingers rested lightly on the wheel, sensitive to every nuance of the wind. Her childlike face, framed by dark, chin-length curls, was a study in relaxed concentration. She was dressed in khaki bush pants and a faded plaid shirt that looked several sizes too big. Her skin, fair and lightly freckled, was bare of makeup.

She'd introduced herself when the plane arrived at the camp, giving him a handshake that was almost mannish in its strength. What was her name? Something Irish—Katy, was it? No—Kelly, that was it. Kelly Ryan.

Jake shifted his legs and tried to look relaxed. "Nice country you have up here!" he said loudly, though he knew she could barely hear him above the engine roar. "Great flying weather, too! Terrific weather, in fact...just terrific!"

Her sharp glance mingled annoyance with wry humor. "Glad you like it!" she shouted back. "If we make it to Juneau in one piece, you can tell your grandchildren about—damn!"

She grabbed the wheel hard as a gust rocked the wings. Her jaw clenched as she battled to stabilize the craft in the ragged wind, but her hands were steady and sure. Kelly Ryan was tough, Jake conceded, gulping back his own fear. Tough and good.

She glanced at him as the plane leveled off. "Are you all right?" she yelled above the engine roar.

Jake nodded, forcing his face into a confident grin. He'd been scared spitless, but he wasn't about to let her know that. "Great roller coaster ride you've got here!" he bantered, but she did not respond. Either she hadn't heard, or she had better things to do than answer.

They were passing over a stretch of water now—Frederick Sound, Jake calculated, remembering the map he'd studied. Kelly flew the plane so low that he could see the whitecapped waves. He could see a fishing boat chugging for the sheltered lee of Kupreanof Island. He glanced at his watch. Twenty minutes to one. No reason to be anxious. There was plenty of time.

His mind rambled through the figures for the SEA-MAR deal. The lumber consignment could make or break the future of his Seattle-based shipping company. But a Japanese firm was after the same contract. The bidding would be close, the competition bloody. Once, Jake would have relished such a fight. Now, even in the face of his company's survival, it was just a job he had to do. A game of numbers. Even if he won, it would be a paper victory, with no Ann to share his triumph.

They were coming up on the point of an enormous island. The Beaver swooped in low, and Jake caught a glimpse of a weathered log house at the head of a narrow inlet, with a floatplane tied to a dock. A lanky old man was standing on the beach. He waved his blue cap wildly as the Beaver passed overhead.

"My grandfather." Kelly shouted the words, and Jake nodded his comprehension. He wouldn't have minded knowing more about the girl—where she came from, how she'd learned to fly—but the engine noise filled the cockpit, making questions impossible. Jake wondered, too, about the old man. There'd been something frantic about the way he was waving his cap. Maybe he'd wanted her to land. Maybe he was worried about the weather.

Jake stared out the side window at the rugged island below. Admiralty Island, it was called on the map in his head. Its sprawling landscape looked as if the Creator had crumpled it in His hand before flinging it into the ocean. He could just make out the only town—an Indian hamlet called Angoon. Elsewhere, no more than a scattered handful of people lived on the island's fringes. Its fog-misted slopes were lush with virgin timber. Creeks gushed through its valleys.

The wind moaned, rattling the fuselage. Kelly was fighting it now, wrestling the controls in an effort to level the pitching wings. Clouds seethed around them—thick, billowy and dark as oil smoke. Sensing the danger, Jake felt a jab of guilt. His own insistence had brought them here. If the girl'd had her say, they'd still be back at the fishing camp, waiting out the squall in safety. They'd been flying over the island for three or four minutes when the wind stopped. The sudden silence was terrifying, like the sucking back of the sea before a tidal wave. Kelly's green-flecked eyes widened sharply. She froze for an instant, poised at the controls. Then, squaring her jaw, she pulled back on the wheel, sending the Beaver into a sickening climb.

The gauges on the instrument panel lurched as the plane leveled off again. Jake looked down at the boiling clouds and forced himself to take long, deep breaths. There was nothing to worry about, he reassured himself. The girl was only trying to get above the worst of the storm. Soon they'd be in Juneau, on solid ground. Maybe if there was time, he'd offer her a quick cup of airport coffee. They could unwind for a few minutes and laugh over their adventure before going their separate ways. He could even apologize for his insistence on bucking the uncertain weather. That was the least she deserved from him.

Jake was starting to feel better when a renewed wind blast hit them like a doubled-up fist. Its power sent the tiny plane skittering sideways like a mosquito. Kelly battled the controls, her jaw set, her small, strong hands white-knuckled on the wheel. Watching her, Jake felt something akin to helpless rage. He had always taken pride in his own strength, his own self-reliance; but now, there was nothing he could do. Everything depended on a girl who looked to be barely out of her teens.

She hesitated, deliberating, then shoved the wheel forward. The Beaver dived into the clouds again at a pitch that made Jake's stomach flop. Gray mist swirled around them, blotting all sense of direction. Rain battered the windshield.

Even at this lower level, the wind was monstrous. It shook the bucking plane, howling like an animal as it raked the wings and fuselage. It occurred to Jake then that they could both die. For himself, maybe it wouldn't be so bad. He'd be going where Ann was; and even if there was nothing, at least his pain would be over.

But the girl—Kelly—was another matter. She was young, with her whole life ahead of her. And her being up here now, risking her neck for *his* business conference, was his own doing. If the worst happened, that was something Jake would carry on his conscience into eternity.

The sound of ripping metal shattered his thoughts. The plane began to yaw savagely. Objects were flying about the cabin—a pen, a screwdriver, a life cushion, Jake's briefcase...

He saw Kelly sawing at the controls. "Stabilizer's loose!" she shouted above the scream of the engine. "Brace yourself! We're going down!"

The Beaver was already plummeting. Jake could feel the sharp angle of its descent in the pit of his stomach. Kelly was fumbling with the radio. He could hear her shouting, as if from a far distance, "Mayday! Mayday!" He seized a tossing life cushion and braced himself in crash position. He should help the girl somehow, he thought. But she had her hands full now, fighting to keep the plane upright for whatever landing she could manage. There was nothing he could do for her. He could only see to himself.

The air whistled around them, and Jake sensed that they were already below the mountains. Strange, how calm he felt, almost as if what was happening had been planned—as if he were coming home.

He pressed the cushion to his face. *"Ann..."* he whispered.

Then he felt the shock of impact, and the whole world went black.

Chapter Two

The plane lay in a wooded hollow, on a bed of ferns and lush, green feather moss. The left half of its overhead wing, ripped off by a dead alder trunk, lay fifty yards to the rear. The right half dangled cockeyed from the crumpled fuselage, attached by one twisted strut. Beads of rain dripped from the mangled propeller blades.

Kelly opened her eyes. Streaks of watery gray light filtered through the shattered safety glass. As her vision cleared, she could make out the silhouette of one grotesquely bent windshield wiper and beyond that, the blurred, inky shadows of the forest. Rain pattered a dim staccato against the plane's metal shell. There was no other sound.

She moaned out loud as she remembered what had happened—the storm. She'd had no business going up in such weather, not even when her passenger had insisted. She should have stood up to his high-handed demands and put him in his place. That's what her grandfather would have done—

Her passenger! Kelly's head whipped frantically to the right. She could see Jake Drummond hanging out of the open door, anchored only by his seat belt. He was not moving.

Ripping off her own belt, she lunged toward him. Only then did she feel the first shock of pain. The side of the fuselage had buckled inward like tinfoil, crumpling over her left leg and wedging it fast.

Twisting her body in the seat, Kelly tried to pull loose. The strain shot arrows up her leg. The leg could be broken, she realized, but there was no time to think of that now. She had to aid Jake Drummond. He could be badly hurt. He could have shattered bones, or be bleeding someplace she couldn't see, or even—

Steeling herself against the pain, she struggled to reach him. Passengers first—Grandpa had drilled that principle into Kelly from the day of her first flying lesson, and by now it was second nature. Drummond's insistence may have gotten them into this mess, but he was her responsibility. His safety and well-being came before her own.

By twisting and clawing, she managed to catch a handful of his damp Pendleton shirt. She clenched it in her fist and heaved her weight backward, trying to drag him inside. But he was a large man, tall and broad shouldered, and the angle was awkward at best. Kelly could not move him.

"Come on!" she muttered through teeth clenched with effort. "You may be arrogant...and demanding...but I'm not giving up on you, Mr. Drummond...! Maybe I can't get you to your precious board meeting...but I can get you back inside this plane, and so help me, I—"

He groaned—a sound, no, a word. A name. *Ann.*

Startled, Kelly froze, her hand still gripping his shirt. She felt a quiver pass through the lean, hard mass of his body. Little by little, he began to stir.

"That's it! Come on!" She tugged at his resistant weight, even more urgently than before. He moaned softly. His back muscles heaved as he gasped, shuddered, then pulled himself painfully to a sitting position.

Kelly sagged into her seat, eyes watching him guardedly. His wet blond hair was plastered to his head. His blue eyes blinked dazedly as he surveyed the mangled chaos of the cockpit. Blood oozed in thin, crimson beads from a half-inch cut on his chin. He looked wild and lost.

"Good Lord...where are we?" he whispered hoarsely.

"Admiralty Island." She forced herself to sound calm. "We've crashed in the forest. Are you all right?"

He fingered his face cautiously, glanced at the smear of blood and shrugged. "It...appears so. I..." His hand balled into a sudden fist. "Damn it, the meeting! Is the radio working? We could call Juneau and—"

"I'll see," Kelly interrupted brusquely. After all, she reasoned, what else would have occurred to him first? Surely not to be glad he was alive, or to wonder whether she was hurt. Not Drummond. He probably had a computer ticking away where his heart ought to be.

She tried the radio. It wouldn't even crackle. "Dead," she pronounced after a couple of futile attempts. "I'm sorry. Something must have broken loose in the crash."

"Can you fix it?"

"I don't know. I can try. But it's an old radio. It's almost as old as the...plane." An involuntary spasm flickered across Kelly's face.

Jake Drummond stared at her, his gaze moving downward to her trapped leg. "You're hurt!" he growled. "Blast it, why didn't you tell me?"

"You seemed to have more pressing concerns on your mind, Mr. Drummond."

His head jerked up. Kelly felt the shock of his eyes, hard and sharp, like splintered blue glass. Those eyes locked with hers in a flash of mesmerizing intensity. Kelly's breath stopped. She'd said too much, she realized, bracing herself for the sting of his retort.

But he only shrugged again, barely easing the tension between them. "I won't even try to answer that one," he muttered. "For now, let's see what we can do about your leg."

Fumbling with his safety belt, he shifted in the seat, then thrust his muscular body across Kelly's lap. She stiffened as his shoulder brushed her breast, but he quickly moved forward, breaking, at least, that unsettling contact.

Kelly stared through the rain-streaked window as his wet weight pressed against her thighs. The sound of his labored breathing filled the cockpit. His scent pricked her nostrils, blending damp wool and, faintly, an after-shave whose leathery aroma bespoke a world of power and sophistication that she neither knew nor understood.

She shrank into the seat, trying to minimize the contact between them. She hadn't been this close to a man in a very long time, but despite the circumstances, her body remembered. The old responses were alive and awake: pulse racing in sporadic bursts, ribs straining with the surge of her breath and that unbidden quiver that rippled in hot little waves from the most intimate part of her. She could almost feel—

Kelly's hands clenched into tight fists as she jerked herself back to reality. *Don't be a fool!* she lashed out at herself. *Didn't it hurt enough the first time?*

She stared furiously out at the drizzle, willing her reactions to cool. Jake Drummond might look like a young

Robert Redford, but to her he was just another passenger.
The only thing that really mattered was getting them both
to safety.

His fingers probed the place where her knee emerged from
its twisted metal prison. Even with the pain, their blunt
pressure sent disturbing tingles up her leg.

"How does it feel?" he asked.

"Sort of numb, except when I try to move. Then my ankle hurts."

"Hang on—" He squeezed lower, jamming his shoulders between Kelly and the bent wheel. Wedged fast, she
stared at the sun-bleached curls at the back of his tanned
neck. He probably played tennis at home, she speculated.
Maybe he sailed, too, in his own sailboat, complete with a
lithe, golden girl in a white bikini. Maybe that was the *Ann*
whose name he'd moaned as he—

"Oww!" She gave a little yelp as Jake Drummond
squeezed past her and slipped back into his seat.

"Sorry," he said. "I think I've figured out how to get you
loose. Have you got a crowbar?"

"No crowbar. There's a red metal toolbox somewhere,
with a hammer and a few wrenches—"

"Where?" He began to rummage behind the front seats.
Biting back pain, Kelly studied him. Yes, he was a compellingly handsome man. His rugged looks would not have
been out of place in a 1950s Western, or behind a TV an-
chorman's desk. Jake Drummond struck her, in fact, as the
kind of person for whom everything fell into place. What he
demanded, he got—even from her, Kelly reminded herself.
But even Drummond had no control over their predicament now.

He found the toolbox under the seat, rifled impatiently
through its contents and shook his head. "We need some-

thing for a lever, to pry with," he said. "Nothing in here's long enough."

"Maybe outside..." Kelly winced again as she turned in her seat. "A stick, or something off the plane—"

"Right." He turned without looking at her, swung out through the Beaver's open passenger door and dropped into the wet, green world outside.

Kelly closed her eyes, giving in, momentarily, to her own fear. It wouldn't do at all, letting Drummond know how weak and scared she felt. She would have to keep her head, to remain cool, detached and professional. Crash landings in the bush were almost commonplace, she reminded herself. Older pilots joked about them, regaling listeners with their hair-raising experiences. Her own grandfather had gone down at least a dozen times in his fifty years of flying.

But this was different. This was Kelly's first crash, and she wanted to cry. She'd been so proud of her own competence; but no truly experienced pilot would have gone up in a storm—not even at the insistence of a passenger with a multimillion-dollar business deal at stake. Now, not only would Drummond miss his meeting, but the plane was ruined, and her grandparents would be frantic when she didn't call in.

Helpless and frustrated, she tugged at her trapped leg. The jabbing pain triggered a sting of tears. She'd tried to tell herself it was all Jake Drummond's fault. But that wasn't true. She was the pilot, and no one had forced her to go up. She had no one to blame for this disaster but herself.

Jake circled the wreckage, his lug-soled boots sinking into the spongy forest floor. He moved with a sense of dazed unreality, as if he'd just stepped out of a space capsule, onto the surface of an alien planet. The world around him was a murky, translucent green. Moss, as thick and soft as cash-here, cushioned the ground and shrouded trees that looked as if they'd stood since the dawn of time. The only sound was the muted drizzle of the rain.

The Beaver lay spattered against the landscape like a crushed toy. Seeing it from outside, Jake found it amazing that he and Kelly Ryan had survived the crash. The fact that somehow, in this green, dripping world, they were still alive, was almost enough to make him believe in miracles.

But this was no time to speculate on how or why. Kelly was still trapped inside the wreckage. He would have to get her out fast. Even in the rain, there was danger of gas fumes meeting a spark from the frayed wires and touching off an explosion. He'd seen that happen in a movie once. But this was no movie, Jake reminded himself. This predicament was all too real.

Jake brushed a cloud of hovering gnats away from his face. Overhead, a metal strut dangled from the shattered wing, held in place by a single rivet. The strut would do as a crowbar, he calculated, if he could twist it free.

He sprang for it, wet palms clutching at the slippery end. The wing's broken edge buckled under the pull of his weight, lowering him slowly back to the ground. The stubborn rivet, however, held the strut fast.

Cursing under his breath, Jake clambered back into the cockpit. Kelly had mentioned a hammer in the red toolbox. Maybe he could use it to break the rivet loose.

He found Kelly hunched in her seat, tugging uselessly at the twisted metal that imprisoned her leg. Her freckles stood out like nutmeg sprinkled against her milk-pale skin. She looked scared, Jake thought. What the hell...he was scared, too.

"Take it easy," he said. "You'll only wear yourself out, trying to get loose with your bare hands."

"Have you got a better idea?" Her dimpled chin thrust defiantly toward him, but her question ended on a shaky note. It wasn't hard to guess that she was hurting. Jake dreaded the thought of what her leg might look like under that twisted mass of metal.

He found the battered tin box and began rummaging through the tools. "There's a strut hanging loose out there," he said, trying to sound confident. "It should make a dandy crowbar. All I have to do is break through the last rivet. Then we'll have you out of here in no time... Aha! Here we are!"

Jake's fingers closed around the handle of a ball peen hammer. "This ought to do the job. You just relax for a minute, and I'll be back with that strut."

Kelly sighed wearily. "You might have better luck with a hacksaw. There should be a small one in there somewhere."

"That'll take too long. I'll try the hammer first." Jake tumbled out of the cockpit again, brandishing the hammer with more bravado than he felt. Back in Seattle, he could command a boardroom with a nod of his head. But he'd never been handy with tools—never really needed to be until now.

Clutching the hammer, he swung it with all his strength against the shaft of the rivet. Nothing. Again and again he tried, the sound clanging eerily above the drizzle of the rain. His frantic blows battered the wing, but the rivet remained intact.

Muttering under his breath, Jake crawled back into the cockpit. He could feel Kelly's eyes on him as he fumbled through the toolbox. At least she wasn't saying "I told you so." But she had to be thinking it—probably thinking he was a stubborn fool, to boot.

Not that it mattered, Jake reminded himself. The only thing that really mattered now was getting the girl out of the wreck and getting them both to safety. After that, he could only hope the SEA-MAR board would give him a second chance.

"Damn!" Jake flinched in sudden pain as his thumb brushed the serrated edge of the hacksaw blade. His hand jerked to his mouth, and he tasted the wet saltiness of his own blood. Not a serious cut, he surmised quickly. But he felt clumsy and awkward. It was not a feeling he liked.

Kelly's eyes were as wide as a startled doe's. Lovely eyes, he realized. They were a deep, crystalline green-brown, like the color of Coca-Cola in those old green glass bottles. Ann's eyes had been gray.

"Are you all right?" she asked, her voice huskily small.

Jake took his thumb out of his mouth. The bleeding had stopped. "I think I just found the saw," he said. "Hope it works better than the blasted hammer."

"I'm sorry I can't help you. In fact, I'm sorry for everything."

Jake had bent to grope for the hacksaw again, more carefully this time. "Don't apologize," he growled. "I was the one who insisted on taking off when we did."

"But I didn't have to give in. The final decision—and the final responsibility—belongs to the pilot. That's what my grandpa always told me. I..." A twinge of pain flickered across her white face. "I should have reminded myself of that before it was too late."

Jake shrugged as he disentangled the saw from a nest of wrenches. "Hindsight's not worth much, Kelly Ryan. You can't go back and change the past."

"No, I guess you can't." She sank back against the seat, her eyes darkening subtly in the shadows of the cockpit.

When she spoke, her voice was husky with emotion. "Get me out of here, Jake Drummond," she said.

With a curt nod, Jake swung outside again. Rain spattered his skin as he angled the thin blade against the shaft of the rivet, clasped the strut with his free hand and, awkwardly, began to saw.

No, he couldn't go back and change the past. The doctor had brought that point home when Ann died. He couldn't go back and spend more time with her, instead of working sixteen-hour days for the future they would never have. He couldn't go back and insist she get the medical checkup that might have caught her cancer in time to save her life. He could only struggle on alone, weighted with guilt and battling self-pity.

At least no one back in Seattle could accuse him of going around with a long face. In the past year, he'd dated several women. He'd even slept with two of them. But those brief involvements, driven by desperation, had only left him frustrated and empty. More and more, of late, Jake had found himself taking refuge in his work. Work was his drug, his anesthetic. It was the only thing that numbed the pain.

The blade of the hacksaw whined as it rasped into the stubborn metal. Jake's body dripped sweat as he rammed his impatience into each stroke. Progress was agonizingly slow, especially when he thought of the dark-haired girl trapped in the wreckage, waiting for him to free her.

Blast it, he'd always thought he could handle anything. But for the past decade, his skills had been honed in the boardroom, on his sailboat and on the tennis courts at the club where he had an executive membership. Even as a boy, growing up fatherless and poor in L.A., he'd had no time for anything but part-time jobs and schoolwork. Hell, he'd never been a Boy Scout! Now here he was, suddenly dropped into the middle of nowhere, with an injured female on his hands and no resources except a box of rusty tools he barely knew how to use. How the devil was he supposed to—

The strut snapped loose so abruptly that it almost hit him in the eye. Jake stood blinking for an instant as the realization sunk in that he'd sawed through the rivet. Rain dripped off his eyebrows and trickled down the back of his collar. He could feel his heart, thudding like a bass drum against his ribs.

He'd won his first small victory. But he still had to get the girl out of the plane and see to her leg. He could only hope it wouldn't be too difficult, that she wouldn't turn out to be too badly hurt.

And he could only hope she wouldn't realize how scared he was.

Kelly stared at the dim hole where the cockpit door had torn loose, gritting her teeth against the throbbing pain in her leg. The crawling black hand on her wristwatch told her that Jake Drummond had been gone about ten minutes. The time that had passed, however, seemed more like an hour.

Knowing that Drummond was a cheechako—a greenhorn—only added to Kelly's anxiety. For all she knew, he could have given up on the strut and wandered off in search of something else to use. He could have gotten lost. He could have stumbled into a patch of spiny devil's club, or even met a grizzly bear. Jake Drummond might be a big-city know-it-all, but he was her passenger—and her responsibility. If anything happened to him, she would never forgive herself.

Kelly was imagining the worst when Drummond's rain-slicked, blond head materialized in the opening. He was brandishing the hacksaw in one hand, the strut in the other. "What did I tell you?" His grin was a mockery of cheerfulness. "Now, just hang on. We'll have you loose in no time."

Kelly groaned her relief. "I'm very glad to see you, Mr. Drummond. But you can drop that fake smile. We both know what a mess we're in."

"Whatever you say." The grin evaporated as he tossed the strut and hacksaw on the empty seat and hoisted his lean weight back into the plane. "It's foggy as blazes out there. Nobody's going to have an easy time spotting us. Are you sure that radio's dead?"

Kelly's eyes closed as another spasm shot up her leg. "I'm sure. Now please stop talking and get me out of here," she whispered through clenched teeth.

"Hold still, then." He squeezed past her to wedge the strut's end under the edge of the twisted metal. Kelly felt his weight again, warm and damp across her thighs. His muscles strained against her as he maneuvered the strut into place.

"I'm not hurting you, am I?" He had twisted to get a better angle, his elbow grazing her breast. She steeled herself against the heat that radiated from the point of contact. Her pulse jumped like a flushed rabbit as sensations she'd struggled years to bury invaded her body like arctic springtime. *Don't be a goose,* she scolded herself. *It's only hormones. That's what Grandma would say.*

Hormones. That, and being alone too long. This rush of bittersweet sensations was purely physical, and Jake Drummond was only a trigger. All the same, Kelly could not suppress a gasp at his touch—a gasp triggered by feelings that had nothing to do with the pain in her leg.

"Sorry. I *am* hurting you," he muttered, his voice coming from somewhere below her knees.

"No. I'm fine." She stared hard at the rain-flecked windshield. "Just hurry, please."

"Hang on." He braced the free end of the strut against the wheel. Kelly gripped the seat as the damp, muscular bulk of his body slid back across her legs. She willed her mind to become a blank movie screen, the projector switched off, the film slashed and tangled on the floor.

As he thrust his weight against the wedged lever, the labored rasp of Jake Drummond's breath filled the tiny space of the cockpit. The crumpled metal groaned as it yielded to his strength. Kelly felt the excruciating pressure ease around her leg. Her breath caught in relief as it lifted. She was free.

"Don't move!" His voice rasped close to her ear. "If that leg's broken, you could make the injury worse."

Kelly wriggled her toes experimentally inside her leather boot. "It . . . doesn't *feel* broken," she said.

"How *does* it feel?" His voice was cautiously flat as he eased the strut out of the way to give her more room. His wet hair and shirt steamed in the closeness of the cockpit, blending with the leathery aroma of his after-shave.

"It . . . hurts." Kelly grimaced as she flexed her ankle and felt a stab of tearing pain. Why now? she thought, sick with frustration. Just when she needed to be strong, when she needed to be in charge, why did she have to be so helpless? "It feels more like a bad sprain than a break," she insisted, trying to sound decisive. "Let's get out of here."

The door on Kelly's side was smashed shut. To exit the plane, she would have to maneuver her way across the cockpit to the opening where the passenger door had torn loose.

"Give me your arms." Jake Drummond was leaning toward her. His eyes were bloodshot, the irises deep turquoise in the greenish light that filtered through the windshield. "Come on—I'll pull, and you can concentrate on keeping that leg out of harm's way."

"No." Remembering what his touch had awakened, Kelly recoiled from his extended hands. "I can do it alone. Just keep clear of me."

Bracing her arms on the seat, she hoisted herself past the foot pedals and over the tumble of gear that had flown forward as the plane skidded to its crashing halt. Jake Drummond had swung out the door again and dropped to the ground. He stood watching, one sun-bleached eyebrow sardonically lifted, as Kelly dragged herself, with effort, across the passenger seat.

"And I suppose you can jump down on your own, too." He stood with legs apart, hands thrust deliberately into his pockets as Kelly eyed the four-foot drop to the ground. Uninjured, she would have no trouble. But the risk of landing on a sprained or broken ankle—

She glared at him, half annoyed, half apologetic. The expression on his face did not change as he reached up to her. "Hands on my shoulders," he ordered. "Careful, now."

His strong fingers closed around Kelly's waist. Ignoring their warm pressure, she clasped his shoulders and felt the solid contraction of his muscles as he lifted her. He swung her tensely out of the doorway. Then, with a subtle shift of balance, he caught her full weight in his arms.

Kelly went rigid against his chest, her heart pounding in sudden, senseless panic. Deep inside, she could feel tiny tendrils of warmth, uncurling like newborn fern sprouts in springtime shadows. Was this all it took—being close to an attractive man she scarcely knew, let alone liked? Sweet Saint Mary, she was worse off than she'd thought!

She forced herself to meet his steel blue gaze. "You can put me down now," she said, masking her agitation with icy control.

His rib cage swelled against her in a long, exasperated sigh, but he made no move to let her go.

"I'll put you down, Miss Kelly Ryan, after we get a few things straight between us," he said in a low, flat voice. "First of all, damn it, stop acting like you think I'm after your virtue. You can trust me. All I want is to get back to Juneau in time to salvage my business."

Kelly flushed beet-red, a trait she'd always detested in herself. "Why, of all the—"

Something in his eyes—something almost menacing—cut off her sputtering protest with the efficiency of a cleaver. "Second," he continued in the same mechanical tone, "I'm assuming all liability for this accident. My company's insurance will cover the cost of the plane and any medical expenses involved in caring for your leg. Third—"

"But it was as much my fault as—"

"Don't be foolish!" he snapped. "As far as I'm concerned it was your skill as a pilot that got us down alive. Aside from that, the responsibility for our being here is entirely mine. Third—"

"Listen, you don't have to—"

"*Third*, we're in this mess together. You're hurt, and I don't know the first thing about getting around in this country. We're going to have to depend on each other, Kelly Ryan. And the sooner we give up this idiot power struggle and start working together, the better off we'll be."

Kelly stared at the muted blue-gray plaid of Drummond's collar, avoiding the cold intensity of his eyes while she weighed his words. For all her pride, his offer to pay for the accident was more than fair, and since the plane was her grandfather's, not hers, she had no right to refuse it. As for the rest... But this was no time for self-examination. Drummond was right; they needed each other. And the only course that made sense was to stop sniping and cooperate.

She forced herself to meet his eyes. "Is that all you have to say?"

"That's all." His arms lay firmly beneath her, supporting her knees and shoulders. "Do we have a truce?"

Kelly paused, with what she hoped appeared to be cool detachment. She was dimly aware that the rain had diminished to a fine mist that formed silver beads on Jake Drummond's eyebrows. Slowly, deliberately, she nodded. "All right. We have a truce."

"Fine," he said, sounding as if he'd just checked off another item on his business agenda. "Now, let's find someplace to get dry and have a look at that leg."

Jake left Kelly half-leaning against the plane while he rummaged through the cockpit for a PVC poncho she'd said was in her gear, and for his own Gore-Tex jacket. The rain had nearly stopped, but the spruce boughs sagged with the weight of fallen raindrops. Without protection, he and Kelly would soon be soaked.

Strange girl, Kelly Ryan, Jake mused as he pawed through the jumble. Not a girl, really—he'd realized that when he looked full into her face and saw a woman looking back at him. Twenty-five or twenty-six, he readjusted his estimate. Proud, stubborn and clearly not very experienced with men. Either that, or she just plain didn't like him. Every time he touched her, she bristled like a suspicious tabby.

Not that he could blame her, after the way he'd bullied her back at the camp. If he hadn't been so overbearing, they'd be safe now. They'd probably just be getting ready to take off. Kelly would be radioing Juneau to notify the SEA-MAR board that he'd been delayed and would need to reschedule the meeting. And the SEA-MAR people, long familiar with such problems, would surely have accommodated him.

Instead, here he was, lost in the fog in the middle of nowhere. The SEA-MAR deal was in the garbage, the plane was smashed, the pilot was hurt; and at this point, the odds of their making it back to civilization could be anybody's guess.

His groping hands had found Kelly's poncho. As he untangled it from the mess, Jake cursed the driving urgency that never seemed to let him rest. The truth was, much as it galled him, he owed Kelly Ryan a full apology—on his knees.

But it was too late for apologies now. Besides, Jake Drummond had his own share of pride. He would not hesitate to pay for the plane, but the price of words was much, much higher. For now, at least, he had said all he was going to say.

Chapter Three

Kelly sat huddled inside her poncho, its long tail protecting her rear from the wet ground as Jake Drummond unlaced her boot. A dozen yards away, the Beaver lay like a crushed insect against the wet, green landscape. It would never fly again, she realized with a sense of loss that raised a lump in her throat. Some parts, like the engine, might be salvaged for later use, but the plane's fragile body was broken beyond repair. Kelly had learned to fly in that Beaver. She felt bereaved, as if she had lost an old friend.

Her eyes blurred as she watched Jake Drummond's suntanned fingers work the worn leather laces. She could have managed the boot herself, she supposed. But a curious numbness had settled over her in the past few minutes. Mild shock, maybe. Or simple sadness as the reality of what had happened sunk in. Whatever it was, Kelly could scarcely summon the desire to move.

At least the same lethargy hadn't affected Drummond. He had taken over with the cool efficiency of a machine. For the moment, at least, Kelly chose to let him.

Pain shot up her leg as he began to work the high-topped boot off her foot. Caught off guard, Kelly yelped like a stung puppy.

"Sorry," he muttered, pausing. "I was trying to be careful, but—"

"It's all right. I just wasn't ready. Try it now." Kelly braced herself against the raw, pulling sensation she knew would come when the boot began to move. Jake Drummond squatted in front of her, his eyes fixed intently on her foot. His fingers were golden and uncallused, the nails immaculate, with small, neat moons. His palms nested her muddy heel as he hesitated, then spoke.

"Maybe we should just leave the boot on. We might be doing you more harm than good."

Kelly studied him furtively from behind the barrier of her knees. His mouth was tense, his hands uncertain. He was afraid, she suddenly realized—afraid of hurting her, afraid of showing his own incompetence in this strange, wild place.

Kelly turned the discovery over in her mind like a new-found marble. Surprise. Jake Drummond, the man with the computerized heart, appeared to have a human side after all.

"The boot's got to come off," she insisted, reclaiming a little of her own lost ground. "If my ankle's sprained, we'll need to wrap it. Come on. I won't cry on you. I'm a big girl."

"I'm well aware of that." He took a deep breath, set his mouth into a determined line and began, by millimeters, to ease the unlaced boot off her foot.

"You've never done anything like this before, have you?" Kelly spoke to take her mind off the ordeal.

"Crash-landing in the Alaskan bush with a beautiful female pilot?" He smiled grimly. "No, I can't say that I have."

Once more, Kelly felt the burn of that hated blush creeping into her cheeks. Drummond was only making a pleasantry, she knew. In truth, she was far from beautiful. She was freckled and snub-nosed, with a figure so ordinary that no man would give it a second glance. Most days, if she looked into a mirror at all, it was only to make certain her face was clean.

In vain, Kelly willed the blush to fade. "That's not what I meant," she said.

"Then what did you mean?" He was maneuvering the boot top gently over the cusp of her heel. His face wore a scowl of concentration.

"This. The first-aid bit."

He chuckled sardonically. "Let's just say that if this had happened in Seattle, I'd be driving you to the hospital emergency room. How are you holding up?"

"All right. You're doing fine." Kelly lapsed into an awkward silence, wishing she could think of something clever to say. A man like Jake Drummond would move in a world of clever women, whose small talk sparkled like fine lead crystal.

"Who is Ann?" She blurted out the question, knowing at once, from the expression that flashed across his face, that she should have left the matter alone.

"What?"

"After the crash, when you were waking up, I heard you say a name. It sounded like—"

"Ann. Yes. She was my wife."

"Was?" A glance at his hand confirmed her earlier impression that he wore no wedding ring.

"She died." The flat, anesthetized way he spoke told Kelly how deeply he felt the loss.

"How?" she asked softly.

"Malignant brain tumor. It was...unexpected. But at least it was fast."

"I'm sorry. When did it happen?" Kelly could have punched herself. Why couldn't she just leave the poor man alone? Maybe he thought she was plotting to entrap him—she, Kelly Ryan, who lacked the wiles to entrap a chipmunk.

"Nineteen months ago. She was young. Only thirty." He had tossed Kelly's boot onto the ground and was working the cuff of her wool sock down her ankle. His face was carefully expressionless, as if he had placed a mask of himself over his own living features. "*Ugh*, that's one ugly ankle," he grunted, as if the exchange about his wife had not taken place. "Rembrandt would have loved those colors."

Feeling slightly ill, Kelly gazed down at the swollen expanse of bruised flesh that ranged from her lower calf to the arch of her foot. "I'd say it was closer to Picasso," she drawled. "Blue Period."

Her jest was rewarded with a toothpaste-commercial grin from Drummond. Kelly could credit her grandpa's dog-eared *History of World Art* for that point—she'd been poring through it since the day she became tall enough to drag it off the shelf. But she noticed that Drummond's smile was forced. His eyes did not match his mouth. And the smile faded altogether as his fingers began their cautious probing of her ankle.

"Look," she said, wincing, "I'm sorry about your business meeting and all. But it's not as if we're stuck here for good. We're on an island. Two days—three days, max—in the right direction will get us to the coast, where we can hail a boat, if not a plane."

Jake Drummond continued his silent exploration of Kelly's leg, intent on the contours of the bone beneath her bruised and tender flesh. "I'm no expert, but it doesn't appear to be broken," he pronounced at last. "You do, however, seem to have one devil of a sprain."

"You're not hearing me," she persisted, annoyed by his lack of response to her suggestion. "That was the worst-case scenario I just gave you. I grew up on Admiralty, and I've got a compass. If I can get a bearing in this fog, I might even be able to guide us to my grandparent's place, or to Angoon—whichever's closer."

He scowled blackly, his palm still cradling Kelly's bare heel. The pressure of his fingers tightened as he spoke. "And *you're* not hearing *me*. You can't walk on this ankle. I say we stay right here and try to fix the radio. Maybe build a signal fire. We're bound to be spotted before long."

Kelly sighed, wishing the man would simply listen to her. "Planes won't be flying in this weather. And even if they were, they wouldn't be able to see us. This fog is thicker than a quilt batt, and it could hang around for a week or more."

Drummond's face was a study in frustrated impatience. "You're sure you can't get that radio working? If I could just notify Juneau, or call back to the fishing camp and have one of my partners—"

"All right, I'll try it one more time," Kelly interrupted, trying to sound calm and in control. "But don't get your hopes up. It's an old radio, and I don't carry spare parts around with me." She struggled to rise. "Now, if you'll just—"

"Oh, no you don't!" His hands were on her shoulders, his eyes locking hers with a cool intensity that made Kelly's stomach flutter. "You're not moving till that ankle's wrapped. There'll be time for the radio later."

He gripped her firmly, as if he expected her to throw him off and bolt for the plane in defiance. Kelly forced herself to meet his blue eyes without flinching, glare to glare. Drummond, she sensed, did not particularly like her. Or maybe it was just that he was out of his element, and he didn't like someone as insignificant—and female—as herself making decisions for him. Well, that was *his* problem. She knew what she was doing, and this wasn't Seattle.

"The first-aid kit is under the pilot's seat," she said. "There should be a roll of adhesive tape in there somewhere."

"Hang on. I'll be right back." He sprang up and strode toward the plane as if he were relieved to be in action once more. Kelly settled back into her poncho with a little whimper. She was getting cold, and her ankle hurt like blazes. She would tinker with the radio just to satisfy Drummond, but it wouldn't do any good. The antiquated device had barely worked *before* the crash. Her grandpa, in fact, had been planning to replace it out of next month's profits. Well, now, at least, he wouldn't have to bother.

She glanced at her watch. It was almost one-thirty. If she and Drummond struck out soon, they could cover as much as ten miles before the late-summer darkness caught up with them and they had to make camp. It would be tough going on her sprained ankle. As soon as the wrapping was done, she'd look for a dead limb that she could fashion into a crutch. It was that, or lean on Drummond all the way—and Kelly Ryan had no intention of leaning on any man.

Seven years ago, as she lay crying her heart out in that bleak hospital room, Kelly had sworn she would never put her trust in another male. She'd done all right for herself since then. But now, suddenly, the danger flags were up. Jake Drummond, for all his high-handed ways, was as dazzling as a diamond; and for the next couple of days, at least, they would be alone together, walking, camping and sleeping.

Oh, she was nothing to Drummond—Kelly was smart enough to realize that. But things happened to men and women in isolated situations. If she lowered her guard, she would be vulnerable, and that was a risk she could not afford to take. She had been too long healing to expose herself again.

She would play it safe, she vowed. She would keep her distance, physically and emotionally. She would be *professional*—cool, detached and very much in charge.

No matter what happened, she would not let Jake Drummond get the upper hand.

Jake's shoulder muscles screamed as he caught the overhead limb and dragged himself higher up the trunk of the dead spruce. He hadn't climbed a tree since he was a skinny fourteen-year-old, and it was a hell of a lot harder than he remembered. Broken limbs jabbed at his eyes. Slabs of rough bark tore his palms. How the hell did Tarzan do it? he wondered, gritting his teeth.

"Can you see anything?" Kelly's husky little voice wafted up from the ground below. Jake had left her sitting on a moss-cushioned rock, performing some kind of witchery with a brass compass that looked as if it could have been used on the *Titanic*. The plan was, he would shimmy up the tree and point out any landmarks he saw, and she would take her bearings off his directions. It had sounded good on the ground. By now, however, Jake was beginning to have his doubts.

"I said, can you see anything?" Kelly repeated the question with a note of impatience. Jake was still trying to figure her out. She was pretty, and obviously bright, but that chip on her shoulder was more like a logjam. First she'd insisted on wrapping her own ankle with the tape he'd found. Then she'd gone through the motions of poking halfheartedly into the radio, before pronouncing it dead. Finally she'd come up with this crazy tree-climbing idea. It was as if she were deliberately trying to keep him off balance.

"Hang on a minute!" he shouted back down at her. "Let me get a little higher. Then I'll have a look around."

"Don't fall!"

"Thanks for caring!"

"I just don't want your broken body on my conscience!"

"I'll do my best to see that it doesn't happen!" Jake muttered a childhood prayer as he heaved himself upward to the next limb. The giant spruce had been dead a long time, and most of its branches had broken off to jagged knobs. He was using these for footholds, while his hands grabbed for the few longer branches that remained. He didn't even want to think about how high he was.

"That's far enough!" she called. "You're making me nervous! What can you see?"

Jake peered into the impenetrable blanket of mist. "Trees and fog!"

"No mountains? No sign of water?"

"If this stuff were any thicker, I wouldn't even be able to see *me!* This is no good! I'm coming down!"

Her sigh of disappointment was audible, even from the ground. "All right, then. We'll just have to head due east and hope for the best."

"We'll have to *what?*" Jake struggled with the challenge of climbing down the tree, which was even more harrowing than climbing up had been because he couldn't see where he was going.

"I can draw a map to show you. The length of the island runs north and south. Most of the boat traffic will be on the east side, between here and Juneau. So our best chance of—"

"Damn it, I know that! It's just—" Jake's boot slipped on the mossy surface. He slid a gut-wrenching six feet before catching a foothold on a protruding knot. For a breathless instant he clung to the trunk, his palms skinned, his heart palpitating. The smell of his own sweaty fear mingled with the cool, damp air. He swore under his breath.

"Are you all right?" Her voice was closer now, about twenty feet below him, Jake calculated.

"Fine." He groped for the next toehold and forced himself to keep moving. "But you and I have to talk, Kelly Ryan. Just give me a minute here...." He scrambled down a dozen more feet, then pushed off and dropped the rest of the way to the ground. Lovely ground. He might have kissed it if Kelly had not been watching.

She was sitting where he'd left her, making a show of whittling away at a long, forked limb with her pocket knife. "Talk about what?" she asked, glancing up at him with elaborate nonchalance.

"Just this." Jake brushed the shredded bark off his moleskin trousers. "*We* are not walking out of here. *We* are not going anywhere."

Her Coca-Cola eyes widened. "But I just told you—"

"*I'm* going. You're staying here while I get help."

She stiffened as his words touched off a sputtering fuse of indignation. "If you think you can just decide to—"

"Look at you." Jake faced her, as resolute and immovable as a granite boulder. "You won't last the first mile with that ankle. Without you along, I'll be able to cover ground three times as fast. It's the only plan that makes sense."

Kelly groaned, fingers raking her crisp, dark curls in a gesture of exasperation. "Sit down and listen, Mr. Drummond. There are some things you need to understand."

When Jake hesitated, she added a tightly restrained "Please."

Reluctantly, Jake lowered himself to a crouch beside her, braced to fend off any argument she might fling against him. The awareness flashed through his mind—maddeningly—that she was even prettier than he'd first realized. The damp air had brought out the soft rose undertone of her skin, and where her mahogany hair brushed her cheek, the contrast was as delicate as a Renoir painting. Her eyes were flecked with tiny dots of gold that—

But this wasn't helping. It wasn't helping at all. Jake assumed a detached scowl. "All right, I'm listening," he growled. "But make it fast. I haven't got much time."

She drew a deep, sharp breath. "Look, I understand where you're coming from," she said. "You've got a big business deal on the line, and you're anxious to get word to Juneau. And yes, it's true that you could travel faster without me. But trust me. You can't hike out of here alone."

"Just watch me, lady."

Kelly shot him the kind of look a schoolmarm might give a smart-mouthed third grader. "Mr. Drummond, whether you like it or not, you're my responsibility. I can't send you off by yourself. You don't know this country. You could get lost—"

"I could take your compass."

"You could get hungry, eat poisonous berries—"

"If I walk fast enough, I won't need to eat at all."

Her eyes narrowed. "And then..." She paused ominously. "Then there are the bears."

"Bears." It was a statement, not a question. Hell, this was Alaska. Of course there were bears.

"Admiralty's a national wildlife reserve. There are more bears here per square mile than anyplace else in southeast Alaska."

Jake felt the hair prickle on the back of his neck, but he feigned an indifferent shrug. "So, there are bears. I saw a gun in the plane."

Kelly sighed wearily. "A pistol. It fires signal flares." She took up her whittling again, and Jake realized that the forked limb was becoming a makeshift crutch.

"Look," she said, "most bears will gladly stay out of your way, especially if you give them plenty of warning. But even an aggressive bear would be less likely to attack two people than one." She glanced up at him with clear, earnest eyes. "It was you who said it. We have to work together. I can't let you go off alone, and you can't leave me here unprotected."

Jake bit back a curse. The girl should have been a trial lawyer, he thought. She had pinned him down with a framework of logic so tight that he had no room to maneuver. The worst of it was, she was right. Even with his company's future at stake, he couldn't leave her alone, injured and without a weapon. No place, not even the wrecked plane, would be safe from a determined bear.

Even together, there would be danger. One glance into those searingly honest eyes of hers was enough to tell him that. But there was no use talking about it now, Jake reminded himself. They would just have to take things one step at a time.

"The sooner we get moving, the better," she said. "I've got a canvas pack in the plane. We can pick out the gear we'll need and carry it in that."

"What about you?" He scowled down at her foot. She had wrapped it from ankle to arch in adhesive tape, and managed to ease the boot back on by leaving off her thick wool sock. But those bruises, darkening so soon after the injury, were not a good sign. She could have torn ligaments or crushed bones—damn it, there had to be more he could do. Why did he have to feel so helpless?

Kelly flipped the knife shut against her khaki-clad leg and thrust it into a front pocket. "Don't worry, I'll be all right," she said, with a critical squint at her forked limb. She'd done a decent job on it, Jake had to admit. She'd cut off the ends to the right length, and planed off the worst of the knots. But as a functional crutch, it was crude at best.

"That's not going to be very comfortable," he said, eyeing the rough fork.

She shrugged her slim, strong shoulders. "It'll have to do. I've never used a crutch before, but I guess I can learn."

Waving away Jake's proffered hand, she stuck the base of the limb into the ground and used it as a prop to struggle to her feet. With the fork braced under her arm, she tried a dozen labored steps. Hop...swing. Hop...swing. Even watching her was painful. When she paused to rest, turning back to face him, Jake caught the glimmer of frustrated tears in her eyes.

"I'll...get the hang of it soon enough," she muttered. "As my grandpa would say, 'It's a long way to Tipperary!'"

"Here." Jake had thrown off his Gore-Tex coat. His fingers were fumbling with the buttons of his wool shirt, his arms shrugging out of the sleeves, his hands jerking the hem of his white cotton T-shirt out of his trouser band. Kelly's eyes rounded as she watched him walk toward her, stripping the T-shirt over his head. She probably thought he was crazy. Or maybe she'd never seen a man's bare chest before. There was, he conceded, a disquieting innocence about the girl—a wild, untouched quality that intrigued him more than he cared to admit.

"Hang on. This ought to help a little." He peeled her fingers off the crutch and began looping the T-shirt over the forked ends. "With some padding you'll be able to lean into it more. It still won't be easy—"

"Here, let me try it." She reclaimed the crutch, her eyes avoiding Jake's bare nipples, which were puckering in the misty air. Thrusting the padded fork under her arm, she took a few tentative, swinging steps. Then, pausing, she slowly nodded.

"It *is* better. Thanks. If only—"

"More padding, right?" Jake was already clambering into the plane. He paused to slip back into his shirt and do up the buttons. No use offending the girl's sensibilities. Besides, he was getting cold.

His duffel bag, which he found after a few seconds of rummaging, was half-filled with dirty laundry. Jake fished out the other two undershirts he'd worn at camp, hoping they'd be enough—he had a feeling Kelly Ryan wouldn't take kindly to his offering her his skivvies. "Here you go!" He tossed them out the open door of the cockpit. "As long as I'm up here, let's figure out what we'll want to carry with us. Have you got any food?"

"Look for a red cotton jacket. I think there's a chocolate bar in the pocket."

Jake blinked. "That's all?"

"Look, I didn't plan this," she said. "But we'll be okay. There are plenty of ripe berries this time of year."

"Great." He remembered her argument against his going alone. "I hope the hell *you* know which ones are poisonous."

Kelly ignored his gibe. "If you've got any bug repellent—"

"Yeah. There's some here in the duffel." Jake's fist closed gratefully around the small aerosol can. The mosquitoes were voracious in this part of the world, and the tiny, biting gnats, known as "no-see-ums" were, if possible, even worse.

"What about blankets?" he asked.

"There's a down sleeping bag rolled up in my pack. I don't suppose you have anything like that, do you?"

Jake sighed. The fishing camp had supplied everything, including bedding. He'd brought nothing of his own except clothes, toiletries and the briefcase he took everywhere he went. Well, he knew who would be freezing at night, and it wasn't the proper Miss Ryan. "I see your pack," he said. "And there's the flare gun. We'll want that, I take it."

"Oh, absolutely!" She'd hobbled to the open door of the plane, where she stood looking up at him with her bare, innocent, strangely disconcerting face. "The flares are under the passenger seat. Oh—and get the tissue roll that's there, too. And the canteen."

"The canteen? Come on, this is the wettest place I ever saw in my life!"

"The water in the streams isn't safe," she said, addressing Jake as if he were a backward child. "It'll give you something called 'beaver fever.' Trust me, you wouldn't enjoy having it."

"Right." Jake hefted the aluminum canteen. It was about half-full. "Matches?"

"In the first-aid kit. Oh—we'll want everything in the kit. Dump it into that plastic bag. The metal box will be too heavy."

"What bag? Oh, that one." Jake followed her directions, reminding himself to keep the load light. He would be the one carrying the gear. Kelly would have all she could do just keeping up.

He retrieved her beat-up canvas pack, with the sleeping bag inside, from the rear of the fuselage. A flash of crimson led him to her red jacket, half-stuffed under the back of the pilot's seat. He rummaged into the zippered pocket and pulled out, with a flourish, one battered-looking Hershey's bar, with almonds.

"Want the jacket?" he asked Kelly.

She nodded. "Thanks. I can wear it under the poncho."

Jake zipped the candy bar back into the pocket. "Then you're hereby appointed keeper of the chocolate. I don't dare trust myself with such a treasure."

A smile flashed across her face as Jake tossed her the jacket—a smile of sudden, dimpled beauty, as ephemeral as the flicker of a hummingbird's wing. So swiftly did it come and go that afterward, Jake could scarcely believe he had seen it at all.

He cleared his throat. "Can you think of anything else?"

"Uh . . . I guess not." She was shrugging into the jacket and did not look at him. Her profile, half-turned away, was as soft as a child's.

Jake finished stuffing the odds and ends into the canvas pack. He hesitated over his own briefcase, then removed the most vital SEA-MAR papers, wrapped them in another loose plastic bag and slid them carefully into the side of the pack. "That should do it, then," he said quietly. "Let's go."

Chapter Four

*T*ough.

That, Jake mused, was the word for Kelly Ryan. She was hobbling ahead like Long John Silver on that crazy makeshift crutch, her little-girl mouth pressed tight with determination. Every step jammed the fork of the limb into her armpit. It had to hurt like hell. But so far, she hadn't even whimpered.

Weighted down with the gear-filled pack, Jake kept his pace even with hers. They'd traveled no more than a few hundred yards from the downed Beaver, but he'd already concluded she couldn't last long. The ground was so spongy that every step was an adventure in balance. Worse, there was no clear path. Everywhere they turned, their way was blocked by moss-draped deadfalls, or by spiny thickets of devil's club—the world's most aptly named weed. The going was hard enough on two good legs. For Kelly, it had to be misery.

Jake's eyes traced her snub-nosed profile, lingering on the stubborn set of her jaw. He remembered the feel of her against his chest when he'd lifted her from the cockpit, her compact body tensed like a cat about to spring. Sensing her discomfort, he had not held her for long. But letting her go hadn't been easy. Her softly understated curves had fit his arms as if they'd been molded there.

Beside him, she slipped on the wet moss. Jake lunged to help her, but she swiftly caught herself with her crutch and moved on without a glance in his direction. A puzzling girl, Kelly Ryan. He could tell she was hurting. But she was pushing ahead as if the devil himself were on her trail. Concerned, Jake nudged her arm.

"Look, it's not too late," he said. "We can always go back to the plane."

"Do you want to get to Juneau, or don't you?" She jabbed the stub of her crutch into the moss and swung her weight forward. "It could be weeks before they find us."

"That's not what I meant," Jake growled, thinking that the SEA-MAR deal was probably down the toilet anyway, so what difference would it make? "Even a couple of days could do wonders for that ankle of yours. If you just could stay off it—"

"I'm staying off it *now*. It's the rest of me that's working." She lunged forward in another awkward, hopping step. Even watching her was painful.

Jake groaned his exasperation. "Kelly Ryan, you're the most stubborn person I've ever known in my life!"

"Thanks. Grandma says it's the Irish in me—from Grandpa's side of the family." She surged ahead, her pert face frozen in a cheerful grimace.

Tough.

Ann had been tough, too, only in a different way. Ann's had been a quiet toughness, a thread of steel underlying a nature that was all softness and femininity. She had been a tender creature, his Ann—a lover of flowers and children and small animals. But tough. Especially in the end.

"Hey, look over there!" Kelly's animated voice shattered his reverie. "Just what I've been hoping to find! A trail!"

"A *trail?*" Jake blinked in amazement. It strained his credulity to imagine any other humans setting foot in this bug-riddled Eden. But the girl was right. Just through the brush lay a narrow footpath, its surface worn smooth with use.

"Come on!" She scrambled awkwardly over a fallen log. "We can move twice as fast along this! All we'll have to do is keep a check on our direction!"

Jake clambered after her, gnawed by an uneasiness he could not explain. A mosquito jabbed his cheek. He slapped it dead, but not in time to avoid one more itchy welt. "What the blazes is a trail doing out here? This isn't exactly Central Park."

Kelly had reached the path and was already stumping along ahead of him on the hard-packed earth. "Of course, we'll have to make plenty of noise," she said, ignoring his question. "Even singing wouldn't be a bad idea. Know any good old fraternity songs? I'll bet anything you were a frat man in college."

Something in her manner triggered a flare of annoyance in Jake. It was bad enough missing his appointment in Juneau, and probably dumping the SEA-MAR contract, as well. It was bad enough being lost in this murky, mosquito-infested forest. The last thing he needed was Kelly Ryan's treating him as if he had some kind of contagious disease.

He strode after her. "Hold it right there! Before we go on, there are a few things you and I need to straighten out!"

She forged ahead as if she hadn't heard.

"Damn it, Kelly!" In a burst of exasperation, he seized her free elbow and whipped her around to face him. Her crutch clattered to the trail as she caught herself against his chest. The amber-flecked eyes that gazed up at him were wide with apprehension, but Jake was too angry to care.

"I've had enough of this!" he rasped, his face inches from hers. "You won't answer my questions. You won't rest. You won't let me help you. Damn it, you won't even look at me when you talk! What the blazes is eating you?"

Beads of mist gleamed on Kelly's thick, black lashes, blurring the defiance that had crept into her eyes. "I don't know what you're talking about," she retorted in a small, tight voice.

"The devil you don't!" Jake's grip tightened on her arm. "You're treating me as if I'd hauled you out here against your will! You're behaving as if you thought I was scheming to drag you into the bushes and have my way with you!"

"Please . . . it's not what you think." Her arm quivered beneath Jake's hand. Her lower lip trembled, and suddenly, inexplicably, it was all he could do to keep from reaching out and brushing its softness with his fingertip—that and more. Jake found himself wondering, suddenly, what it would be like to kiss her: to nuzzle and nibble those delicate pink petals until she whimpered, then to crush her mouth with his, to plunge in his tongue and plunder the dark, moist nectar of her mouth. . . .

Damn!

Jake brought himself up short. What was the matter with him? A minute ago he'd been on the verge of shaking some sense into the girl. Now, suddenly, all he could think of was those satiny, full-blown lips and how sweet they would taste.

What the hell, maybe she was right about him. Maybe on some subconscious level, he *was* scheming to drag her into the bushes and—

Disgusted with himself, he broke off the thought. Who could blame Kelly for being on edge? The poor girl was injured, scared and in pain. And here he was, behaving like a Neanderthal.

"I'm sorry," he muttered, his hand dropping from her arm. "It hasn't exactly been a great day for either of us. If I've done anything to alienate you, or make you nervous—"

"You've done nothing." She spoke in a husky whisper. "Please understand, it's not you. It's me."

Jake sighed as the anger drained out of him. "Look, you can trust me, okay? All I want to do is get us both out of here."

For a long moment she met his gaze, her eyes as deep as the forest around them. Then, as if the effort were too much for her, she turned away. "Forgive me," she murmured. "As I said, it's not you. I just don't warm up to outsiders easily, that's all."

Stepping back, Jake bent to pick up her fallen crutch. "There's not much I can do about that," he said. "But right now, you're hurt and I'm lost. Neither of us has a great chance of making it back to civilization alone. Until we're out of this mess, we've got to depend on each other. The least we can do is try to get along."

Kelly hesitated, then exhaled sharply. "You're right, and I apologize. I'll try not to be such a trial to you." She stood balanced on her good leg in an attitude that reminded Jake of a rain-soaked sparrow. Only her eyes moved as he held out the crutch. What was behind those lovely, guarded eyes? he wondered. Was she just shy, or was there more to Kelly Ryan than he realized?

"Truce?" He proffered the rude crutch as a peace token.

"Truce—again." She accepted it with a forced little smile that held no trace of the radiance he'd glimpsed earlier.

Noting the absence, Jake handed himself a private chal-lenge. Before the day ended, he would coax at least one real smile out of her.

Turning away, she swung back onto the path with such energy that Jake had to stride to keep up.

"Just for your information, I wasn't in a fraternity," he said. "I was too busy studying and waiting tables at the lo-cal pizza joint to have much of a social life."

Kelly gave him a swift, serious glance. "Well, you may want to sing anyway, or yodel, or recite Shakespeare or whatever it is you do."

"Why?" A sense of foreboding lifted the hackles under Jake's collar.

"This nice, smooth path we're walking on is a bear trail," she said. "And we don't want to surprise any bears."

Jake swallowed. She was enjoying this, he thought sourly. Dragging newcomers out in the bush and scaring them silly was probably the Alaskan state sport. However, he wasn't about to argue.

"I hope you like Hank Williams," he said loudly. "I know most of his songs by heart because my mother was the ultimate fan. If she'd had her way, in fact, my name would have been Hank Williams Drummond. Luckily, my father intervened."

He glanced at Kelly. No smile. "Any requests?" he asked cheerfully.

"No, but you might ask the bears."

"Very funny," he grumbled in mock irritation. "All right, then. Here goes." Taking a deep breath, Jake launched himself into a full-volume, if slightly off-key, rendition of "Hey, Good Lookin'."

Hank Williams he wasn't. But if he could put Kelly at ease by making a fool of himself, it was worth a try. If nothing else, at least they ought to be safe. His singing was bound to scare off any bear within earshot.

Jake finished the first song, then rumbled his way through "Your Cheatin' Heart" and "I Can't Help It If I'm Still in Love With You." His untrained baritone, so deep it amounted to little more than a growl, was no match for Hank Williams's immortal country tenor. But even Kelly had to admit that Jake Drummond was a good sport.

Which was a lot more than she could say for herself.

What was wrong with her? Back at the crash site, she'd resolved to be professional, competent and detached. Now, here she was, behaving like a petulant little girl. No wonder she was getting on Jake's nerves. No wonder he'd finally lost patience with her.

There was no excuse for her behavior. But at least she wasn't fool enough to deny what was causing it. She was scared. Plain running scared. And she didn't know what to do about it.

For the past seven years, Kelly had managed to keep her emotions frozen under a protective layer of ice. Oh, it wasn't that she'd been a manless hermit. A couple of earnest young rangers on the island had been regulars at her grandparents' house. One of them had taken her to a few movies in Angoon and kissed her, awkwardly, on the front porch swing before the Forest Service transferred him to Denali. The other had seemed as fond of her grandma's moose stew and hot cinnamon buns as he was of her—not that Kelly had much cared.

There were plenty of men on her charter flights, too, and they often made passes. Most of them, however, had wives back in the Lower Forty-eight; and even the single ones were only interested in a souvenir romp with their female bush pilot. Kelly had become adept at brushing them off. In fact,

she felt fairly comfortable around men—as long as she remained in control.

But Jake was different. She had sensed it from the moment he climbed into the plane.

What was it? Oh, Jake was a dazzler—drop-dead handsome, with an aura of power that was almost tangible. Like
Richard Cory in the old poem, Jake Drummond glittered
when he walked.

But that alone was not enough to send her heart into a
skittering panic every time he got too close to her. Kelly had
met other men just as good-looking and just as successful.
Once she'd even flown Kevin Costner to an exclusive lodge
on Chichagof. She'd managed the job with little more than
a flutter of her feminine pulse.

With Jake it was something more. Kelly was not even sure
what that something was. She only knew, instinctively, that
Jake Drummond had the power to hurt her as she never
wanted to be hurt again in her life.

A raven croaked raucously from the top of a dead spruce,
and Kelly realized that Jake had stopped singing.

"So much for critics," he said, with a flash of his one-
thousand-candlepower grin. "I think my voice has just been
designated an environmental hazard. It's your turn to entertain our furry friends."

Kelly lurched forward on her crutch, ignoring the
wrenching pain in her shoulder. "I'm not much of a singer,"
she said, her mind scrambling. "But I can recite one of the
poems my grandpa taught me."

An extralong stride brought him up behind her. "Then by
all means, go ahead. The bears and I are all ears."

Self-consciously, Kelly cleared her throat and began,
haltingly, to recite "The Cremation of Sam McGee" by
Robert Service.

The poem went on and on, and so did Kelly, dramatically recounting the saga of the Southerner who froze in the Alaskan wilds, only to revive when his companion kept a deathbed promise to cremate his last remains.

Jake broke into applause as she finished, his throaty laughter weaving a small nest of coziness around Kelly's heart. For the space of a breath, she allowed herself to enjoy the feeling, to bask in its warmth. Then, with a toss of her head, she forced it away.

"Your turn again," she said crisply. "You don't know any Lyle Lovett songs, do you?"

"So you've had enough of old Hank?" His eyebrow quirked sardonically. "Okay, you win. But let's give the bears a break for now. As long as we have to make noise anyway, I'd just as soon talk."

"Talk?" Kelly's pulse skipped nervously. Keeping a safe emotional distance hadn't been so hard when he was singing, or when she was reciting. But *talking* was different. Talking meant questions and answers. It meant learning things she'd be better off not knowing, or skirting her own secrets, fearful of saying too much.

"Frankly, Kelly, I'd like to know more about you," he said, and Kelly's heart slammed.

"I hope you don't want to hear the story of my life," she muttered. "Believe me, it's pretty boring."

"Boring? Growing up on an island full of bears? Learning to fly a bush plane?"

"Oh, that part hasn't been boring. But I've never even traveled outside Alaska. I've never done anything..." She grimaced as her crutch tip struck a stone. "...anything the least bit important."

"Important how?" he persisted.

She shot him an exasperated glance. "Important. Like making a contribution—making a difference for someone.

That may not fit your definition of the word, but it fits mine.''

"That's a fine definition, Kelly.'' His voice deepened huskily as he spoke. "But you're wrong about not making a difference. I'm alive right now because of you.''

Kelly swung forward on her crutch, feigning a nonchalance she did not feel. "That doesn't count. You just happened to be along when I saved myself, that's all.''

"You don't give yourself much credit, do you?''

It was more of a statement than a question, and Kelly chose not to respond. She was muddle-tongued enough already. Every time she opened her mouth, she ended up sounding like a fool.

She remembered the leggy, elegant women she'd seen in the magazines her grandma got in the mail. Jake Drummond would know women like that. He would probably meet them at parties and yacht races, and on the tennis courts. And the things they said to him would be just right—smart and funny.

Kelly felt as smart and funny as a marsh toad.

"Last time I heard 'The Cremation of Sam McGee' I was in sixth grade,'' Jake was saying. "It took me all the way back to Miss Shannon and her geography lessons on the far, frozen North. If you don't mind my saying so, your delivery was a lot livelier than hers.''

"Is this your first time in Alaska?'' Kelly asked lamely.

"It is. But I was fascinated by the place as a kid. *Call of the Wild, White Fang*... I read them all.''

"You'd enjoy my grandpa,'' Kelly said. "He was born in Fairbanks, and he's spent most of his life up here. When it comes to history, he's a real treasure trove.''

"You live with your grandfather?''

"With him and my grandma. They raised me. My parents drowned in a boating accident when I was a baby. I don't even remember them."

Jake fell into silence for a moment. Then, as if he'd suddenly remembered the need to warn the bears, he quickly shot her another question.

"So how did you come to take up flying?"

"My grandpa. He was a fighter pilot in World War II. When he got home, he worked sixteen-hour days in a salmon cannery to buy his first Beaver." Kelly swallowed hard, thinking of the precious, shattered craft they'd walked away from. "If you owe your life to anyone, it's him, Jake. I learned from the best."

"I could have guessed that from the way you handled the plane." Jake paused to shift the weight of the pack, then closed the gap between them in three hard strides. "Thank you, by the way, for finally calling me by my first name."

Again that infuriating blush heated Kelly's cheeks. Surely he'd noticed it—he was looking right at her. She braced herself, but the teasing comment she'd expected did not come. The dazzling Mr. Drummond, she conceded, knew how to be a gentleman.

"I apologize for having been so formal," she murmured, embarrassed by her own crimson face. "It's the way I was raised. My grandpa always called his passengers 'Mister'— and I mean the men of course. He made sure I did the same. It was more businesslike, he always said."

Jake moved in a half step closer—so close that when he spoke, his voice tickled like a bumblebee in her ear. "Well, Kelly, I think it's safe to assume that our relationship has moved past the business stage."

Kelly's blush deepened to the color of wild raspberries. Jake Drummond was almost behaving as if he *liked* her. But that made no sense. He was just being nice, that was all.

None of those elegant, witty women he *really* liked were handy, so he was just—

"Oh!" Kelly's crutch had caught in a tree root. Propelled by her own momentum, she lurched to one side and sprawled facedown on a mat of green moss and tiny, purple twayblade orchids. Unhurt but mortified, she lay still, tears stinging her eyes.

"Are you okay?" Jake crouched beside her, probably thinking what a clumsy fool she was. One hand rested patronizingly on her shoulder.

"Yeah, I'm okay," Kelly muttered, spitting out a shred of moss. "Just let me up. I'll be fine."

"Here." His hand gripped her arm and, despite Kelly's struggling determination to rise by herself, pulled her to a sitting position.

"You're sure you're all right?" His eyes scanned her anxiously, reflecting genuine concern.

Kelly blinked away tears, her cheeks blazing. "Yes, I'm sure," she said, trying hard to sound dignified. "That moss was as soft as a mattress."

A fleeting smile quirked a corner of his mouth. "Hold still," he said, fumbling for his hip pocket. "Your 'mattress' left some mud on your face."

"So, what's a little mud?" Kelly attempted a tentative smile. Her fingers found the damp spot on her left cheek and began a furious rubbing.

"Wait—you're just making a smear." Jake had come up with a clean white handkerchief. He moistened it with water from the canteen. His free hand captured Kelly's chin.

Kelly's heart stopped.

"This'll just take a second," he murmured, his fingertips igniting sparks along the curve of her jaw. She froze, senses quivering as the crisp linen stroked at her cheek. His eyes were much too close, she thought. She could see all the way into their silver blue depths. She could see things she had no wish to see—like traces of the long, cold pain that settles in as the first shock of grief wears away. She could see anger, bewilderment, all the emotions she knew so well.

Nineteen months, he had said, since his wife's death.

Kelly lowered her gaze to the safer territory of his firm, slightly cleft chin. Groping for some distraction, she tried to imagine the kind of person Ann, his wife, might have been. For a man like Jake Drummond, choosing a woman would have been like selecting from a box of gourmet chocolates. Ann, of course, would have been lovely. Lithe and graceful, with flawless skin and high cheekbones, like the models in the magazines. She would have worn clothes with designer labels, and given the most elegant dinner parties in Seattle, with heirloom china and real silver, and fresh, long-stemmed roses on the—

"Ouch!" Kelly flinched as the fabric scrubbed raw flesh.

Jake drew back a little, his fingers still bracing her chin. "Sorry. Underneath this mud, you've got a nasty scrape. Hold still—I'll do my best to clean it without hurting you."

Wetting the handkerchief again, he dabbed gently at Kelly's cheek. She closed her eyes to shut out his nearness, but it didn't help. The absence of sight only made her more acutely aware of him—the shallow rasp of his breathing, the leathery aroma that was part after-shave and part warm, clean male scent.

Kelly tried to concentrate on the forest sounds around her: the subtle patter of water dripping from leaves, the raucous scolding of a squirrel. She fought to banish Jake Drummond from her mind. But it was no good. She could feel his eyes on her face. She could feel his breath on her skin. A trickle of perspiration slid down her neck to pool in the hollow between her breasts.

What she needed, Kelly scolded herself, was an ice-cold dunk in a glacial lake.

The handkerchief paused in its cleaning, then withdrew, to be followed by a breathless silence. Kelly was afraid to open her eyes. Her thoughts skittered like cornered mice as Jake's fingertips braced her jaw. She counted her own heartbeats, struggling to keep her emotions from veering off course.

Just when she couldn't bear it any longer, his hand released her. Kelly heard him clear his throat. "That...seems to be all of it. Hang on, I think I saw some salve in the first-aid kit."

Her eyelids fluttered open. He was crouched an arm's length away, shrugging out of the pack.

She could not stand another minute of this.

"Don't bother with the salve," she said quickly. "It'll take too long. We need to get moving."

"Your face—"

"It'll be fine. It's only a little scrape. Let's go."

Nodding as if he understood—although, of course, he didn't—Jake eased himself to his feet. Looming above her, he reached down to pull her up.

Kelly hesitated; then, steeling herself, she caught his big, hard hand. As his fingers closed around hers, she willed herself not to feel their warmth. All Jake Drummond wanted was to get to Juneau. To an outsider like him, she was nothing more than hired help.

As Kelly regained her feet, she spotted the crutch. It had bounded under a salmonberry bush when she fell. Wriggling her hand out of Jake's clasp, she pointed toward it.

"If you'll just get me my—"

"No."

Kelly stared at him in shocked silence. His eyes were steel—no, steel could be bent, she corrected herself. Jake's eyes were granite.

"But how do you expect me to—?"

"No more crutch, Kelly," he said in a flat, determined voice. "I've spent the past hour watching you hobble along on that miserable contraption. Every step hurts you—it hurts me just to see it! And now, you just took a nosedive into the bush. That's enough."

"Of all the presumptuous, high-handed..." Sputtering impotently, Kelly made a lunge for the crutch. But Jake was faster. In a single motion, he seized the laboriously carved limb and snapped it over his knee.

Somehow Kelly managed to keep from falling a second time. She danced on one foot in the middle of the bear trail, eyes darting in helpless rage from the splintered crutch to the man who had broken it.

Jake scowled back at her, unmoved. "Don't ask me to apologize," he said in that same maddening, expressionless tone. "I just did you a very big favor. Sooner or later, you'll realize that for yourself."

"I take it you plan to carry me the rest of the way," Kelly said coldly.

"Not unless you can fit yourself into this pack."

"Then what—?"

Jake bridged the distance between them with a single stride. His smile glittered with irony as he offered Kelly his arm.

"Your crutch, milady," he said.

Jake moved carefully along the trail, his left arm supporting Kelly's waist, her right hand gripping his shoulder. Pressed against his side, she matched her steps to his like a partner in a three-legged race. She was cooperating, but

Jake knew she wasn't happy about it. Her body was taut with resentment. Her angry silence was worse than a tirade.

Not that he blamed her. Kelly was a fiercely independent woman. The last thing she'd want would be to have a man take charge of her by force. But Jake was not sorry. She had needed his help. Now, for all her stubborn pride, she had no choice but to accept it.

Too angry, still, for conversation, she limped along at his side. Every step pressed the soft curve of her breast against Jake's ribs. The contact was no heavier than the brush of a cat's paw. But Jake had to admit it was getting to him. The slightest touch sent a chain reaction of hot little spasms flashing along the nerve path to his loins. After nearly an hour of this torture, the strain threatened to burst the crotch of his one hundred and fifty-dollar moleskin bush pants.

Jake had battled the sensation every step of the way. He had sung all the Curly and Will songs from his mother's old *Oklahoma* record. He had recited Antony's speech from *Julius Caesar,* and as much as he could remember of Hamlet's soliloquy. He'd even tried to scare himself to distraction by keeping still for minutes at a time, defying a nine-foot *Ursus arctos* to materialize around the next bend in the trail.

But it was no good. Libido was winning over logic. The hell of it was, there wasn't a damned thing he could do about it.

Kelly limped along beside him, wrapped in a stubborn silence that even the threat of bears could not dispel. She had left the burden of noisemaking to Jake, as if she didn't care one way or the other. Maybe he *had* been too hard on her, Jake reflected morosely. Maybe he could have found a more diplomatic way to get rid of the crutch—or at least a kinder way. She didn't deserve the high-handed treatment he'd given her.

But she deserved the alternative even less.

He had almost kissed her.

It had happened back there on the trail, as he finished wiping the mud from her scraped cheek. Her eyelids had been tightly closed, her chin cradled tensely in the cup of his fingers. For the space of a long breath, Jake had paused to gaze at the square-cut prettiness of her face. His eyes had traced the sooty line of her lashes against her porcelain cheek, then drifted lower, to linger on the luscious mauve rose of her mouth.

The urge that seized him had been so powerful, it almost took his breath away.

Jake had come fearfully close to giving in. He had leaned nearer, his senses swimming in the delicate, old-fashioned fragrance that warmed on her skin. Her kiss, he thought, would be as sweet as springtime.

Kelly's face had blurred as he closed the scant distance between them. Only then had he noticed it—the tear, gleaming on her cheek like an opalescent jewel. He could see where it had trickled between her lashes, leaving a thin, wet trail on her skin.

That tear had stopped him like a slap in the face.

Once more now, Jake reexamined his motives. Yes, it would have been delicious, kissing Kelly. It would have been sheer heaven, enfolding her gentle curves in his arms, pressing her soft warmth into his body.

And what then?

Was he ready to live with the consequences?

Assuming Kelly didn't slap his face, was he ready for a serious relationship with a girl whose life was so far removed from his own?

Or was he ready to make a game of it, playing along until he got back to Juneau, then waving her a breezy goodbye?

Either way, it wouldn't work, Jake concluded for perhaps the eleventh time. He wasn't ready for any kind of long-term involvement. The loss of Ann was still too fresh.

And Kelly wasn't the kind of girl for games. She was too tender, too vulnerable, too innocent not to be hurt.

Jake was no Sir Galahad. Even now, he was tempted to grab her in his arms and kiss her till she whimpered. But that wouldn't do. He would only end up hating himself—and sooner or later, Kelly would hate him, too.

So he would play the gentleman. He would be polite and kind and patient. And he would ignore those damnable flashes of heat that curled downward into his vitals every time Kelly brushed against him.

He did not know how many hours lay between them and safety. He only knew that every minute with Kelly Ryan would be an exercise in willpower.

And if he weakened, heaven help them both.

Chapter Five

Jake's muscles groaned as he shifted the weight of the pack on his shoulders. For hours now, he'd been slogging through a dripping, green world that never seemed to change. His feet were sore and soggy. His back ached. His face, for all the repellent he'd smeared on every inch of exposed skin, felt like one giant mosquito bite. Gnats circled dizzily before his eyes.

Beside him, Kelly was humming a spiritless rendition of "The Marine Hymn." Her silent spell had long since fizzled out, but she'd been far from friendly. The closest thing they'd had to a real conversation had been a chilly exchange about what to do if they met a bear.

"The worst thing you can do is run," she'd declared with a nonchalance that gelled Jake's blood. "That would be like giving the bear an invitation to chase you, and they're a lot faster than they look. The odds of your getting away wouldn't even be worth figuring."

"Not even if I left you behind as an appetizer?" Jake had teased, faking a jocularity he did not feel.

She'd shot him a we-are-not-amused glare. "Your best chance, if there's time, is to get up a tall tree. Big bears don't usually climb. They're too heavy." Kelly had allowed herself a melodramatic pause. "Of course, the bear could always shove your tree over, or shake it till you fall out."

Jake's nerve endings had jangled like alarm bells. Kelly Ryan was *enjoying* this, he'd told himself. She was probably *trying* to scare him. Hell, for all he knew, the bears on this island played poker and carried union cards.

"Okay," he'd affirmed, trying to sound chipper. "So what do you do if there's no tree handy?"

"You stand your ground—try to show the bear you're not afraid. With luck, it won't charge."

"And if it does?"

"You stay where you are and hope the charge is a false one. More often than not, it will be."

Jake had exhaled shakily. "What if the bear means business?"

"At that point, if you've got a gun, you shoot. Otherwise, you drop facedown, play dead and hope the big bruiser doesn't chew you up too badly."

She *was* enjoying this, Jake had reflected darkly. She was probably watching out of the corner of her eye to see how badly he was squirming. Well, he wouldn't give her the satisfaction. Ten years of boardroom politics had taught him one thing: don't let anybody see you sweat.

"What..." His voice had squeaked like a fourteen-year-old boy's. He quickly cleared his throat. "What about the flare gun? I know it couldn't stop a bear, but it might at least help scare one off."

Kelly's face had pursed thoughtfully. "It might," she'd conceded. "At least, it wouldn't hurt to keep it handy. Bend over, and I'll dig it out of the pack."

They'd found and loaded the flare pistol. Now, here was Jake, trudging along the trail with the ridiculous weapon clenched in his right fist, his left arm bracing Kelly's trim waist. He still found her nearness disturbing. But at this point, he told himself, his tortured body couldn't have managed a response if she'd stripped to her underwear and danced the hootchy-kootchy. He was too uncomfortable, too nervous and too exhausted.

He was also hungry, Jake realized. He'd been too keyed-up about the SEA-MAR conference to eat much that morning. Now hunger's sharp teeth were gnawing into the hollow of his stomach. What would Kelly take, he wondered, for her fifty percent interest in one slightly mangled Hershey's bar?

He was tempted to ask. But something about the determined set of her jaw told him it wouldn't do any good. Kelly was holding up much better than he was. She'd soldiered along for hours without complaint, and showed no sign of being tired. Blast her, she even *looked* fresh. The cool mist had brought out the pink in her cheeks and curled her hair into damp little ringlets around her face. And the mosquitoes had scarcely touched her; but then, why should they, when they'd been so busy with *him?*

Jake had always set his sights on sophisticated girls, and there were plenty of those in Seattle. But most of the women he knew would have been reduced to sodden, whining wrecks by a place like this. Kelly was one of those rare females who seemed to be made for the outdoors. She bloomed in this setting, like a wild rose.

He wondered if anyone had ever told Kelly Ryan how pretty she was.

Someone should, he reflected, since it was so obvious that she didn't know. She seemed to shrink into herself every time he looked at her, as if there was something she didn't want him to see. More than once today, Jake had fought back the temptation to grab the girl and *show* her how blasted desirable she was. Even now, he caught himself imagining the feel of her in his arms, the small of her back arching against his palm, her sweetly rounded breasts straining against his chest. He imagined tasting the swollen buds of her lips, then, with aching restraint, nibbling a path along her jaw to tease and tug at the delicate, pink curl of her ear. He imagined loosening the first button on her flannel shirt and sliding a tentative fingertip along the satiny ridge of her collarbone; then, as he kissed her, easing his hand lower, to stroke the—

A low, rumbling growl shattered Jake's fantasy.

He went rigid, hair bristling on the back of his neck, heart slamming his ribs. "Listen!" he hissed. "Did you hear that?"

She stared up at him, her eyes as round as quarters. "Hear what?" she whispered.

"Something . . . growled."

Kelly's lips tightened, but she said nothing.

"Stay close!" he whispered, drawing her protectively against his side. "Keep moving, and listen!"

With Kelly pressed against him, he crept along the trail. The flare pistol lay cold in the clutch of his sweating hand. His mind swam with fear as he tried to imagine protecting her from a charging bear. He could boost her partway up a tree, he calculated, then turn and fire the flare into the monster's face, giving her a chance to climb before—

His throat clenched as he heard the growl again. But this time, Jake suddenly realized, he'd not only heard, but *felt* it, as a small rumble that quivered through Kelly's ribs.

She shot him a furtive glance, the now-familiar pink tide creeping under her skin. Jake's knees melted with relief as he realized what was happening.

"I take it you're hungry, too," he muttered, chagrined.

Kelly nodded, blushing furiously as she struggled to contain her embarrassment. Her lips twitched. Her cheeks puckered. Then her eyes crinkled at the corners and, like a sudden burst of sunshine, she began to laugh.

Caught off guard, Jake stared at her. Kelly's laughter was hearty and unrestrained, yet as delicate as the half-remembered tinkle of a glass chime his mother had hung in her summer garden. It almost made the whole damned lousy day worth something, hearing her laugh like that.

"You had me so damned scared." Jake felt a warm, giddy response bubbling up inside him. He tried to speak calmly, but she was getting to him. His own self-control was straining at the seams. His ribs ached with the effort of holding it in.

Then suddenly, it didn't matter. He was laughing with her, his emotions effervescing as if someone had popped a cork. Here he was, stranded in the middle of nowhere with an injured female, a major business contract down the sewer, his feet aching, his mosquito bites itching, his belly a gnawing pit, with nothing to eat but a blasted candy bar. And he was laughing.

"I scared *you?*" She sagged against him, helpless with mirth. "You heard me, and you thought…" She pressed her hands to her face, her body shaking so hard that Jake feared she might be getting hysterical. If they'd been in Seattle, and Kelly had been a different kind of woman, he might have seized the moment and gathered her into his arms, held her tight against his chest, maybe even kissed her. But that wouldn't do here, he reminded himself. Not with Kelly Ryan. Kelly wasn't the sort of girl a man played games with.

She deserved a man who played for keeps, a man who could love her with all his heart.

The last thing she needed was a pass from a stranger who had no heart to give.

So he let himself laugh with her. He laughed until his ribs ached and his eyes watered. He laughed until, at last, they faced each other, spent and trembling.

Gazing down at Kelly, Jake felt something stir and shift inside him, as if a heavy black weight were straining to float free. Seized by a sudden urgency, he willed the weight back into its place. It was too soon, he told himself. Too soon to let go of the grief that had been his anchor for the past nineteen months.

Kelly's eyelashes were wet. Tears of laughter glistened on her flushed cheeks. Jake's resolve softened at the sight of her. It would feel very natural to reach up and brush those tears away, he thought. Surely she wouldn't take it for anything but the innocent gesture it was meant to be.

But no, he reminded himself, it wasn't worth the risk. Kelly had let down her guard for the moment, but the wrong move from him would snap those barriers right back into place. The distance that remained between them was safe and comfortable. Leave it be, Jake told himself.

He settled for giving her an awkward little cuff on the shoulder. "What do you say we break out that Hershey's bar? Next thing you know, I'll be growling along with you." Glancing away, Kelly blotted her tears on her sleeve. Her hand fumbled for the pocket under her poncho, then paused resolutely. "Not yet," she declared. "Once the candy bar's gone, we'll have nothing in reserve. We'd better save it."

Jake shrugged his assent. A mouthful of chocolate would have tasted like heaven about now, but if Kelly could be tough, so could he.

"In that case, how about a nice filet mignon with sauce béarnaise?" he said. "Or would mademoiselle prefer noodles Romanov and fresh strawberry cheesecake?"

Kelly flashed him a wry grin. "Right now, I'd settle for a burger and fries. But since there's no McDonald's handy, we'll just have to forage."

"Forage?" Jake glanced around at the woods with a pointed lack of enthusiasm. Nothing he saw struck him as appetizing. The bushes looked woody and bitter. The moss-bearded trees sported doughy, oozing clumps of fungus that he wouldn't have tasted on a million-dollar bet.

"It won't be so bad." Kelly was nudging him forward. "Come on. We can find things as we walk. I'll show you what to look for."

Jake bit back a skeptical retort. As far as he was concerned, feeding off the land had nothing on a good four-star restaurant. But he sensed a softening in Kelly, an unfolding of trust and confidence that was as delicate as a flower. To wither it with a blast of sarcastic humor—he was capable of being crass, but not that crass.

His hand found the circle of her leather belt and curved to support her waist, even as his mind steeled against her nearness. "Lead on, then," he declared. "My hunger is in your hands. Whatever you find, I'll eat!"

Kelly rewarded him with a heart-melting smile.

Half an hour later, the drizzle began again. Kelly tugged up the hood of her poncho. Beside her, she could feel Jake hunching into his Gore-Tex coat. The rain was plastering his wet, blond curls to his head. He looked cold and tired, she thought. And the fiddlehead fern shoots they'd found to munch on probably hadn't slaked his hunger any more than they had her own. She was tempted to offer him the chocolate bar—but no, they had a long way to go. Later on, they might need it even more.

They had fallen into a dangerous silence—dangerous because of the bears, and for other reasons, as well. Silence gave Kelly time to think. It gave Jake's nearness a chance to work into her body, stirring up sensations that had no business being there.

Jake's arm was looped under the poncho, his hand tucked warmly at her waist. It hadn't been a bad idea, his breaking her crutch, she conceded. By now, her shoulder would have been in agony from throwing her weight onto the crudely forked limb. But substituting Jake for the crutch was like being flipped out of the frying pan and into the fire. Every press of his hand, every subtle shift of his lean torso against her side, sent tingles of awareness shooting from the point of contact to Kelly's brain. The fact that she was so tired only seemed to worsen the condition.

"So tell me about your business," she said, groping for an impersonal topic to break the silence.

He exhaled raggedly. "Not much to tell. We do contract shipping between the West Coast and the Pacific Rim. The company's not really big yet, but we're growing. We have hopes—at least we did until today."

"I'm sorry."

"It wasn't your fault." Jake's voice carried a bitter edge. "The meeting was a long shot anyway. We were bidding against a Japanese firm three times our size. Our only chance was to convince the SEA-MAR folks that they'd be better off shipping with an American company."

"Maybe they'll give you another chance." Kelly clasped at a thin straw of hope. SEA-MAR was one of several companies that represented the interests of the Tlingit tribe, whose lands were rich in timber, fish and minerals. The Tlingits, of all people, understood the vagaries of wind and weather in this country. Surely, if they suspected that the plane was down—

"I can't count on that." The raw edge of Jake's voice slashed into her thoughts. "They're under no obligation to wait for me, especially when the Japanese have already made them a decent offer."

"But you can't just give up!" Kelly insisted. "Those two men I met at the camp—your partners—if they get word you didn't make it, maybe one of them could go in your place and—"

"No. That's not how it works. Shamus and Roger took me on twelve years ago because I had an MBA, and they wanted someone who knew how to do the proposals and spreadsheets that would bring in big contracts. They run the shipping end of the business, but they're not negotiators. That's *my* job." Jake's jaw tightened as he stared into the peppering rain. "They were counting on me, and I let them down."

"And I just wrecked my grandpa's airplane. We're a sorry pair, Jake Drummond."

He made an odd little sound that could have been either a snort or a chuckle. "You're all right, Kelly." His hand tightened perceptibly around her waist, sending Kelly's pulse rocketing into overdrive. "I'd like to know more about you," he said.

"Oh, no, you don't!" She shrank into her hood to hide the telltale pink flush. "You can't wriggle off that easily. It was you we were talking about, not me."

She felt the shrug of his shoulders and the loosening of his hand. "So we were," he muttered.

"You mentioned you'd lost your wife." Kelly plunged ahead, seized by a sudden desperation to widen the distance between them. "Do you have children in Seattle?"

"No children." Jake's breath caught as he spoke. "She...we tried, but Ann wasn't able to have them. We were looking into adoption when she became ill."

"I'm sorry," Kelly said softly. "She must have been beautiful. At least, that's how I imagine her."

"Here." Jake handed her the flare gun, freeing his right hand to fumble for his wallet. Fishing it awkwardly out of his hip pocket, he flipped it open to reveal an expensively finished studio photograph.

Beautiful? The word was an understatement, Kelly thought as she watched the rain bead on the plastic that covered Ann Drummond's picture. Her wistful gaze traced the contours of Ann's thoroughbred bones, the elegant neck, the loosely coiffed hair, light brown and artfully tousled, the eyes, deep gray and arrestingly honest. Even in a rain-blurred photo, it was evident that Ann's beauty had been more than physical. Hers was the beauty of a warm, confident character, the self-assurance of a woman who had known she was loved.

"She's lovely," Kelly murmured as Jake folded the wallet and slipped it back into his pocket. "You must miss her very much."

His jaw tightened as he stared ahead into the drizzle. "I keep busy," he said. "It helps, but only a little."

"You haven't found anyone else, then?"

"No." Jake spoke the word with stark finality, and in the silence that followed, Kelly sensed the closing of a door. He had given her a glimpse into his pain. It was more than enough for both of them.

"What about you?" he said, picking up the pace and pulling her forcefully along with him. "I imagine a girl as attractive as you would have a pretty hectic social life."

"Not really." Kelly feigned an indifferent shrug, deliberately ignoring the compliment. He was just making a pleasantry, she told herself. Besides, she'd seen Jake's idea of an attractive woman, and she knew how she measured up. Compared to Ann Drummond's swanlike beauty, she was as plain as a chickadee.

"I'm always busy," she added lamely. "Between the flying business and my studies, I don't have much time for socializing."

"Studies?" His curiosity was merely polite, Kelly thought. It couldn't be more.

"I take correspondence courses from the University of Alaska. If I can stick with the program, I'll have my teaching certificate in a couple of years."

Jake drew back a little to study her, his blue eyes narrowing. "Uh-huh, I can picture you as a teacher," he said. "I can see you in front of a classroom full of kids, making all those wiggly little boys behave."

"Nice try," Kelly responded, "but you have the wrong picture."

"Then suppose you give me the right one."

"Oh, it's just..." She paused, suddenly flustered. She could feel the dream stirring again—the dream she'd nurtured in her heart for almost as long as she could remember. A dream as small as hers would mean nothing to a successful man like Jake, she reminded herself. But all at once that didn't seem to matter. The dream was *hers*. It was radiating now, bursting out of her, and she had to give it voice.

Kelly spoke in a rush of words. "I want to be a teacher, but not in a regular classroom. There are kids all over Alaska whose homes are too isolated for them to go to school. Kids living out in the bush, on islands, in native villages... The only way for many of them to get schooling is to have a teacher fly in every few weeks to help them with their lessons. To you, that may not sound very important, but it's what I've always wanted to do. That's the kind of teacher I want to be."

Her throat was tight by the time she finished speaking. She glanced at up Jake, half-afraid he would laugh at her intensity. But no, it was all right. The eyes that probed hers were warm with interest.

"Earlier you said something about making a difference. I take it this is what you meant."

Kelly nodded. "Oh, I love flying. I never want to give it up. But hauling rich sportsmen and their gear around the backcountry...it's just a job. It doesn't *last*. Kids do."

Jake slogged silently along for a moment, lost in thought. The forest was so still that Kelly could hear the rain dripping from the saturated spruce boughs, and the resonant chuck of a raven from the crown of a dead hemlock.

"I have only one question for you," he said at last.

"What's that?"

"Why wade through two more years of correspondence courses when you could get your degree so much faster going full time, on campus?"

"Oh, but I couldn't do that!" The response exploded from Kelly's lips. "It's impossible!"

"How long would it take you?"

Her mind raced through the calculations. "A year, at most. Less if I carried a full credit load. But—"

"Then, what's stopping you? If it's money—"

"No!" Kelly protested vehemently. "That's not the problem at all!"

"Then, why not just do it?" His voice dropped persuasively. "What's getting in your way?"

"Oh..." She sagged as the comfortable old excuses slid into place. "It just wouldn't work. There's my grandparents—they aren't as strong as they used to be. And there'd be no one to fly the charters—"

"Who'll fly the charters when you become a teacher?" Jake pressed his argument with the tenacity of a bulldog. Kelly stared down at the trail, wishing he would just back off and leave her alone. Jake Drummond didn't know anything about her, or about her past. He had no idea what it would cost her to pull up roots and strike out on her own.

"It's a question you'll have to resolve sooner or later," he argued. "Why wait? Why not resolve it now?"

"You don't understand." Kelly fought back a flash of strangling panic. He was suddenly too close, too insistent on driving her where she could not even think of going. She pushed away from him, stumbled on her weak ankle and lost her balance.

He caught her with his arm, pinning her abruptly against him. His eyes pierced her like steel probes.

"What is it, Kelly?" His voice was a raw whisper. "What the devil are you so afraid of?"

Gathering her courage, she forced herself to meet the full impact of his gaze. "I'm not afraid of you, if that's what you mean."

"I don't believe you."

The words struck Kelly like a gauntlet across the face. Impelled by her own outrage, she seized the back of his neck with one hand and jerked his head downward. Her mouth closed on his in a brutal, emotionless kiss.

That, at least, was what she'd intended. But the first shock of Jake's rain-cooled lips went through her like an electric current. She felt him stiffen. Then his hand tightened on the small of her back, flattening her hard against him. His mouth warmed, molding hungrily to hers.

Kelly's response surged like a wet, hot tide. Time hung suspended as she clasped his head. Her fingers taloned his rain-slicked hair as she fought against emotions that pounded like the sea. She was making her point, that was all, she reminded herself dizzily. But this couldn't go on. If she yielded, if she gave in . . . Marshaling her strength, she wrenched herself away from him. Jake let her go. They faced each other an arm's length apart, both of them flushed and unsteady.

Kelly's breath came in little gasps as she struggled to speak. "That was just to prove a . . . point. Nothing more. Now will you believe I'm . . . not afraid of you?"

"Afraid?" His eyebrow quirked in sardonic amusement. "After a demonstration like that, I'd wager you're not afraid of anything in the world," he said. "My apologies."

"Then the subject is closed."

"Absolutely."

Turning down the trail again, he offered her his arm. Kelly limped to his side, accepting the inevitable. She needed Jake's physical support, just as he needed her knowledge of the island. Beyond that, she reminded herself, there was no bond between them. None whatsoever.

All the same, as his arm slipped under her poncho, Kelly's pulse surged like an engine readying for takeoff. The discreet pressure of his fingers at her waist set off spark-showers all through her body. She could feel her nipples puckering inside her bra, shrinking into hard little knots.

This could not go on.

"I hope I didn't shock you," she said, feigning nonchalance. "I don't usually kiss a man on the first date."

Jake managed to combine a chuckle with a groan. "Let's just say that if you did, I've never had a more pleasant shock. I only have one question."

"What's that?" She steeled herself for another clash of wills.

Jake's blue eyes rounded innocently. "Does this occasion call for breaking out the Hershey's bar?"

It was Kelly's turn to groan. "No! Absolutely not!" She pummeled his ribs with softly doubled fists, grateful for the release it gave her. "Forget about chocolate!" she stormed good-naturedly. "On this trek, we're only eating natural, wholesome foods, like fiddleheads and acorns and wild morels and—"

Jake kissed her again.

This time there was no chance to brace against her reaction. His arms caught her hard against him. His lips captured hers with a sureness that made her head swim. Kelly whimpered, squirming feebly in an effort to break away, but her resistance was no more than a sham. She had *wanted* this. She had wished for it, against all common sense and reason.

Jake's devilish mouth teased and sucked and nibbled, drawing her out of herself until she was lost in a world of dark, moist sensation. The rain pattered softly around them. Kelly felt it on her closed eyelids as her hood fell back. Her lips tasted raindrops sweetened by his skin. She quivered as long-buried yearnings stirred inside her. Deep in her body, desire throbbed like a swollen spring bud, aching to blossom.

No! She couldn't let it happen....

It was the rough contact of his tongue that finally reawakened her fear. The first warm thrust triggered an avalanche of panic that overrode everything, even her need. Kelly's pulse broke into a rabbity scramble as she began to struggle in earnest, twisting and pushing in his arms.

He released her so abruptly that she swung outward with a little cry and stumbled against the base of a massive spruce. Hot-faced and ashamed, she crouched there, tears stinging her eyes.

Jake's arms had fallen to his sides. He stood gazing at her across the breadth of the trail, his expression blending confusion and concern.

"Kelly, if I've hurt you—"

"You haven't. None of this is your fault."

"Look." His breath whooshed out in a burst of frustration. "I'm sorry I misread you. If I hadn't thought you *wanted* me to kiss you—"

"What else *could* you have thought?" Her anguished whisper cut off his words. "I told you, it was my fault, not yours. You did what any red-blooded male would do under the circumstances."

Dismayed, he shook his head. "Whatever you're thinking, Kelly, I would never have taken advantage of you. As corny as it may sound, I respect you too much for that."

"Respect?" The word hissed out of her like an epithet. "You don't even know me, Jake! You don't know anything about me!"

"I know enough," he said gently. "I've seen your resourcefulness, your courage—"

"Oh, stop it!" Her fist struck the tree trunk, knuckles scraping on the rough bark. Above her head, a jay burst out of the foliage in a squawking explosion of feathers. Startled into silence, Kelly watched the bird as it fluttered into the mist. This was no time to behave like a hysterical fool, she reminded herself. Whatever had happened between them, Jake was still her passenger, her responsibility. It was up to her to put this idiocy aside and get them both to safety.

Setting her jaw, she eased her weight onto her feet, braced her legs and took a tentative step. Beneath her, the injured ankle twisted, shooting hot arrows through her body. Kelly bit back a gasp of pain and forced herself to keep moving. She had to be strong. She couldn't let herself depend on—

"Oh!" The cry burst out of her as her leg buckled. Helpless against the pain, she pitched sideways. The ground rushed up to meet her.

Suddenly Jake's strong hands were there. She felt them catching her, lifting her, bracing her elbows as she stood again. He held her decorously, as if she were some priceless porcelain object that might shatter at his touch.

"It's all right, Kelly," he murmured, his voice a rasp in her ear. "There may be things about you I don't understand, but you don't have to worry about leaning on me. Nothing else is going to happen, I promise. You have my word on it."

For the space of a breath, Kelly hesitated. Then, unable to doubt the truth of his words, she sagged wearily against him. As his arm circled her waist, her eyes blinked away a blur of tears.

"Come on," she whispered. "Let's move it, Drummond."

Chapter Six

The August sun hovered above the horizon, gleaming through the low-lying fog like an iridescent balloon. Darkness was still hours away—Jake had been in Alaska long enough to anticipate that. All the same, his body had begun to protest every step. Every exhausted cell and fiber argued that it was evening, time to rest.

Kelly plodded beside him in weary silence. They had chatted companionably through most of the afternoon—safe, neutral topics like politics, books and art. For a young woman who'd spent her life on a remote island, she was surprising well-informed. She was also articulate, incisive, even witty, as long as their conversation steered clear of personal matters.

And it did. Jake made sure of that. Their clash back on the trail, when he'd kissed her, had left them both drained and frustrated. They existed now in a state of armed truce, hoarding what little strength remained for survival. Neither of them was up to another skirmish.

The rain had thinned to a silvery mist. Kelly had slipped back the hood of her poncho. Her skin glowed like mother-of-pearl in the eerie northern twilight. She looked beautiful, Jake thought; and in spite of everything, he found himself aching to draw her into his arms again and warm his lips against the rosebud sweetness of her mouth.

He cursed himself back to his senses. Kissing Kelly had been delicious, but he'd never met a more misreadable female in his life. He had sworn not to touch her. But what was he supposed to think, when she'd grabbed his neck and kissed him till his toes curled in his boots? It made some kind of sense that she would want to be kissed back. It had flashed through his mind, in fact, that Kelly Ryan might be a lot more worldly than she appeared. So he'd followed his instincts—and ended up feeling like a first-class heel.

He didn't need those kind of games, Jake counseled himself. From now on, he'd stick with women who didn't mind letting him know what the score was. Girls like Kelly, who bombarded a man with mixed signals, would be strictly off-limits.

"Jake! Look!" Her cry startled him out of his musings. He was instantly alert, nerves jangling, eyes blinking dazedly into the murky shadows.

"What is it?" he muttered. "I don't see a thing!"

"It's blueberries!" She was dancing like a puppy. "A whole thicket of them—see? A dozen yards ahead and to your left!"

"Blueberries..." Jake's tired tongue tripped over the word. "And next you'll be telling me there's a five-star hotel around the next bend, complete with king-size beds and a hot tub in every—"

"Oh, will you stop that? Just *look!*" She was pointing now, hopping excitedly on her one sound leg. Jake peered into the mist-blurred shadows of the forest. He could just make out the dark, leafy clumps of berry bushes, sagging under the weight of juicy, ripe fruit.

"I'll be damned!" he muttered, stumbling like a drunkard toward the berry patch and pulling her with him.

"Wait!" She clawed at his sleeve, resisting urgently. "We can't just dive in! You and I aren't the only creatures who like blueberries!"

Jake froze as her words sank in. He stared into the fog, half expecting to see a nine-foot bruin come barreling out of the bushes. But he saw nothing, heard nothing, except the drip of fallen rain from overhead spruce boughs.

"Here." Kelly had found a fist-size green cone on the trail. "I'll toss this into the berry thicket. You keep the flare gun handy, and be ready to sprint for the nearest tree."

Jake checked the flare pistol, wondering how many years it had lain unused in the plane. A drop of sweat trickled down his temple as Kelly's arm curved tensely back from the shoulder.

She knew how to throw. The spruce cone whined through the air, arched over the berry clump and dropped squarely into its center. For a split second nothing happened. Then pandemonium broke loose. Instinctively, Jake thrust Kelly behind him. He swung the flare gun toward the thicket as sound and motion exploded from the foliage.

Birds. Nothing but birds.

Jake's knees sagged as the covey of squawking brown quail scattered into the trees. From behind him, Kelly's breath eased out in a long, low whistle.

"It's okay," she said softly. "If there was a bear in that thicket, we'd have met him by now. Come on, let's get some berries."

The blueberries were prime—swollen with summer ripeness and clustered so thickly that their wet weight threatened to snap the fragile bushes. Savoring the anticipation, Jake picked a single berry and rolled it on his tongue. It was exquisitely cool, its silk-suede skin barely containing the juice inside. At the first slight pressure it burst, showering the inside of his mouth with sweetness.

Suddenly ravenous, he stripped off a handful of berries and tossed them into his mouth. He saw that Kelly was doing the same thing. Her cheeks were as round as a chipmunk's. A dainty blue trickle had escaped the corner of her mouth to thread a path to her chin. She wiped it away with the back of her hand, her green-flecked eyes dancing with a pleasure that was almost—damn it—erotic.

Jake forced himself to concentrate on filling his belly. He had eaten canned blueberries, frozen blueberries and blueberries in pies. He'd even sampled fresh ones from Seattle's Public Market. But he had never experienced the bursting freshness of berries right off the bush. Never had he imagined anything could taste so sinfully good. Maybe it was because he'd been trekking all afternoon in the cool, damp air. Maybe it was just because he was so hungry. Or maybe the whole experience had something to do with Kelly.

His sidelong glance met her eyes. She grinned, showing off a tongue tip that was stained a dark purplish blue. If he were to kiss her now, Jake fantasized, her mouth would taste like the berries—darkly sweet, rich as summer wine.

What, he wondered idly, would the rest of her taste like?

Kelly glanced shyly away, almost as if she sensed what he was thinking. "Don't gobble down too many of these," she cautioned. "I know they're wonderful, but on an empty stomach—"

"I get the picture." Jake paused in his eating. His eyes lingered on a droplet of berry juice that clung like a jewel to the edge of her lower lip. He imagined capturing her chin with his fingertips, then bending gently down to lick away the tiny dot of sweetness from . . .

What in blazes was he trying to do, drive himself crazy?

"Those birds had me going for a minute," he said, groping for a distraction. "I thought we'd found ourselves a bear for sure."

"So did I." She laughed thinly. "But I did admire the way you stepped in front of me with that silly flare gun. Most of the men I know would've been halfway to Angoon by now."

Unexpectedly, he warmed to her praise. "Maybe you know the wrong men. Or maybe the others know more about what they'd be dealing with. I've never seen a bear in the wild. In fact—" Jake managed a wry chuckle. "In fact I'm beginning to wonder if these so-called bears of yours are some kind of bogeyman you Alaskans invented to scare green cheechakos like me."

For a long moment Kelly did not answer him. Her eyes were staring intently at the ground. "Come take a look," she said, her voice a tight-throated whisper. "This is something you ought to see."

Moving to her side, Jake followed the direction of her gaze. There, pressed into the soft earth at the base of a bush, was a single footprint.

It looked, at first glance, like the mark of a rounded human foot. Only it was bigger, Jake realized, comparing it to his own size eleven boot. *Much* bigger.

He felt the tingle along his arms as the hairs stood on end. "How fresh do you think that print is?" he muttered between clenched teeth.

"Pretty fresh. See, there's hardly any rainwater in it. And judging from his track, I'd say he's a big one—nine feet, at least."

Jake swallowed hard. "I don't know about you, but I just ost my appetite for berries. Let's get the hell out of here." He grabbed Kelly's arm, battling the natural urge to run. The bear, in all likelihood, would know exactly where they vere. Their best chance of escaping in one piece lay in an unhurried getaway.

Kelly trembled against him as they picked their way back o the main trail. Her earlier talk about bears had been flip-vant and filled with bravado. But right now, she was clearly s scared as he was.

A surge of protectiveness welled up in Jake's chest. He ound himself wanting to gather her in his arms, to stroke ner dark, damp curls and reassure her that everything would be all right as long as he was here to take care of her. But vhat a joke that would be. Except for the next-to-useless flare pistol, he was unarmed. He was also lost, cold, tired and completely out of his element. Jake had never felt more helpless—except on the day the doctors showed him the re-ults of Ann's brain scan.

"Does it bother you to talk about your wife?"

Kelly's question jolted him, coming as it did from out of nowhere, with no tie to anything they'd been saying or do-ng. He stared at her, not knowing how to answer.

"If it does, we can talk about something else," she added wiftly. "But we do need to keep up some kind of dialogue or the bears, and unless you feel like doing Hank Williams gain—" Her breath caught in a nervous little hiccup. "It's ust that her picture is so lovely. I can't help wanting to know more about her. For instance—"

She broke off, dismayed by the expression on his face. "I guess it *does* bother you, doesn't it? I'm sorry. I have this way of dredging up things that are better left alone. My grandma does it, too. It must be genetic."

"No, it's all right," Jake heard himself saying. "It's just that I'm not used to talking much about Ann. It's hard. And it never seems to get any easier, even after nineteen months."

"Maybe talking would help you."

"Help me? Lord, do I look like that much of a basket case?"

Her eyes softened. "There's a lot I may not know, Jake, but I'm not blind. When a man's hurting as much as you are, it shows."

Jake stared into the mist-enshrouded forest, struggling to evade the burning honesty of Kelly's gaze. He'd been running away from the anguish of Ann's loss from the moment he stumbled out of her hospital room. Over the past nineteen months, work and more work—fifteen-hour days, six-day weeks—interspersed with frenetic socializing, had become his routine and his refuge. He'd scarcely allowed himself time to *think* about Ann, let alone talk about her.

Well-meaning friends had collaborated in his avoidance. In their concern, they'd tiptoed around Ann's death, as if they were trying to deny she'd ever lived. They'd refused to let him alone, tugging him out of his solitude with their urgings to come play tennis, to drag himself to the yacht club parties, to meet and bed new women. Anything but dwelling on Ann. Anything but dealing with the pain.

Now here was Kelly, in her innocent wisdom, inviting him to talk.

Oh, he knew where she was coming from. Talking about Ann would be a surefire way to douse the spark that had flared between them earlier. Ann's lovely ghost would be the perfect chaperon—all-seeing, all-knowing, never leaving them alone.

Was that what Kelly Ryan wanted? Fine. Maybe he just ought to let her have it.

"So, where would you like me to begin?" Jake's voice carried a sharper edge than he'd intended. Kelly's waist strained against his hand.

"You don't have to do this," she said quietly.

"No, it's fine," he protested, knowing he'd stung her, and not particularly liking himself for it. "Just understand that it won't be painless."

"I understand." She paused to fish the ancient brass compass out of her pocket and recheck their direction. Then she fell into step with him once more. "Tell me about— Oh, why not start with how you met her?"

"How I met her." Jake exhaled raggedly, relieved that Kelly had at least started with something easy. "It was seven years ago, in Seattle. I presented a bid to her father's lumber company. Ann was filling in for his receptionist that week. We got the bid, and I asked her out to help me celebrate."

"And where did you go?" Kelly's voice was as gentle as rain.

"I took her to this great little seafood place on the Sound. Bruno's, it was called—it closed a few months later, and we never had the chance to go back. But the food was wonderful. I had lobster. She had swordfish...." Jake's throat tightened as the memory washed over him—moon-silvered waves lapping the rocks; the lonesome cry of foghorns; white candles on the table, their flames miniaturized in the gray velvet mirrors of Ann's eyes.

Suddenly, as if a dam had burst, the words came. They poured out from the floodgates of his memory—all the good times he and Ann had enjoyed together. Summer afternoons on the Sound, with cold beer and pastrami sandwiches and wind billowing the sails of their boat. The killer tennis matches which she'd won as often as he had. The hillside house, a wedding gift from her parents, which Ann had decorated to perfection. The parties. The friends. The laughter.

Kelly listened sweetly through it all, her jade-flecked eyes deep with understanding. If Jake hesitated, her soft-spoken questions would nudge him on, freeing yet another rush of bittersweet memories.

He knew he was talking too much, probably boring her, probably, in fact, being a complete pain in the butt. But Kelly didn't seem to mind. Her gentle acceptance surrounded him with warmth, drawing him out of his long, cold silence.

She could not know what a precious gift she was giving him.

"So, what did Ann do while you were working so hard? Did she have a career of her own?"

Kelly forced herself to keep asking questions. It wasn't easy, but it was working. She was already seeing Ann Drummond through Jake's eyes—Ann's beauty, her warmth, her graciousness and her accomplishments. More to the point, she was beginning to understand just how much Jake had loved—and *still* loved—his wife.

The rest of her strategy was easy. All she had to do was compare her own tattered inadequacies with Ann's perfection. From there, the truth loomed as large and undeniable as a mountain. Jake's kiss had been nothing more than a stray impulse. He could never be interested in someone like her. Not after Ann.

"She didn't really need a job," Jake was saying. "A lot of what I earned went back into the business, but Ann's grandfather was one of Seattle's big lumber barons. Before he died, he set up trust funds for each of his granddaughters. He was more than generous."

Jake's eyes narrowed, as if he were shutting in some emotion he did not want Kelly to see. "Ann did manage to keep busy. She did full-time volunteer work, most of it with underprivileged children. She used to say it was the next best thing to having kids of her own."

Kelly remembered then what he'd told her earlier, about his wife's not being able to bear children. Throwing tact to the wind, she forced herself to ask another question.

"If Ann wanted a family so much, why didn't you try to adopt sooner?"

She had pushed too hard. The glance Jake flashed her was shot with pain. Turning away without an answer, he stared into the trees. His silence was so deep that Kelly could hear the sob of wind in the spruce boughs. She could hear the muted crunch of their boot soles on the mossy trail. The wan daylight was almost spent. Before long they would need to start thinking about shelter for the night.

"Ann wanted to adopt." Jake's voice was flat, without expression. "She brought it up again and again—begged me, almost. But I kept putting her off. I was giving so much time to my work, I didn't feel up to being a father, too. Or maybe I was just afraid. My own father had died when I was two. I had no role model, no one to show me what to do—"

Where he supported her waist, Kelly felt Jake's hand quiver. His face, however, remained as impassive as stone. "That was where I failed her," he said. "She wanted a baby so much. It was the one thing I could have done to make those last years happier for her. But I was too damned selfish—"

His throat rippled in the fading light as he struggled to keep his emotions in check. "Finally I made an effort to see things her way. We went to an adoption agency and filed the papers—she was so damned excited about it, I felt like a heel for having made her wait so long." He paused, his breath catching in his throat. "Three weeks later we found out she was dying."

Jake's ribs jerked as he fought for self-control. Kelly pressed close to his side, knowing it would be useless to say anything. Words were only words. They had no power to wipe out the past or change the unchangeable. No one knew that better than she did.

They moved ahead like robots as the twilight crept around them. Kelly knew they should stop and try to build some kind of shelter for the night. But her exhausted body would obey only one command—that of putting one foot in front of the other. Her injured leg had long since gone numb. So had her mind.

The sharp hoot of an owl startled her back to her senses. It was darker than she remembered, and the moon lay like a cold silver disk above the trees. What on earth had happened? Had she been walking in her sleep?

"I think I see something!" Jake's taut voice hissed in her ear, and she realized he had been supporting her weight, all but carrying her spent body along the trail.

"Where? What is it?" Kelly went rigid against him, her eyes probing the moonlit darkness.

"Off that way." He nudged her to the right. "Through that tall clump of trees. Tell me my vision isn't playing tricks."

Kelly blinked the sleepiness out of her eyes. Through the feathery black silhouettes of spruce, she caught the unmistakable glint of moonlight on placid water—one of the myriad lakes that dotted the island. If she could figure out which one...

And then she saw what Jake was really looking at. A solid block of shadow, its flat, regular planes oddly out of place in a spot so wild.

"It's a cabin!" She broke loose from him, lurching on her swollen ankle. "A Forest Service cabin! Come on!"

"Then I'm not crazy." Jake stumbled after her, catching her arm. "Would there be anybody inside? A radio—?"

"Not likely. These little places are built for emergency shelter, that's all, and most of them are pretty primitive. But we should at least be able to get inside."

They circled the tiny, windowless log cabin to reach the front, which faced on the moon-silvered lake. As Kelly had guessed, the place was deserted. But the door, secured by a stick jammed into the hasp, was easy to open. It creaked inward on its rusty hinges, beckoning them into the inky darkness beyond.

"Hang on." Jake had dropped the pack on the stoop and was rummaging inside for the flashlight. Finding it, he cast a penetrating beam into the cabin's black interior.

A wood mouse streaked across the split-log floor and disappeared into a crack, but there was no other sign of life. The darting light revealed bare log walls, a set of high, empty shelves, a rusted cast-iron stove and, along one wall, a set of built-in bunks, one above the other. The whole cabin smelled of dampness and mold. Kelly shivered as thunder played tag across the far hilltops.

"At least it's got a roof and four walls," Jake muttered. "I can't say much for the decor, and the room service isn't quite up to first-class, but all in all, it has a certain ambience that—"

"Oh, will you just be still and get in here?" Kelly limped across the threshold, eyes following the exploring beam of Jake's flashlight. "And it's got something else! Just look!"

The light beam wavered. "I don't see what—"

"In that far corner—see—it's dry wood! A whole lovely, wonderful stack of it!"

Tired as he was, Jake chuckled at her enthusiasm. "Well, don't just stand there gaping, woman. Let me at that stove!"

Even with dry wood on hand, firing up the stove was far from easy. The cabin had not been used in a very long time. The stove's metal flue was blocked by a large, soggy, deserted bird's nest, which Jake had to climb on the roof to dislodge. While he was busy, Kelly discovered a hatchet in one dark corner and began splintering kindling off the chunky fire logs.

They'd been incredibly lucky to find this place, she reflected. Lucky in more ways than one. There weren't that many cabins on the island, and from the air, at least, she was familiar with all their locations. Maybe tomorrow, she'd be able to recognize the shape of the lake or spot other landmarks she recognized. Then she would know exactly where she and Jake were. She would know how to get herself and her passenger to safety.

And that, Kelly reminded herself, was all Jake Drummond could ever be to her—her passenger. She would return him to Juneau, and that would be the end of it. They would never meet again, which was just as well. They were two very different people, from two very different worlds.

How could she have kissed him, back there on the trail? What kind of madness had come over her?

Overhead, she could hear Jake's boots scrambling on the roof. The stovepipe rattled as he probed for the nest. Jake hadn't been so bad, once he'd gotten off his high horse, Kelly mused. He had been helpful, cheerful and a damned good sport. Given half a chance, she could almost *like* him.

He had kissed her, too. More than just a casual peck. If she hadn't pulled away, they could have been in serious trouble....

She brought the hatchet down full force, splintering a thick chunk off the side of the log and driving the blade into the wooden floor. Jake had spent the rest of the afternoon talking about his beautiful wife, Kelly reminded herself as she worked the hatchet loose. And she was being an idiot.

Pausing to rest, she picked up the flashlight from where it stood on its base and let the beam wander idly over the interior of the cabin. The light flickered on the narrow bunks, one built low, the other several feet over it.

At least the sleeping arrangements were above reproach. There would be no awkward moments, no silly innuendos. They could climb into their separate bunks and drift into innocent slumber, like two five-year-olds at a sleep over.

Kelly's thoughts scattered at the sound of Jake scrambling off the roof. A moment later, he stumbled in through the front door. His face and jacket were streaked with black soot, but he was grinning triumphantly.

Kelly feigned a scowl. "I thought you were going to *reach* into the flue, not climb into it."

"I did what had to be done! No bird's nest ever got the best of Jake Drummond!" He squatted in front of the open stove. "Hey, you haven't stoked it! Here I am up there, risking life and limb, and you're down here manicuring your nails!"

Kelly tossed a chip at him. "Haven't you ever laid a fire, Drummond? We needed kindling, and I've been cutting some. Now stand aside!"

She took his place in front of the stove and began a careful layering of chips, splinters and logs. By the time she'd finished, Jake had dug the match tin out of the pack. "You do the honors," he said.

Kelly lit one precious match and touched it to the splintered wood. The flame flickered tentatively, then caught the air as she blew on it. Slowly it began to spread. Within minutes the logs had started to blaze, flooding the small cabin with crackling warmth.

Jake had closed the door and was shrugging out of his wet coat. "Hey, I'm impressed. This little place is almost cozy. Now if we just had some hot cocoa with marshmallows...."

"Oh, no you don't!" Kelly slid the plastic poncho off her head, leaving on her dry jacket over her flannel shirt. The candy wrapper crackled as she patted her pocket. "You're not sweet-talking me out of this chocolate bar, Jake Drummond. I'm saving it for an emergency."

She found a handy nail and hung the poncho on it, then turned back to look at him. Her breath caught. Jake was standing in front of the open stove, rolling up the sleeves of his soft woolen shirt. In the cabin's warm darkness, his whole form seemed to rise out of a pool of firelight. Flame gilded his arms, his face, his wind-tousled hair. Kelly blinked, dazzled by the sight of him. Jake Drummond, the Golden Man—as glittering and unattainable as the sun.

The magic lasted only an instant. Then Jake turned away from the firelight, breaking the spell. His blue eyes glinted sardonically. "Define 'emergency,'" he said.

It took a split second for Kelly to realize he was still talking about the Hershey's bar. "Emergency. As in life-threatening circumstances," she retorted with a thrust of her chin.

"That works for me. I threaten your life, and you give me the chocolate."

Kelly stifled a giggle. "Absolutely not."

"Do you plan to sleep in that jacket?"

"If I have to."

"Stubborn little twit, aren't you?" He scowled in mock ferocity, then shrugged. "Sit down and stick out your foot. I want to have a look at that ankle."

She plopped onto the floor in front of the stove where she could bask in its delicious warmth. Crouching in front of her, Jake cradled her boot between his knees and began loosening the laces. He had become the Golden Man again, his blond curls gleaming like molten flame in the firelight. Kelly drank him in with her eyes.

"How does it feel?" He was working the collar of the boot down over her heel, his touch cautious.

"Sort of numb," Kelly muttered. "Could be worse."

"Swelling's gone down some.... Guess we can just leave the tape on it for now. But your toes feel like little blocks of ice. No wonder you're numb. Here, I'll warm you."

His fingertips began a gentle massaging of Kelly's foot, beginning at the toes and working inch by inch, with exquisite skill, up through the instep. The sensation was...slow heaven. Kelly closed her eyes as the warmth trickled up her leg. Little by little she felt the tension leaving her body. Her breath eased out in a long, contented sigh.

"How does that feel?" Jake asked, his thumbs working a soothing pathway along her arch.

"My...other foot is getting jealous."

"We can fix that." He braced Kelly's other boot between his knees and untied the laces. Shoe and sock slipped off in a single motion.

"Mmm!" A moan escaped Kelly's lips as his fingers began their devilish work. This time there was no injury to worry about. Jake unleashed the power in his hands, kneading her foot with deep pressure and long, sensual strokes. Kelly closed her eyes, transfixed by the sensations that rippled up her leg to invade her torso, kindling pools of silken heat in dark, forbidden places. Her nipples puckered into aching nubs. Oh, this wasn't a good idea. Not a good idea at all.

"How does it feel?" he murmured.

Kelly exhaled shakily. "Where did you learn to do this?"

"My mother had arthritis in her feet. The doctor taught me how to massage them for her. I did it for years."

"Well, all I can say is, I hope this didn't do to your mother what it's doing to me!"

His hands froze in midstroke. He stared at Kelly for an instant, taken aback by her frankness. Then he shook his head. A corner of his mouth twitched, to be followed by a burst of half-embarrassed laughter.

"Kelly Ryan, you're a breath of fresh air!" he exclaimed. "But I think, if we know what's good for us, we'll stop horsing around and get some sleep. Okay?"

"Uh-huh." Heart pounding like a rabbit's, Kelly retrieved her missing sock and tugged it back onto her naked, tingling foot. She felt deliciously warm, disturbingly content.

Jake glanced at the beds. "You can have the bottom bunk—I'll take the top. And since you're its owner, I guess the sleeping bag is all yours, too."

Catching the pack by a loose strap, he dragged out Kelly's down bag, and tossed it onto the lower bunk. Then he unfolded his cramped legs and eased his way to a standing position.

For a long moment he stood in the glow of the fire, stretching and basking like a big, tawny cougar. Kelly avoided him with her eyes as she unrolled her sleeping bag, shook it to fluff the feathers and laid it on the thin, faded mattress that served the lower bunk. Shedding her jacket, she wriggled into the snug down cocoon. Exhaustion washed over her like a flood. She closed her eyes.

Jake was unlacing his boots. Kelly heard them thud to the floor, one, then the other. Only then did he turn around to climb into his own high bed.

The wood frame creaked under his weight. Kelly heard his muffled curse. She opened her eyes to find him halfway out of the bunk, staring at the mattress.

"What's wrong?"

He sighed wearily. "Nothing. Go to sleep."

"Jake?" She sat up, blinking in the firelight.

"It's just that the roof's been leaking above the bed. The mattress up there is a soggy, mildewed mess." He swung to the floor again and padded over to the stove. "Don't worry, I'll be fine right here. I'm tired enough to sleep on a bed of nails."

Kelly tugged at the zipper on her sleeping bag. "At least take this—"

"Forget it. I'll be fine," he growled, stretching his six-foot frame on the hard floor. His shoulder bones bumped against the splintery surface as he struggled for a comfortable position.

Kelly snuggled into her warm down cloud. She closed her eyes, but sleep would not come. The image of Jake, trying to rest on the rough, cold boards, nagged at her conscience. There was one solution to the problem, but...

Don't even think about it, Kelly Ryan!

Twisting determinedly toward the wall, she screwed her eyes shut and tried to sleep. She could hear the scrape of Jake's belt against the wood as he shifted position. The frustrated rasp of his breathing filled the cabin's small space.

It was no use. Kelly couldn't stand it any longer.

She sat up and unzipped her sleeping bag all the way to the bottom. Squirming out of the way, she spread the unfolded bag over the bed like a quilt.

"Jake?" Kelly slid under the warm layer and flattened her body against the wall, leaving most of the bed space empty. Jake lay with his back toward her, blanketed in stubborn silence.

"I know you're awake," she said. "Turn around and look at me."

Muttering under his breath, Jake sat up. His hair was mussed, his eyes bloodshot.

Kelly raised the edge of the sleeping bag in unmistakable invitation. "We're both over twenty-one, and we're wearing all our clothes," she said. "Don't be an idiot."

Chapter Seven

No sane man could have refused Kelly's offer.

Jake eased himself onto the narrow bunk, drawing a mental line of demarcation down the middle of the mattress. Kelly was being kind, that was all. Her motives for inviting him into her bed were above questioning. He would behave himself as a proper guest.

Not that he was worried. He was exhausted—utterly spent in every muscle, nerve and fiber of his body. Misbehavior, Jake assured himself, was well beyond his capacity tonight.

He stretched himself full-length along the outside edge. The bed was warm, and soft, compared to the floor, at least. The down sleeping bag that covered him was sweet with that flowery, innocently sensual aroma he'd come to link so intimately with Kelly.

Jake closed his eyes, floating in a contentment that was as strange as it was unexpected. Cradled by Kelly's fragrance, and lulled by the silken sound of her breathing, he experienced a feeling of peace, a sense, almost, of having come home.

"Kelly?" he whispered, unsure of whether he was awake or dreaming.

"No pillow talk," she murmured foggily. "Just go to sleep."

Jake lay still, his mind probing the darkness around him. For the past nineteen months he had dreaded the time before sleep. That was when the memories came back, the lost joys, the bittersweet regrets.

But tonight was different. This darkness seemed almost friendly, its silence free of loneliness and pain. Jake had not been able to drift off like this since Ann . . .

The fire smoldered away to hissing red coals. Where light had been, shadows flooded the little cabin. Somewhere, far off in the night, a wolf howled at the phantom moon.

Jake stirred and opened his eyes. Kelly slumbered against him, curled into a little ball of warmth. Slowly he became aware that he had curved his own body to accommodate hers. They lay nested like spoons, oblivious to the heat that simmered along their line of contact.

Oblivious, that is, until now. Jake suddenly became aware that his fatigue was gone. Where Kelly's firm rump pressed his groin, he threatened to burst the zipper of his moleskin pants.

Groaning inwardly, he tried to ease away from her. But there was no place to go. The bunk was too narrow, and he had no desire to risk waking her by tumbling out of bed.

Trying to shift his position only made matters worse. The slightest move sent bursts of rocket fire jolting through his tormented loins. For all his agony, however, Jake knew better than to try midnight seduction on a girl like Kelly. His only alternative was to lie absolutely still and hope the madness would pass.

Kelly whimpered, stirring fitfully in the darkness. Jake ground his teeth as she moved against him with tiny, broken cries. Seconds passed before it occurred to him that something was wrong. She was trembling in her sleep. Her ribs jerked as silent sobs racked her body.

"Kelly?" Forgetting his own discomfort, Jake reached out for her in the darkness. His arms enfolded her, gathering her head and shoulders close against his chest. She came to him without resistance. Her hair was like silk against his cheek. Her tears were wet through his sleeve.

"It's all right, girl," he whispered tenderly. "You're having a bad dream, that's all. It'll go away."

Turning in his arms, she buried her face against his chest. The move eased the excruciating pressure on Jake's groin, but that was no longer his main concern. He cradled her gently against him, murmuring small comforts as she cried.

"Shhh..." His lips brushed her temple; he tasted the salty musk of her tears. "It's all right, Kelly.... I'm here. I won't let you go."

Her hands clutched at him like a frightened child's. What could be troubling her? he wondered. Kelly Ryan was one of the most fearless young women he had ever known. She was so competent, so open to life. What terrors tormented her in the dark night, when her defenses were down?

But what was he thinking? She'd had one hell of a traumatic experience *yesterday*. Going down in a tiny plane, crashing in the wilderness, would give anybody bad dreams. In fact, he could probably expect a few of his own in the nights ahead.

Bending closer, Jake nuzzled a lingering kiss in the middle of her forehead. Her skin was like cool satin, inviting his touch as she snuggled against him. Her soft, even breathing told him the nightmare had passed.

With a contented sigh, he shifted his position so they could both lie more comfortably. The fire in his loins had dimmed to a glow. Its urgency had bloomed into a tenderness so deep it almost brought tears to his eyes.

Kelly nestled against his side, as if needing his protection. Jake drew her closer with a sigh. In the warm darkness, he could hear the low crackle of embers in the stove. He could hear the scamper of a small animal running across the roof, and the growl of approaching thunder.

As the first raindrops pattered on the shingles, Jake closed his eyes. Drifting now, he let their rhythm carry him into slumber.

He awakened to morning birdcalls. Gray fingers of daylight probed through chinks in the logs, casting pallid sun dots on the floor. In the cold, silent stove, the fire had burned away to ashes.

Kelly slept in the circle of his arms. Her eyelashes lay like black silk fringes against rose-petal cheeks. Her dark curls spilled across Jake's sleeve. Beneath the flannel shirt, her breasts undulated gently in rhythm with her breathing. Jake battled the temptation to brush one with his hand, to cup its living softness and feel the delicate rise and fall against his palm. Or, even more enticing, to undo each of the tiny brown buttons that held her shirt, and—

But no, it would be a disaster. How could he expect to control his actions? He could not even control his thoughts.

Giving in to a lesser temptation, Jake brushed a furtive kiss along her hairline. Her skin was as sweet as morning dew. His lips lingered, then reluctantly moved away.

Oh, he had no illusions about himself and Kelly. In the real world, they had nothing in common. Their relationship, what there was of it, would end with their rescue. From that point, their lives would resume separate paths—paths that would probably never cross again.

But for all that, he owed her a tremendous debt. Her flying skill had saved his skin, but that was only the beginning. Kelly Ryan had blundered into his self-pitying, workaholic existence and forced him to take a second look. She had reawakened him to life.

How lovely she looked, how soft, lying there with the morning light on her face.

This wasn't helping, Jake scolded himself as he slid his trapped arm carefully out from under her neck. Another minute, and he wouldn't be able to keep his hands off her.

Kelly sighed in her sleep as he eased out of bed, but her eyelids did not even flutter. Yesterday's ordeal had exhausted her. He would leave her to rest until she awakened on her own.

Pinpricks tortured Jake's benumbed arm as he crept across the cabin, found his boots and slipped quietly through the front door. As he crossed the threshold, his breath caught in surprise. He stepped outside into a low-lying cloud that shrouded the cabin like a thick, white cocoon.

He had toyed with the idea of some close-by exploring, but the fog was so heavy, he could barely see ten feet from the door. Last night, in the moonlight, he and Kelly had seen a lake. This morning he could hear the sound of water lapping the reeds near the shore, but the lake itself was curtained in mist.

Lacing up his boots, he slipped behind the cabin to take care of his physical needs. By the time he returned, the first sliver of sun had edged above the horizon. The cloud had already begun to thin, dissolving into cottony wisps as the daylight warmed.

No sound came through the half-open doorway of the cabin. Still reluctant to wake Kelly, Jake stretched, rubbed his unshaven chin and settled himself on the low rock stoop to watch the morning.

It felt strange, just sitting like this. Most days, he hit the ground running—off to work, off to the club for an early-morning handball game, off to a board meeting, the airport, the boat marina, cramming activity into every spare minute. How long had it been since he'd simply sat still and watched the sun come up? Jake could not even remember, but it felt all right. It felt . . . fine.

By now, through the thinning fog, he could see the lake. It was surprisingly small—more like an overgrown pond than what he'd expected to see. The water was deep and still, a dark mirror for the slanting rays of sunlight that filtered through the trees. Clumps of horsetail rimmed the shallows.

An ancient hemlock rose from the far edge, its long-dead trunk twisted like a gnarled hand. As Jake watched, a dusky shape on the topmost limb stirred, fluttered and took wing—a heron, he realized, as the large bird, legs trailing like ribbons, flapped into the dawn. What had made it leave so suddenly? Was it possible that something had startled it? What if—?

Then Jake saw. And his heart froze in his chest.

Lumbering out of an alder thicket was a bigger bear than he had ever dreamed of, let alone seen. Its color was a rich, cinnamon brown, and it moved with the majesty of a czar, the absolute lord of its domain.

Either the bear had not noticed Jake, or it simply didn't care. Its pace was unhurried, even leisurely, as it paused to browse on a clump of salmonberries. Late-summer fat rippled beneath its prime coat. Muscles shifted like granite slabs along its massive neck and shoulders.

Jake's throat had gone dry as parchment. But strangely enough, he felt no fear—not even when the bear paused at the water's edge and swung its huge, dish-faced head directly toward the cabin. He was dimly aware that the water was no barrier at all, that the bear could cross the distance between them in seconds, and that even braced and barred, the cabin door might just as well be made of toothpicks.

But for all that, Jake's overriding emotion was not fear, but awe, mingled with a sense of destiny. It was almost as if life had led him here, to this place, this morning, and the sight of this splendid animal. A sense of peace crept over him, an assurance that the bear meant no harm—that he and Kelly would be safe.

As if his thoughts had summoned her, he felt Kelly's presence in the open doorway behind him. She crouched at his shoulder, scarcely breathing as they watched the bear together.

Her right hand crept forward to clutch Jake's upper arm. He felt the quivering pressure of her nails through his sleeve. His opposite hand moved slowly across his chest to capture her fingers and press them into his flesh.

The bear's nose swung in a wide arc, casting for the scent of danger. Satisfied, it lowered its head to the water. It drank in great, lapping gulps, like an oversize dog, until at last, thirst slaked, it gave the air a parting sniff, wheeled and lumbered off into the trees.

For the space of a long breath, Jake could not move. He sat clutching Kelly's hand to his arm, his heart pounding. No words would come together in his brain. The one action that did come to mind—sweeping Kelly into his arms and ravishing her with kisses—was something he dimly recalled having promised not to do. Still, from the way her fingers trembled, she clearly needed kissing. Maybe just this once...

He was on the verge of breaking his word when she pulled back her hand and moved away from him. She was almost on her feet before she spoke.

"I know exactly where we are now," she said quietly. "And I know where we need to go. If everything goes exactly right, you could be back in Juneau before the end of the day."

Jake could never have anticipated the impact of her words. A physical jolt went through his body. His pulse rate jumped. His muscles tightened like coiled springs. Tension clenched the back of his neck as the morning's magic fled and reality rushed in. He remembered the business, the SEA-MAR contract, the missed meeting. Maybe the Tlingit board had gotten word that the plane was down. Maybe, if he got back in time, there would still be a chance.

Kelly smoothed a circle on the wet earth and used the tip of her pocket knife to sketch out a crude map. "This is Admiralty Island," she said. "Here's the south end of it, where we saw my grandfather. And right here—" She jabbed the point into the ground for emphasis. "Here is where we are right now."

"How sure are you?" Jake leaned over the map, his voice hoarse with the effort of reining in his excitement.

"Positive. This cabin, this little dark lake—I've never been here before, but I've flown over them a hundred times. I know the whole island from the air. There's no other place like this."

"Then we can't be more than a few miles from the coast!" Jake strained forward like a runner at the starting gate. Kelly glanced at him in hidden dismay. For a little while, last night and this morning, she had almost believed she was seeing the *real* Jake—thoughtful, funny, even tender. But apparently she'd been wrong. The real Jake

Drummond was the brusque, impatient man she'd met at the fishing camp. Now, with the prospect of rescue in sight, he was back.

"How long before we can be there?" he demanded.

Kelly answered mechanically, masking her emotions. "Four or five hours, I'd say, if we keep up a steady pace. Of course, we ought to think about breakfast first. I saw a couple of fish jump out there in the lake. If we can rig some kind of trap and scare them into it, we should be able to—"

"That could take all morning," Jake interrupted. "What if a boat comes along the coast, and we're not there to hail it because we were fishing?"

Kelly shrugged. "Have it your way. I can be ready to go in ten minutes."

"Fine." He swung back toward the cabin door, then hesitated. "How's your ankle this morning?"

"Still swollen, but much better," Kelly said, wondering if he had any ideas about striking out on his own. "I'll still need some help, but we should make faster time than yesterday." She impaled him with a determined glare. "Don't even think about leaving me here. We've been over that before, and it isn't an option."

Before he could respond, she turned away and limped for the bushes that edged the far side of the cabin. Considering where she was headed, and the fact that her feet were jammed into unlaced boots, she managed her exit with a fair amount of dignity.

"Kelly."

She kept moving, pretending not to hear.

"Kelly, turn around and look at me." Jake's voice was too insistent to ignore. Kelly halted and made a show of glancing casually over her shoulder.

He was standing on the stoop where she had left him, one hand extended slightly toward her as if nothing had changed. Jake Drummond, the man with the computer-chip heart.

"What?" She flung the question like a gauntlet.

"Just this. I would never go off and leave you here. The idea hadn't even entered my mind."

For the space of a heartbeat, Kelly let his words touch her. She remembered last night after that terrible dream, how he'd cradled her in his arms, his warm lips skimming her hair, while she pretended to be asleep. Just for an instant, she allowed herself to believe that she might be becoming important to him. But it was no good. She tossed the illusion away, before she could become too attached to it.

"I just wanted to make sure," she said with a shrug. "The coast isn't very far, but you don't know this island. There's no guarantee you wouldn't get lost."

Ignoring the edge in her voice, he swung back toward the door. "I'll be inside, packing up the gear. Hurry."

"I said ten minutes. That's what you'll get—at least you will if we don't waste any more time talking."

Kelly pivoted on her sound foot and hobbled off toward the bushes, her eyes stinging. She *would* hurry, she resolved. In fact, she could hardly wait to get to the coast and signal a boat. The sooner Jake Drummond was out of her life, the happier she'd be.

She was trembling now, but whether from anger, fear or relief, she could not have said. She only knew that she had nearly let her guard down. She had almost allowed herself to trust an outsider again. And it would have been a disaster.

What if Jake had wanted to make love to her last night? What would she have done?

Hot quivers flashed through her at the very thought of it—Jake's naked, golden body entwined with hers in the firelight, his strong hands molding her breasts, his legs tangling wildly with hers as they—

But she was a fool to wonder. Jake *hadn't* tried to make love to her, or even shown any sign of wanting to. He had only held her, as he might have held a frightened child.

And even if he *had* tried, she wouldn't have let it happen. Foolish she might be, but she wasn't crazy.

Kelly combed her hair with her fingers, jerking at the tangles till her eyes watered. She hadn't asked for this—not any of it. Not the plane crash. Not being stranded alone with the most compellingly attractive man she'd ever met. Not the emotional tug-of-war that even now was threatening to tear her apart.

But *she would get through this,* she vowed. She would carry on with her head held high, and finish with her dignity—and her heart—intact.

This was not a matter of ego. It was a matter of personal survival. If she let Jake Drummond destroy her, Kelly knew, she would never have the courage to face life again.

As the sun mounted the sky, the weather began to clear. Jake gazed hopefully at the emerging blue patches, ears straining for the drone of a search plane.

Kelly moved along beside him, her eyes fixed on the trail. Her ankle seemed considerably better. Where she had needed his supporting arm yesterday, she now managed with a light—and chilly—hand on his shoulder. Jake found himself missing the close physical contact, but at least they were making faster progress. Even his empty stomach was forgotten in the headlong push for the coast.

Kelly called for a pause to check the compass. The land was more level here than where they'd crashed, but the coastal forest was so lush and rainy that even the bear trails were overgrown. It was beautiful country, but Jake had had his fill of being cold and damp. Next time he took a vacation, he vowed, he would try someplace like Cabo San Lucas.

"How much farther would you say it is?" he asked her, trying to fill the awkward silence between them.

She frowned, her eyes looking at the trees, at the clouds, anywhere but at him. "Not far. Maybe a couple more miles. But there's another storm coming in. A big one."

Jake glanced at the sky, which he could have sworn was still clearing. A new storm could delay their rescue for hours, even days. "How the blazes can you tell?"

She hesitated, put off, perhaps, by his demanding tone of voice. He could have phrased the question more gently, Jake chastised himself. The tension between them wasn't Kelly's fault. It was his. The hell of it was, there was nothing he could do.

He wished he could make her understand how it was with him—how, with rescue a near reality, the weight of responsibility had fallen on him like an avalanche. People's jobs were at stake; people's futures hung in the balance—men, women, families, all depending on the outcome of *his* performance. For a few hours, he'd almost been able to forget that. But it was no longer possible. If there was one chance in a hundred of salvaging the SEA-MAR contract, he had to fight for it. He had to get back to Juneau as soon as possible.

He looked at Kelly. Her chin was fixed in that stubborn little thrust he'd come to know so well. He knew she was hurt, but there was no way to make things better. Not without hurting her even more later on.

"So how can you tell about the storm?" he asked, making an effort to sound less impatient.

She began to walk again, her hand quivering on his shoulder like a grasshopper about to jump. "It's not easy to explain. People who live long enough on these islands develop a sixth sense, almost, about the weather. Something in the air. A smell. A prickly feeling, like an electric current. Somehow, we just *know*."

Jake scowled at a patch of sky, desperately willing it to grow larger, to prove her wrong. "And I suppose you can predict cold winters by the coats of woolly-bear caterpillars, too," he muttered.

Kelly shrugged. "So don't believe me. You'll see."

As if her words were prophetic, a fresh breeze struck Jake's face. A shuddering sigh rippled through the spruces. Overhead, the clouds began milling like cattle before a stampede.

Something in the air. Jake felt it, too—the crackle of impending danger.

"Come on!" Seizing her arm, Jake broke into a stumbling sprint that carried them a hundred yards before he realized that neither of them could sustain the pace. He halted abruptly in the lee of an elephant-size glacial boulder. Kelly's momentum swung her against him. She crashed into his chest and clung there, panting and frightened.

In the course of their run, the breeze had become a staggering gale, so fierce it threatened to rip them off their feet. Kelly's hair lashed her pale face. Jake wrapped her in his arms. They clung together, feet braced apart against its tearing force.

"We've got to keep going," he gasped. "If we can make it to the coast and send up a flare—"

"There's no time!" she shouted above the howl of the wind. "We've got to find some kind of cover! I've seen storms like this—"

Lightning cracked across the boiling sky. Rain began to
fall, pelting curtains of water that drenched them where they
stood. Raindrops washed down Kelly's face, plastering tendrils of hair to her skin. Jake fumbled the poncho out of the
pack and got it over her head, but she was already soaked.
She shivered against him as he guided her to the most sheltered part of the huge, granite monolith—a crevice just wide
enough for their two standing bodies. Here they would be
out of the brutal wind, but not the rain. It gushed through
the top of the crack, torrenting down on all sides of them.

"Here." Kelly struggled out of her plastic poncho. Lifting her arms, she spread it tent-fashion over both their
heads. Its folds fell around them, shrouding them to the
waist in translucent, olive-drab darkness.

Their bodies bumped in the tight space—breasts, hips,
knees and more. Resigning himself to the inevitable agony
her nearness brought him, Jake gathered her in his arms.
She was shivering beneath her wet jacket.

"Just hang on," he muttered. "This storm can't last forever. We're bound to get out of here soon."

Kelly's only response was the chattering of her teeth. Jake
tightened his arms, surrounding her with his own soggy
warmth. He thought about the words he'd just spoken—
hell, he didn't know what he was talking about. The storm
could last for days. They could be stranded right here.

Alone, he might have chosen to wade out into the deluge
and strike for the coast. But Kelly was chilled, hurt and exhausted. She was in no condition to cover the distance, not
in this weather. And there was no way he could leave her
behind.

Tucking her small, wet head beneath his chin, Jake forced
all thoughts of the SEA-MAR meeting from his mind.
"Take it easy," he whispered against her hair. "I'm here,
Kelly. I'll warm you."

* * *

Kelly closed her eyes. She could feel Jake's heart drumming against her ear in a low counterpoint to the rain. He had unbuttoned his Gore-Tex jacket and opened the front to enfold her in its dry warmth. His arms held it around her.

She pressed her face to his shirt. The soft wool tickled her cheek. It smelled of wood smoke and man sweat, and ever-so-faintly of the leathery after-shave Jake had worn when he boarded the Beaver. That had been twenty-four hours ago. It seemed more like twenty-four days, Kelly reflected as she inhaled the comfortingly pungent scent. No, it seemed more like a lifetime.

She lifted her head. "Jake, I'm sorry," she whispered above the rain's wild patter.

"Sorry for what?" His throat moved against her hair. She felt his voice as a growl against her temple.

"Everything. I'm sorry the plane crashed. I'm sorry I got hurt and slowed us down. I'm sorry you're not back in Juneau right now, celebrating your new shipping contract."

"What a crazy girl you are!" His voice was determinedly cheerful. "If I hadn't been so muleheaded about taking off in bad weather, none of this would have happened."

"I knew better than to try it. I should have stood up to you. But you were so damned bombastic and self-important. I was almost looking forward to getting you up in that turbulent air and seeing you lose your cookies!"

"Were you, now? Well, it didn't happen, did it?"

"No," Kelly conceded with a little laugh. "You're tougher than you look, Jake Drummond."

"You're a pretty tough lady yourself, Kelly Ryan."

His arms tightened around her. Deep in Kelly's body, their gentle pressure thawed rivulets of response. She felt the stirring of hungers too long buried, the ache of needs too long imprisoned; and suddenly she was too tired, too lost and too scared to hold them back anymore.

Unbidden, her hands slid around his rib cage until she was holding him beneath his coat. Jake's breath caught with a hard gasp. His heart jumped against her ear. A shudder went through him as his own hands began to move.

Kelly's lips parted as his fingers found the hem of her jacket and slipped underneath to splay on her back. Their warmth shot like flame through the worn, wet flannel of her shirt. She moaned softly, her spine arching like a cat's to his touch as his strong hands kneaded each cold-clenched muscle, leaving it warm and pliant. Neither of them spoke, but the wordless, primitive dialogue of their breathing filled the darkness and blended with the pounding rain.

Half-dizzy, Kelly buried her face against his shirt. Jake had barely touched her, but she was liquid inside, molten with her own heat. Surely he would stop. He would laugh, make a joke or even say something sardonic and hurtful. Then the torment would end, as it always did.

But not this time. His right hand abandoned her back. His knuckles grazed her breast as the fingers fumbled for her chin. Kelly's heart stopped as he nudged her face up to his. His mouth brushed her trembling lips, softly, with such exquisite restraint that she could have cried out with the pain of it. Wild with need, she stretched upward on tiptoe, wanting more.

Jake groaned in frustration. "Damn it, Kelly, I gave you my word," he muttered. "I promised you nothing would—"

His noble speech ended in a gasp as her hand caught the back of his neck. Hungrily, she pulled his head down to hers. He responded with a quivering moan, and then his mouth crushed her eager lips.

Kelly felt her whole world spinning like a Chinese rocket. She arched upward in the darkness, opening to his kiss as he caught her close. His hands—*sweet heaven, yes*—they were tugging at the hem of her shirt, pulling it loose from the waistband of her khakis. She whimpered as his fingertips slid up her back, their touch like rough, cool silk on her bare skin.

A frantic voice inside her clamored that this was crazy, that this was the last thing she should be doing. But its rationality foundered in the whirlpool of her own desire. Kelly knew she was out of control, but she could no more stop herself than she could stop a waterfall from plunging off a precipice—no more than she could stop the beating of her own heart.

Their lips clung and parted. Jake's breath came hard as he caught her closer. Kelly nestled her face in the warm hollow of his throat and gave herself up to the tactile bliss of his moving hands. Inch by inch, his fingers separated the wet flannel from her skin, warmly massaging each curve of her spine. She closed her eyes, scarcely able to breathe as they hesitated, then slid upward under the back of her bra.

Outside the glowing darkness of the poncho, the rain drummed a steady patter. Kelly's heart jumped as Jake's hand explored the sensitive flesh beneath the elastic. She arched against him with a tiny moan.

"Kelly—" His lips moved against her hair.

"It's all right," she whispered. "I understand. This is now. And now is all there is."

There, she had said it. She had absolved herself of any expectations. He would know that he didn't have to stay, didn't have to feel guilty when he walked away from her. She had made everything safe for them both.

Jake murmured something she could not quite hear. His mouth caressed her temple, her closed eyelids. Then, suddenly, his breath went raw. His fingers eased forward beneath the stretchy cotton knit to stroke the swelling outer curve of her breast.

Kelly tensed. Then her breath rushed out in a torment of ecstasy as her flesh melted into his palm. Her head fell back as his hand formed a tender cup that moved in silken circles, molding, shaping her softness. Her teeth pressed into her lower lip as his thumb found the sensitive areola of her nipple and gently teased it to a throbbing bud. Heat waves rippled through her body, fed by the secret flame that blazed between her thighs.

Through layers of clothing, the iron-hard pressure of his desire swelled against her belly. Aching for release, Kelly strained upward, butting with her hips, frantic for that sweet-hot contact, that—

No!

She stiffened in his embrace as long-dormant alarms screamed in her head. She had to stop. She couldn't lose control—not after what had happened before.

"Kelly?" Jake had noticed the change in her. His hand stilled on her breast, then swiftly withdrew. His arms dropped to his sides.

"Kelly, if I've done anything to hurt you—"

"Hurt me?" With a brittle laugh, she squeezed away from him in the tiny space and began stuffing her shirt back into the waistband of her trousers. "Not yet, you haven't. But we've got to get out of here, before we both end up sorry."

"Listen," he said, looking pained. "If it's me you're worried about—"

"Jake, it isn't you." Kelly's voice trembled. Her fingers felt as thick as her grandma's dumplings as she struggled to work the damp shirt under her belt. "Oh, believe me, it isn't you. You'd be safer dancing a tango with that bear we saw this morning than crammed in here with—"

"Hey! Give me some credit, lady! You didn't exactly have to knock me down and tie me up, did you?" Jake's attempt at lightness fell flat. Abandoning the effort, he lifted the hem of the poncho and peered glumly out at the storm.

"What's it looking like?" Kelly asked.

"Rain's about the same. But I'd say the wind's let up a little."

"Then let's go!" She jerked up the zipper on her damp jacket. "Come on, we can make it!"

"Kelly, you're wet, you're cold—"

"Wet, I'll concede. Cold?" She shrugged. "Cold is something we could both use right now."

"You're hurt, too. And your ankle's getting worse again, I could tell when we got here."

"Jake, please." The look she cast him was so fraught with desperation that he shook his head.

"All right," he said softly. "If you're that anxious to get out of here, we'll try it. But we'll take it easy, okay?"

"Okay. Let's go." Kelly jerked the poncho down over her head and plunged out in front of him, into the driving rain. She needed to get away from here, away from the torment of this man's nearness. She needed to get home, where she felt safe.

Her first half-dozen strides carried her well ahead of him. Then her weak ankle buckled beneath her weight. She lurched forward, and would have fallen if Jake hadn't sprung to catch her.

She felt his arms around her again, hands gripping her shoulders, fiercely this time. Rain and tears blurred his expression, but his voice, when he spoke, grated with suppressed anger.

"I said we'd take it easy! I don't know what's eating you, Kelly Ryan, but if you don't slow down, so help me, I'll sling you over my shoulder and carry you!"

Kelly slumped against him in resignation. For a few seconds she allowed herself to rest, gathering all that was left of her strength. Then, squaring her shoulders, she forced herself to look into Jake's stormy blue eyes. She had to be strong, she reminded herself. She had to show him he couldn't hurt her.

"I'm all right." Her whisper grated with determination. "I can make it. I'll be fine."

Chapter Eight

Jake saw the world through cold, gray curtains of water. Rain pelted on his bare head and drizzled down the back of his upturned collar. It seeped through the seams of his "waterproof" boots, turning his thick wool socks into mushy mats that squished with each step he took.

Time had blurred since he and Kelly left the shelter of the rock, but he wild-guessed that at least an hour had passed. Maybe even two. By now, the coast had to be very near, but the trees still walled them in on all sides.

He glanced at Kelly where she trudged beside him, lost in the hood of her poncho. Damn it, he'd give anything to know what was going on inside that pretty, stubborn head of hers. Back there in the crack of the boulder, she'd ignited like tinder in his arms. Now she seemed as cold and remote as the moon.

Oh, he could understand at least some of it. Kelly was warm and womanly. She'd responded to him exactly the same way he'd responded to her, and the chemistry had been like touching a match to gasoline. But she wasn't stupid. She had more sense than to get involved with someone like him—an outsider, who would soon be on his way. If he could have chalked up her reaction to an attack of good judgment, he wouldn't be so troubled now.

But there'd been more to it than that. When she'd pulled away from him, he'd glimpsed something in her eyes. It was pain, he realized—an anguish as sharp and profound as his own.

He remembered last night, how he had held her as she sobbed in her sleep. He'd thought it was the crash, but no, he realized now, it had to be more than that. Something was haunting Kelly Ryan.

"Listen! I hear something." Kelly's words, the first she'd spoken in the last half mile, broke into his thoughts.

"What?" Jake was instantly alert. His ears strained to hear above the dull patter of the rain. "I don't—"

"Shh! Listen." She was quivering with excitement. "Jake, it sounds like—"

He touched a finger to her mouth as his own ears caught the sound. Even muffled by the trees and the rain, it was unmistakable now—the low, throbbing drone of an outboard motor. But it was getting fainter, Jake suddenly realized. It had moved past them and was traveling away.

"Come on!" Jake seized Kelly's waist and began running toward the sound, dragging her with him.

"No!" She struggled to stop him. "We won't make it in time! We've got to shoot off our flare!"

The loaded flare pistol had been stowed to keep it dry. Kelly ripped it out of the pack, aimed it straight up and pulled the trigger. The flare screamed into the rain-black sky. Clouds flashed ghostly fire as it burst overhead in a shower of sparks, then died away into a stillness that was broken only by the drumming rain.

They could no longer hear the sound of the motor.

Jake reached out and gripped Kelly's hand. Her small, rough fingers curled between his as they both held their breath. Maybe the boat had been too far away for anyone on board to notice the flare. Maybe there'd been no boat at all. Maybe they had both imagined the sound because they'd wanted so badly to hear it.

Rain trickled down Jake's face. It dripped off the end of Kelly's nose where it stuck out past the edge of her hood. She turned her face toward him and attempted a tremulous smile that didn't quite work.

"Oh, damn!" she whispered. "Damn, damn, damn!"

Jake gave her shoulder an awkward squeeze. "There'll be another boat," he said.

"But not another flare. That was our only—"

She broke off, transfixed by something in the distance. "Jake! The boat! I think it's coming back!"

Jake cupped his ears, straining to hear above the rain. The drone of the motor was as faint as a fly buzz, but it was getting stronger by the second.

"Come on!" He plunged ahead, sweeping her up with him, half carrying her toward the beach. By now, the throb of the motor was clearly audible, drowning out even the heavy beat of the rain. They burst out of the trees to see a small wooden dory, with a lone man at the tiller, bucking the choppy waves offshore.

"Hey! Over here!" They knew the man had probably seen them, but all the same, they danced and yelled like lunatics. As the dory made for shore, Jake sprinted forward and caught the line to drag its bow onto the gravelly beach.

The lone boatman cut the outboard and raised it clear of the bottom. Beneath the hood of his yellow slicker, his face was broad and young and dark. Tlingit, Jake quickly surmised. And not a stranger. He was grinning broadly at Kelly.

"Hey, this is my lucky day! Half the boats in Angoon are out searching for you, and I win the prize! Your gram and gramps are going to be mighty happy about this!"

"You don't know how grateful we are to see you!" Kelly leaned over the gunwale and gave him a tired hug. Looking on, Jake felt an unexpected twinge of jealousy. Was the young Tlingit just a friend, or was he more? And why should it make any difference? What the hell—they'd been rescued, hadn't they?

Kelly remembered her manners. "Jake, this is Eddie Willis, from Angoon. We went to school together. Eddie, meet Jake Drummond, my passenger."

Passenger. A safe and proper description if there ever was one, Jake groused. Kelly hadn't even seen fit to introduce him as her friend.

Eddie's grin flashed again as he extended a hard, brown hand. "Climb in, you two, and let's head for the barn. I've been fighting this damn storm all afternoon, and there's another one due in tonight that's supposed to be even worse. Come on. I can use you to help bail out the rain."

Kelly was unsteady on her feet, as if the ordeal had finally caught up with her. Eddie took her hands and helped her into the dory, leaving Jake to shove the craft off the gravel bar and vault into the bow. The outboard sputtered to life, then roared as Eddie gunned it to full speed. The small dory bounded over the whitecaps on a course that paralleled the beach.

"Where'd you go down?" Eddie shouted above the noise.

"I'm not sure. It was so foggy." Kelly looked pale, Jake thought. She huddled into her poncho, and when she spoke, each word seemed to tax her strength. Jake fought the urge to slide close to her and wrap her in his arms. That wouldn't

lo, he reminded himself. They weren't alone in the wild anymore. They'd been rescued, and he was still trying to figure
out Kelly's relationship with their rescuer.

Eddie wiped the salt spray off his face. "How'd the plane
hold up?"

Kelly shook her head. Her expression left no room for
doubt about the Beaver's condition, but she seemed too exhausted to say any more.

Jake took up the conversation for her. "Kelly did a great
job of landing, but from the looks of the plane, we were
damned lucky to have walked away. It was pretty well de-
molished. Even the radio was gone. We weren't able to let
anybody know what had happened."

Eddie steered the dory around a jutting rock. The little
boat bounced from wave to wave with a repetitive, jarring
smack. "Oh, we knew, all right. Kelly's grandpa got the last
distress call and radioed Juneau. When you didn't come in,
everybody knew you'd gone down. Hell, you were even on
the six o'clock news last night."

Jake went limp as relief washed over him. The SEA-MAR
board would know, then, why he hadn't shown up for the
meeting. There was still hope that they would put off their
decision, that they would give him a second chance.

He glanced around the boat for any sign of a radio. There
was none. "I'll be needing to make some calls," he said.

Eddie squinted at him through the rain. "You could do a
phone patch from Angoon. But Kelly's place is closer. We'll
be there in a couple of hours, if this damned weather doesn't
get any worse. Kelly's grandpa's got a radio—a real an-
tique, but it works. Meanwhile, man, this boat's filling up
with rain. There's a can under your seat. Be my guest."

Glancing down, Jake saw that water was sloshing around
his boots. He grabbed the floating coffee can and started
bailing. It felt good to be occupied. Anything was better

than sitting idle, with his mind racing at ninety miles an hour.

He took a second to glance at his watch. It was two o'clock. It would be four by the time they got to Kelly's. First thing, he'd have Kelly's grandfather radio Juneau and get word to the SEA-MAR board. Then he'd try to reach Shamus and Roger at the fishing camp. After that he'd—

But he was moving too fast. If he had any sense, he would slow down and give himself time to sort out the past twenty-four hours. He would reflect on everything that had happened, everything he had discovered about himself. If he flung himself right back into the race, he would lose it all.

Even Kelly.

He glanced at her over his shoulder, where she sat hunched on the thwart. His heart contracted with worry. She was too quiet, too pale. She needed rest and good, warm food. That, at least, was not far off. Afterward, maybe if there was time . . .

But he had already lost her, Jake realized. Whatever he and Kelly had shared, it was already part of the past. Even now, the demands of their separate worlds were rushing in to claim them.

Jake put himself to bailing once more, trying to shut out the emptiness that had settled over him since their rescue. It was over, he reminded himself, and there was no way to go back. He had no choice except to move ahead, to plod on toward a future that suddenly loomed as bleak and color-less as the rain.

Kelly felt the cold all the way to her bones. She huddled under the poncho, striving to control the chatter of her teeth. She had no wish to call attention to herself and be fussed over. Right now, all she really wanted was to get home and get warm.

Eddie's old Johnson Seahorse droned in her ears, the sound mingling with the spank of waves on the bow and the steady drizzle of the rain. More storm to come, that was what Eddie had said. All planes would be grounded for the duration. Even the twice-weekly ferry might not run if the channel was too rough. Jake could be stuck in Angoon for days.

But that was his problem now, she reminded herself. She'd done her job. She'd gotten her passenger to safety. From here, he could manage fine without her.

She could see Jake out of the corner of her eye. He was bailing rainwater out of the boat—much more energetically, Kelly thought, than the job called for. He had not spoken to her since the dory pulled away from the gravel bar—scarcely looked at her, in fact. But his message was blasting through loud and clear. They'd come back to the real world now. He'd remembered who he was. And once again, drab little Kelly Ryan was no more to him than hired help.

A chill went through her as a fresh wind gust struck her face. Just hang on, she told herself. You'll be home soon. Then everything will be all right.

She closed her eyes. Yes, she was going home. Home to her warm bed, her grandma's hot scones and her grandpa's stories. She would be safe there. And she would try to forget everything that had happened in the past two days.

Everything.

By the time they rounded the last bend before Kelly's place, the storm Eddie Willis had predicted was already howling over the horizon. The dory rode the waves like a bronc buster, flying over the crests with bone-jarring whacks. Jake gripped the gunwale with one hand and the bailing can with the other as he struggled to empty the hull.

Kelly clung to the thwart, her face a pale blur beneath the hood of her poncho.

As they skirted the point, Jake recognized the long floating wharf with the Beaver moored to one side. And he recognized the lanky old man in the blue baseball cap. He was leaning into the wind like a weathered scarecrow, peering anxiously into the rain.

As the boat came into view, the old man pulled off the cap and began waving it in the air. Seconds later, Jake saw a woman in a red rain slicker come running out of the big log house to join him on the wharf. The two stood there together, clinging anxiously as the dory chugged into the cove.

Kelly pulled back the hood of her poncho so they would recognize her. She waved one arm, and the elderly couple responded with a frenzied dance, hugging each other, jumping up and down so excitedly in the battering wind that Jake feared they would topple into the water.

The dory bucked waves all the way in. Eddie Willis snubbed the boat up to one of the old tires that cushioned the pier and threw out a line. By the time he had it knotted, Kelly had scrambled out onto the wharf. Her grandmother, a trim, pepper-haired woman in her late sixties, burst into tears of relief as she caught her close.

"Kelly! Oh, thank heaven!" she murmured. "I spent the whole night praying for you!"

Jake had climbed out behind Kelly. He filled the awkward moment by introducing himself to Kelly's grandfather. The old man clasped Jake's hand in a bearlike grip and shook it so heartily that the knuckles cracked. "Frank Ryan," he rumbled. "And this is a happy day for all of us!"

Jake cleared his throat, dreading the news he had to break. "I'm afraid your plane's beyond fixing, Mr. Ryan—"

"Call me Frank, young man."

"Did you hear me, Frank? Your plane is a total loss. But I've already told Kelly that my company's insurance will pay for a new..."

Jake's voice trailed off as he noticed the tears in the old man's blue eyes.

"Thank you kindly," Frank Ryan said. "The important thing is having Kelly back. But I've logged a lot of miles in that old Beaver. A new plane just wouldn't be the same. We'll salvage what we can of her, and take it from there."

Frank's wife had broken loose from Kelly to hurry to the end of the wharf, where Eddie Willis was already untying the dory. "Eddie! You can't leave yet!" she shouted above the wind. "Come on in—I've got coffee and fresh cinnamon buns—"

"Can't take the time!" Eddie yelled back. "Storm's blowing in! My wife'll be worried if I'm not back!"

My wife. Jake felt the lightness of relief as the words sank in. The young Tlingit was married. He had no claim on Kelly. Not that it would make any difference, Jake reminded himself. *He* had no claim on Kelly either.

His concern shifted, however, as he realized the boat was leaving without him. "Hey! Wait!" he shouted. But Eddie had restarted the motor and could not hear him. His hand waved a cheery farewell as he edged clear of the pilings and swung the dory for home.

"I'll radio Mary Sue and tell her you're coming!" Frank bellowed after him. But those words, too, were lost in the roar of the old outboard. The storm was picking up. Rain swept out of the sky in stinging, horizontal sheets, driven by a wind so fierce that Jake had to lean into it to stand. The dory hugged the contours of the shore, keeping to the shallows.

"He'll be all right," Frank said. "Come on, let's get ourselves inside."

Kelly and her grandmother were already struggling toward the house, their bodies bent against the storm. Jake lengthened his step to catch up with Frank's whip-lean figure.

"Look—" he shouted above the wind. "I'd planned to go into Angoon and stay. I didn't mean to impose—"

"Impose? Horsefeathers!" the old man rumbled. "Doris and I are always glad for fresh company. We're happy to have you!"

"Eddie said you had a radio. I hope you won't mind helping me contact a few people."

"All in good time, lad. But first we need to get you fed and warmed up." Frank Ryan strode up the landing at a pace that left Jake trailing behind with the pack. Through the gray sweep of rain, he could make out the house, a rambling structure built of stone and weathered logs. It nestled amid an ancient fall of glacial rock, so well placed that it seemed to rise naturally out of the land. A wooden walkway zigzagged upward from the pier, ending in a broad, sheltered porch. Smoke curled from the massive rock chimney.

The house struck Jake as a haven, a shelter that had weathered countless storms over the years and would survive many more to come. This, then, was where Kelly had grown up. No wonder she seemed so reluctant to leave.

By the time Jake and Frank staggered to the front door, the wind had become a yowling wildcat that raked the trees and clawed at the water. The two men stomped the wetness from their boots and followed the women inside, bolting the heavy door behind them.

Jake was instantly wrapped in warmth. The blaze that crackled in the big rock fireplace radiated cheerful heat into the room. The mouth-watering aromas of cinnamon, coffee and fresh-baked bread floated out of the kitchen.

Kelly and her grandmother had vanished. Jake felt an unexpected pang of loss. She had been so constantly beside him that it seemed strange now, having her gone. In the next instant, however, his ears picked up the sound of running bathwater. Kelly, he realized, had been whisked off to a hot tub—the very thing she needed in her chilled condition. It was all right. He would see her again. They would still have a chance to say goodbye.

Following Frank's example, Jake shrugged out of his wet coat and hung it on a rack beside the door. Then he peeled off his muddy boots, placed them on a rubber mat and padded over to the fireplace in his stocking feet.

The Ryans' living room was a journey into the past. The rugged leather furniture and brass hurricane lamps would not have been out of place in a Humphrey Bogart movie. The walls were lined with old flight maps and books—shelves upon shelves of well-thumbed books. Their titles ran the gamut from aeronautics to opera.

Photos in vintage frames crowded the mantel. One showed a dashing, younger Frank in a World War II Army Air Corps flight suit. Another captured Frank and Doris on their wedding day—he in uniform, she in a pastel suit with an orchid corsage. The picture next to it— Jake's throat tightened as he realized what he was seeing. A tall young man who resembled Frank stood beside a pretty, petite, dark-eyed young woman. The toddler they held so proudly to the camera was a beautiful little girl with mischievous eyes and a tumble of dark curls.

Kelly.

Frank had come up behind him. "That picture was taken just a few weeks before they died," he said. "Ray, our boy, was the only child we were able to have. Kelly's all that's left of him."

Jake cleared his throat. "You'd have been proud of her out there, Frank. She was cool. She was competent. She flew that plane like an angel. And after we went down, her first concern was for my safety."

"That's the way she was taught." The old man's voice betrayed his emotion as he reflected on what he had almost lost. The moment might have become awkward for both of them if Doris had not come bustling in from the kitchen.

"There, I've got Kelly thawing out, and I've radioed Angoon and—" She stopped short and shook her crisp, pepper gray curls. "For heaven's sake, Frank, the man's probably starved half to death, and here you are standing around talking! Come on, into the kitchen with both of you! That's an order!"

Jake needed no coaxing. He followed Doris's trim figure, clad in a smart, pink jogging suit, through the swinging doors and into the kitchen. There, the table was already set with cups, saucers, utensils, an old-fashioned percolator of steaming coffee and a pan of fresh-baked cinnamon rolls. The aromas swam in Jake's head. He hadn't realized until now how hungry he was.

"The bathroom's all yours as soon as Kelly's out of the tub," Doris was saying. "Meanwhile, let's get some nourishment down you. Sorry it's not something more substantial. I've got some meat loaf and potatoes in the oven, but they'll be a while yet, so dig into what's here."

Jake sank into his chair as she filled his cup with a dark swirl of coffee. Doris Ryan was a few years younger than her husband, with a pert, square-cut face. Her eyes were her most striking feature. They were a deep, emerald green, and as Jake took his first sip, their directness suddenly impaled him.

"So, how did you and Kelly survive the night?" Her tone was casual, even friendly, but there was no way Jake could have missed the message. He swallowed the coffee too fast, almost scalding his throat.

"We were lucky. We found an old Forest Service cabin. There were...uh...two bunks in it." All true, Jake tried to reassure himself. Just the same, he felt as if he were seventeen again, and had just shown up at 2:00 a.m. with his fifteen-year-old prom date.

"Kelly's a professional. Nothing happened," he added, damned grateful he didn't have to fudge more than a little. Doris's knowing, green eyes would have seen right through him. Maybe they already had.

"Have some cinnamon rolls, Jake." Frank shoved the cast-iron baking pan across the table. Jake used a handy spatula to lift out a single saucer-size roll, fragrant with cinnamon and wonderfully sticky. The first bite was heaven, or would have been except for the riveting presence of Doris's eyes.

"Kelly told me she sprained her ankle in the crash," Doris remarked. "It still looks swollen. How did she manage to walk?"

"Oh...she needed some help the first day. But she managed. Your granddaughter's a tough girl. I...gained a lot of respect for her out there." Jake squirmed inwardly, feeling like a bug under a magnifying glass. What was he supposed to say? That he hadn't been able to keep his hands off her? That—damn it—he'd come closer to falling in love with spunky little Kelly Ryan than with any other woman he'd met since Ann's death?

He took another sip of bitter, black coffee, washing away the sweetness in his mouth. Doris, he realized, was nudging him toward a confrontation with his own feelings for Kelly. And he wasn't ready. Not now. Not yet. Maybe never. They were two very different people, he and Kelly. They had different lives, different goals. They were all wrong for each other.

When he looked up at Kelly's grandmother again, he saw that her expression had softened. "I'm sorry," she said, bending close to refill his coffee cup. "You must think I'm a nosy, terrible person. It's just that when it comes to Kelly, I'm like a mother bear with a cub. We're fairly old-fashioned around here, and she's awfully precious to both of us."

"I understand," Jake said, taking another bite of cinnamon roll. And he did. He understood Doris's feelings perfectly, he told himself.

The feelings he didn't understand were his own.

Kelly stretched in the tub, gazing at her breasts through drifting clouds of bubble bath. She was beginning to feel alive again. Her skin had taken on a glow in the warm water. Her nipples rose out of the lavender foam like smooth, shell-pink islands—very different from the puckered little nubs they'd become when Jake's palm had cupped her flesh, his skilled fingers stroking, exquisitely stroking—

Stop it!

Kelly opened her eyes wide, filling her sight with the familiar reality of the bathroom. It was over, she reminded herself forcefully. She was home. Jake Drummond might be stuck here until the storm blew over, but in his mind, he had already left Admiralty Island. Every thought, every emotion was focused outward. Kelly Ryan was already part of the past. To put it more succinctly, she was history.

Days from now, he would be back in Seattle. He would probably be regaling some pretty society blonde with his adventure. And if he even mentioned the quaint little bush pilot who'd shared it with him, it would only be in passing.

She sat straight up in the tub, water from her soaking hair trickling down her back. The bath had accomplished its purpose. She was warm. She was clean. It was time to get out, before her mind began to wander again.

She used her toe to jerk the chain on the rubber plug. The bubble mounds swirled in lazy circles as Kelly stepped out onto the mat and rubbed herself dry with a rough, white towel.

Oh, blast him, why had Eddie taken off and left Jake here? She'd already had more of Jake than she could handle. She needed time to herself—time to get over him and recover her balance.

She remembered her grandmother's knowing eyes as she'd glanced up from running the bathwater. Grandma hadn't said a word—hadn't needed to. One look had been enough to tell her something was different. She was probably in the kitchen right now, grilling Jake until he squirmed with embarrassment. Heavens to Betsy, would Doris Ryan ever realize her granddaughter was a woman of twenty-five, not a naive seventeen-year-old?

Kelly twisted the towel around her wet hair and flipped it into a turban, then shrugged into the white terry robe that hung on the door. It would probably be a good idea to get dressed before showing herself. But if she knew her grandmother, things could be getting entirely too hot in the kitchen by now. Jake might be in serious need of rescuing. She couldn't afford to wait until things got worse.

It was the only thing to do, Kelly told herself, opening the bathroom door. Besides, she had yet to apologize to Grandpa for crashing the Beaver. He needed to know how sorry she was, and the sooner she told him, the better.

From his small, cluttered office adjoining the kitchen, Frank had radioed the charter flight agency in Juneau. His contact there had promised to phone the SEA-MAR board and get back to them. Now, for Jake, there was nothing to do but wait.

He tried to sit calmly at the table, sipping coffee and chatting with Frank and Doris. But waiting had never been his strong point. Every tick of the kitchen clock grated like sandpaper on his raw nerves.

Outside, the storm clawed at the house, rattling the window frames and soughing mournfully along the eaves. Rain battered the thick glass panes, blurring the trees and water outside. Grateful as he was for the shelter, Jake could not help feeling like a caged animal. He fought the urge to get up and pace the floor.

"Sounds like you've got an awful lot riding on this SEA-MAR meeting," Frank said, breaking off a hunk of cinnamon roll and shaping it between his big, rough fingers.

"I have. This contract could make my company's future. At least, it could if the Tlingits haven't already awarded it to the Japanese. I'm hoping the board will at least agree to—"

The rest of the words died in Jake's throat as Kelly walked into the kitchen.

She was wearing nothing but a terry-cloth robe that cuddled her body like a soft, white cloud. The towel on her head framed the elfin perfection of her face, setting off her glowing skin and dark-framed eyes. A tendril of hair had escaped to curl wetly along the shell-pink contour of her cheek.

Her beauty stopped Jake's breath.

She hurried at once to her grandfather, standing beside his chair with stricken eyes. "Grandpa, I'm so sorry about the Beaver. I know how much that old plane meant to you. I should never have taken it up with a storm coming—"

"It wasn't her fault, it was mine," Jake cut in swiftly. "I didn't want to wait. I insisted she fly me back to Juneau right then—"

"Now, stop it, both of you!" Frank rumbled. "What's done is done. Kelly, the important thing is that you're safe. I won't deny that I set quite a store by that Beaver, but she's only a machine. I've already told Jake, here, that I plan to salvage as much as I can. Maybe if I can get some replacement parts, there'll be enough of her to rebuild."

"In any case, you can send the bill to me." Jake sighed, wishing the stubborn old man would just settle for a new Cessna and be done with it. A brand-new plane would be safer for Kelly to fly, and probably less costly, to boot.

"We'll talk about that later," Frank growled. "Meanwhile, you sit down, Kelly, and get some food in your stomach before you keel over on us. Go on, now."

Jake drank Kelly in with his eyes as she edged around the table. He remembered seeing Elizabeth Taylor in one of her perfume ads, wearing nothing but white terry cloth. The costume was much the same; but with all due respect to the divine Liz, she didn't have a patch on Miss Kelly Ryan.

That elusive scent, the one that had so bewitched him earlier, drifted with her like an aura as she moved. Jake could almost imagine opening the front of her robe and burying his face in—

Damn!

Kelly slipped into the empty chair across from Jake, her collar loosening around her shoulders as she settled into place. Nothing showed. The robe, in fact, covered her quite modestly. But each shadow, each hidden curve, stirred a memory in Jake's mind. He remembered the feel of her in his arms, the silk of her skin beneath his hand.

The kitchen suddenly seemed very, very warm.

Doris turned away from the sink, where she'd been rinsing some vegetables. A worried frown flickered across her face as she glanced from Jake to Kelly. All she said, however, was "Dinner will be ready in an hour, dear. I know you're starved, but you'll be sorry if you fill up on sweets."

"Let me worry about that, Grandma." Kelly speared a cinnamon roll with her fork and took a none-too-delicate bite. She closed her eyes as she savored the taste, her expression so innocently sensual that it stirred hot sparks in Jake's loins. He could only hope that what he was feeling didn't show in his face. If it did, Doris would be after him with a shotgun.

He forced his mind to concentrate on the upcoming moment of truth with SEA-MAR. Any minute, now, he would know. If the board had delayed its decision, he was back in action. If not... But he would deal with the devastation if and when it happened, not before.

In any case, he would not try to contact Shamus and Roger until he knew. With luck, they hadn't heard the news broadcasts. They might not even know he was missing. But he couldn't count on that. In all likelihood his partners would be worried sick about him.

"Jake, the bathroom's free if you want to clean up," Kelly was saying. "There's no shower, but I promise you the tub will feel wonderful."

Jake glanced up at her. A jewel of crystallized sugar had stuck to the edge of her full, pink lower lip. He stifled the impulse to lean across the table and remove it with the tip of his tongue. What the blazes was wrong with him? Every time he looked at Kelly, his brain seemed to drop below his beltline. Maybe he'd been out in the wilds too long, and was reverting to caveman mentality.

"Thanks, but I'll wait for the return call," he said. "I won't be able to relax until I know what's happening."

At that moment, as if triggered by his answer, the antiquated radio in Frank's office began to crackle. Jake went rigid as a tinny voice filtered through the static. "This is Moon Dog calling Eagle . . . Moon Dog calling Eagle . . . Come in, Eagle."

"That's it! That's our call!" Frank was on his feet, lurching for the office door. Jake would have been right behind him, but Kelly motioned furtively for him to stay put.

"Handling the radio is Grandpa's job," she whispered. "Stay out of his way and let him take care of it."

Jake settled uneasily back into his chair. He knew what Kelly was trying to tell him. The old man's eyesight might keep him from flying, but the radio remained his domain. That was as it should be, Jake told himself. Even so, it was torture, trying to sit still and be calm while Frank fiddled with the dials and shouted into the microphone.

". . . What's that, Moon Dog? Come again, I'm not reading you! Over."

The reply sputtered through the static, so faint that Jake could not make it out from where he sat. Kelly's eyes held his across the table. He could sense her worry, her unspoken support.

"Now, make sure I heard you right," Frank was shouting. "Friday at fourteen hundred hours, if the weather clears. And we check back if it doesn't. Over."

The receiver crackled again. Kelly's eyes were dancing now, her body almost bouncing off the chair with excitement. Jake held his breath, afraid to start believing too soon.

"That's it, then! Thanks kindly, Moon Dog! Over!" Frank replaced the microphone and strode out of the tiny office, beaming from ear to ear. "It's all right, lad! The SEA-MAR folks knew you'd gone down, and they put off their decision. You've got another appointment day after tomorrow, at two. Now, all we need to do is get you there.''

Jake went limp with relief. His knees turned watery as the tension drained out of him. It was all right. He hadn't missed his chance.

Kelly's eyes met his across the table—luminous, joyful to their golden depths. Jake sat perfectly still, warmed by their glow. The two of them had fought and sniped and argued from the crash site to the coast. Not until now did he understand how real her concern for him had been.

Her undisguised happiness had caught him off guard. He bit back his emotions, suddenly torn. Where had it come from, this unexpected sense of sweetness? He had almost stopped caring; even the challenge of the SEA-MAR contract had been no more than a job he had to do. Suddenly, with Kelly there to share the good news, it was as if—

But no, it was all wrong. It had been Ann who'd given meaning to his victories. Only Ann. How could it ever be the same with someone else? Jake's mind began a frantic scramble to build up the walls, protecting the pain that had become part of who he was.

Kelly reached for the coffeepot, mercifully breaking the spell. "I guess I can uncross my fingers now," she said.

"I'd feel better if you kept them crossed through Friday." Jake eased his aching body out of the chair. He felt exhausted, like a marionette whose strings had been cut. "We need to get word to my partners. After that, if you don't mind, I'd like to take you up on that offer of a bath."

"I'll get right on your call," Frank said, ducking back into his office. "It shouldn't take long. I've never had any trouble getting through to folks at that fishing camp."

"Thanks," Jake said, turning away from the table as he spoke. "I want you to know how much I appreciate—"

The words stopped in his throat as he glimpsed the fleeting expression on Doris's face. Even now, it was gone. But in that instant, when he'd turned and caught her unguarded, the fear in her eyes had chilled him like a gray winter wind.

Chapter Nine

Jake opened his eyes. He was in a strange bed, in a strange room, with log walls and blue gingham curtains framing a rain-splashed window. The small, brass clock on the nightstand said 7:45.

Morning.

He raised his head, his confusion clearing as he came fully awake. He remembered last night: the cinnamon rolls and Doris's tasty moose meat loaf, and Kelly, pink and glowing in white terry cloth. He remembered shaving with Frank's razor, lazing in the hot bath and discovering, by chance, that the sweetly sensual aroma he'd come to identify so closely with Kelly was nothing but old-fashioned lavender bath salts, the same kind his mother had used when he was small.

Freud might've had something to say about that, Jake mused. Not that Kelly smelled the least bit motherly. In fact, there was something indecently sexy about the way Kelly

Ryan's chemistry mingled with an innocent substance like lavender that—

"Oho! So you're finally awake!" Frank's head popped in through the bedroom door, cheeks ruddy from the morning wind. "We were beginning to wonder if you'd died on us in the night! Your clean duds are right here. Throw 'em on, and I'll rustle you up some breakfast." He tossed Jake's freshly laundered clothes onto the foot of the bed. Jake sat up and reached for his T-shirt.

"How's the weather out there, Frank?"

"Clearing some. But according to the FM station in Sitka, there'll be more rain rolling in this afternoon."

"Any chance of my getting to Juneau before then?"

"Nope. I'm just winding up an engine rebuild on that other Beaver down at the dock. We got her hoisted in the other day, but just bolting everything in place is a good half day's work. There's the ferry, but it doesn't run till day after tomorrow."

Jake yanked the shirt down over his ears, trying to hide his anxiety. "Could I help you with the engine? I've never worked on a plane, but I've tinkered with my share of old cars."

"Maybe. I usually count on Kelly for that. But Doris says she needs her help canning snap beans this morning. 'Twixt you and me, I think she just doesn't want the girl out in the weather till she's rested up. My wife's a fine woman, but when it comes to Kelly, she can be as fussy as a biddy hen with a chick."

Jake swung his legs off the bed and reached for his clean boxers. "I'd hardly call Kelly a chick. She's as strong and capable a woman as I've ever met."

Frank's eyes narrowed. "That she is, lad," he said gently. "But there's more to Kelly than you know."

Questions leapt into Jake's mind, but Frank had turned from the doorway, his guarded expression warning Jake against asking more. "Wander down to the kitchen when you're ready for breakfast" was all he said.

When he had gone, Jake finished dressing. A quick glance outside revealed that last night's storm had diminished to a gusty drizzle. Between the weather and the disabled plane, he would be stuck here till tomorrow. There was nothing to do but make the best of it.

Remembering his manners, he remade the bed and straightened the room. It was a small room, clearly reserved for overnight guests. The patchwork quilt and homemade curtains lent it a coziness, but the only sign of regular use was the narrow pine desk, its top crowded with papers, pens, books and an old manual typewriter.

Mildly curious, Jake picked up one of the books, a slim, paperback volume, heftily titled *Bloom's Taxonomy of Educational Objectives.* Only then did he realize he was looking at Kelly's correspondence course material.

He remembered her plan then, and how her voice had rung with conviction when she talked about it. Now here it was. Kelly's dream. Tied up in this clutter of scribbled notes and dull textbooks. Another couple of years, she'd said. Two more years of wading through dreary stuff like this, and Kelly Ryan would be a certified teacher.

He thumbed through another book, this one as thick as his wrist, with print that was almost microscopic. Kelly wanted her dream badly, Jake realized, and suddenly he burned to give it to her, tied up in a pretty gold ribbon. But some things couldn't be given, he reminded himself. They could only be earned.

All the same, it was a pity she couldn't make it easier on herself. A few months on campus would make the dream come true a lot sooner. And it would certainly be less tedious than digging through a mountain of correspondence courses.

He'd suggested that to her, Jake recalled. But she'd put up so much resistance that their conversation had almost ended in a fight. What was standing in Kelly's way? he wondered. She'd said her grandparents needed her, but Frank and Doris seemed very self-sufficient. As for money, she'd insisted it wasn't a problem, and Jake believed her. Charter flying paid well enough.

But something was holding Kelly back. What was it? Jake puzzled. What had he glimpsed in her eyes yesterday, when she'd pulled away from him?

"Hey, Jake, your flapjacks are on the griddle!" Frank's voice echoed up the hallway. "Better step on it!"

Jake took a few seconds in the bathroom, then hurried to the kitchen. Frank was tending bacon, eggs and flapjacks on the big, white butane stove. Doris was busy at the sink, washing glass mason jars for canning.

He sat down at the single place setting and glanced around for Kelly. She was nowhere to be seen. Maybe she was still in bed, he mused. That, or she was avoiding him this morning. Her attitude toward him seemed to change almost hourly. He never knew quite what to expect from her.

"So how did you sleep?" Doris asked in a friendly voice.

"I didn't even twitch," Jake responded, digging into the plate Frank had set in front of him. "Thanks for the bed, and for this great breakfast. Are you always this good to strangers?"

"Oh, we welcome company," Doris said. "It can get pretty lonesome out here, can't it, Frank?"

"Doris just likes seeing a handsome young face at the table," Frank kidded. "Gives her a nice change from looking at this old mug all the time!"

"Stop that!" Doris flipped him playfully with water from the sink. Frank retaliated by whacking her trim bottom with the end of a dish towel. Their affectionate horesplay encouraged Jake to be bolder than he might have been.

"What about Kelly?" he ventured. "Doesn't this place get pretty lonesome for her, too?"

Frank and Doris glanced at each other. An uneasy silence had fallen over the kitchen.

"Oh, Kelly does all right," Doris said brightly. "She's got a few old school friends in Juneau, and she's dated a couple of the Forest Service boys here on the island. Nothing serious, but sooner or later, I suppose..."

Her voice trailed off as the back door opened and Kelly walked into the kitchen. She was dressed in blue jeans and her grandfather's oversize canvas coat. In her arms, she carried a hefty basket, piled with freshly picked string beans.

Seeing Jake, she smiled. Except for faint shadows under her eyes, she looked wonderful, he thought. Crisp, damp curls framed a face that was pink from the morning chill. Raindrops jeweled her skin, and the mischief had returned to her eyes.

She was beautiful. Damned beautiful.

"Jake's going to help me work on the plane this morning," Frank said. "That'll free you up to help your grandma."

"I didn't know you were a mechanic, Jake." Her interest seemed slightly impersonal, as if she'd already blotted the past two days from her mind.

"A mechanic, no, but I drove old cars for a lot of years," Jake said. "I got pretty good at keeping them running. But Frank's in charge today. I'll just be there to hand him the wrenches." He paused for another forkful of Frank's delicious flapjacks, swimming in fresh blueberry compote. "I hope you plan on flying me out of here tomorrow morning.''

Kelly nodded, her manner almost businesslike. "According to Sitka, we're supposed to get a window in the weather about then. You and Grandpa get the plane fixed, and I'll manage the rest." She tossed the coat onto a chair, dumped the beans into a colander and joined her grandmother at the sink.

Watching her, Jake reflected glumly on the day ahead. If he had his way, he and Kelly would spend it together. They would put on raincoats and walk along the rocky beach—and maybe if he found the courage, he would take her hand and tell her how lost and confused he was, and how much he needed someone like her.

Or they would curl up in a nest of pillows before the fireplace and talk for hours about Kelly's life, her dreams and her fears. If her grandparents weren't nearby, he might even draw her dark head to his shoulder and brush a kiss across the bridge of her pert, freckled nose, then—

But what was the use? He knew how the day would go. He and Kelly would spend the long hours staying out of each other's way. They would invent means of avoiding one another. They would make polite excuses, masking what had happened between them as if it had never taken place.

It was as if they had already said goodbye.

Kelly snapped another bean and stuffed the pieces into the mouth of the glass mason jar. Pausing, she wiped a hand across her damp forehead. The kitchen was a fog of steam. On the stove, the pressure cooker hissed like a fat steel dragon. Rows of finished jars lined the countertop, their brass lids pinging as they cooled.

Her grandmother turned away from testing a stubborn seal. "It was good of you to help me, dear," she said. "I probably should have let you rest. You do look tired."

Kelly brushed her hair back from her face. "I certainly don't mind helping," she said. "But you're not fooling anybody, Grandma. If I weren't here, I'd be down there working on the plane with Grandpa and Jake. You're just trying to keep me out of trouble."

Doris Ryan's eyebrows lifted, but only a little. She was accustomed to Kelly's frankness. "Sweetheart, I just don't want to see you hurt again," she said.

"Grandma, I'm not—"

"Listen to me, Kelly. I've known you all your life, and I'm not blind. You're dangerously close to falling in love with that man."

In love.

The words jolted Kelly like a slap.

No, her mind clamored. She couldn't possibly be falling in love with Jake Drummond. It was true that he'd stirred her physically—true, even, that she'd been touched by the loneliness in him. But *love?*

The idea was almost a joke. Love was beyond anything she and Jake had shared. Love was trust and intimacy and giving. Love was the current that flowed between her parents in the photograph, between Frank and Doris.

Between Jake and his lovely Ann.

Kelly shook her head in swift denial. "You're wrong, Grandma. Jake's an attractive man, and I'll admit there've been a few sparks. But I'm not seventeen anymore. I've got more sense than you give me credit for."

"Does he have someone else? Someone back in Seattle?"

"Jake's a widower. He showed me a picture of his wife. She was...breathtaking." Kelly dropped a sterilized lid onto the mason jar and reached for more beans from the dwindling pile. "He's still in love with her. I don't think any woman alive could compete with such a beautiful ghost."

"Oh, Kelly!" Her grandmother's dismay was so heartfelt that Kelly glanced up from her work, meeting the full impact of those sharp eyes. What she saw there was so startling that she dropped the bean she'd been about to snap.

"Grandma, you *like* him, don't you?" she said.

"Of course I like him. He's charming. He's thoughtful. And he's as handsome as a movie star, to boot. Why do you think I'm so worried? Oh, sweetheart, why don't you find someone who won't break your heart? One of those nice ranger boys..."

Kelly forced herself to laugh. But the sound came out hollow, and she knew her grandmother wasn't fooled. "Maybe I'm not ready to find anybody yet," she said. "Maybe there are other things I want to do with my life."

"Then why not strike out and just *do* them? There's no reason why you couldn't spend this winter at the university finishing your degree."

"That's what Jake told me." Kelly's tense hands snapped a fresh bean into three pieces and plopped them haphazardly into the jar. "Everybody's trying to run my life these days."

"Kelly, this is your home. You know how much we love having you here. But you can't spend the rest of your life on this island. In a few years, your grandpa and I will be gone. If you can't break away, you'll be all alone. Try it now, while you're still young. Have new experiences. Meet new people."

"What about the charter flights?" Kelly choked back a surge of fear. She knew the emotion was unreasonable, but she couldn't stop the panic. It welled up in her throat until she seemed to be drowning in it.

"We don't need the business," her grandmother was saying. "The money we've saved for our retirement is plenty for us. Anytime you want to—"

Kelly's heart had begun to pound. She forced herself to speak calmly. "I appreciate that, Grandma. But for now, it makes more sense for me to stay here and finish my correspondence courses. When the time comes . . ."

She let the words trail off as she busied herself filling the last jar with the last of the beans. Her grandmother watched her in silence, her eyes filled with concern.

"And speaking of correspondence courses," Kelly continued cheerfully, "I promised myself I'd have that term paper on Reading Recovery ready for Monday's mail plane. That means I'd better hit the books for the rest of the afternoon."

"Go ahead, then, dear. I'll clean up." Her grandmother's chipper response sounded strained, Kelly thought as she strode determinedly down the hall to the spare bedroom. Grandma meant well, but this time her perceptions were way off target. The idea that Kelly Ryan, once burned and oh-so-wise, would be foolish enough to fall in love with a man as unattainable as Jake Drummond—

But she wouldn't even waste time thinking about it, Kelly resolved. What she needed this afternoon was a stiff dose of reality medicine, in the form of homework.

Plunking onto the worn leather chair, she opened two books to their marked places and cranked a fresh sheet of paper into the antiquated Smith-Corona. Her thoughts fluttered this way and that, like sparrows pecking for crumbs, as she fixed her eyes on a relevant paragraph.

Concentrate, she ordered her reluctant brain. But the letters on the page might as well have been Arabic for all the meaning they held. Nothing would sink in.

Her gaze wandered to the bed where Jake had slept last night. On leaving, he had tugged up the covers and gone through the motions of smoothing them, but the spread was lopsided, as if he'd done the job in a hurry. Without thinking, Kelly got out of the chair, leaned over and pulled it even, tucking a fold under the pillow to make a neat roll.

Jake's warm, clean scent lingered in the bedclothes. Something stirred in Kelly's chest as she remembered sleeping in his arms, cradled by that scent. She struggled now against the urge to fling aside the blankets, bury her face in the sheets and fill her senses with the comforting, tantalizing male aroma that was so uniquely his.

Love?

She pressed her palms to her stinging eyes. No, this wasn't love, she told herself. It was only the cry of a heart too long empty, the yearnings of a body too long untouched.

For the past seven years she had kept her emotions packed in ice. She had fled from involvement, hiding away on her island, dating men who never threatened her safety and telling herself it was enough. Why? Because she'd been young and foolish once. Because she'd been hurt so deeply that the risk of ever loving again was more than she could stand.

Then the plane crash had shattered her secure little world. She had found herself alone, under conditions of danger and intimacy, with the most magnetic man she'd ever met—and her brittle facade had melted like frost in a warm chinook wind.

Drifting to the window, she parted the curtains and stared out at the gray weather. The worst of the storm had passed, but a mist of rain lingered in the air, and wind roughened the leaden water in the channel. Down by the dock, she could see the Beaver, with Jake and her grandfather toiling over the exposed engine—getting wet, no doubt, as well as tired, cold and dirty.

By now, Jake's head would be crammed full of Frank Ryan's old flying stories. He was probably getting bored—but no, Kelly realized, Jake would listen with genuine interest. He was like that. For all his big-city glitter, Jake Drummond didn't have a pretentious bone in his splendid male body.

A smile tugged Kelly's mouth as she remembered some of the funnier moments over the past two days. Jake, sliding down the tree as if it had been greased. Jake, scaring off the bears with his off-key Hank Williams imitation. Jake, nearly jumping out of his skin when her stomach growled.

She remembered the night in the cabin—how he'd climbed up on the roof to dislodge the bird's nest and come down looking like a chimney sweep. She remembered his dismay at finding the soggy mattress in his bunk, his noble effort to sleep on the floor—and the amazement that had flashed across his face when she'd invited him into her bed.

Love?

But that question was beside the point, Kelly reminded herself. By this time tomorrow Jake would be out of her life for good. Her only claim on him would be the memory of what they'd shared.

Blast love! She *liked* him! Jake had blundered into her life and shaken everything loose. He had roused her to anger, to desire, to laughter. He had brought her face-to-face with herself.

And here she was hiding in the house, too cowardly to enjoy the time they had left.

Without consciously willing it, she felt herself moving. She was in the hall now, grabbing for her old work coat. Could she do it? she asked herself. Could she accept Jake's going and savor their relationship for the brief interlude that it was?

There were no easy answers, but for her own sake, Kelly knew she had to try. Otherwise she would shrink into herself again. She would spend her life running, hiding, shutting herself off from pleasure because she was so afraid of the pain that would follow.

The front door slammed behind her as she burst out onto the porch. From somewhere inside the house, she thought she heard her grandmother's voice. But Kelly could not stop to listen. Her feet were already skimming the wooden walkway, carrying her swiftly down to the dock.

"Now just hold this steady while I tighten it down."

Frank's instructions blurred in Jake's mind as he glanced up and saw Kelly running toward them, her limp barely noticeable now. For an instant he thought something might be wrong. Then he saw the grin on her face.

"What's up?" he called out.

"Nothing." Her cheeks were pink. Her wind-tousled hair glistened with rain as she jogged out onto the dock and stopped alongside them. "I was through in the kitchen and thought you two might need some help, that's all."

Frank scowled in mock sternness. "Sure it's all right with your grandma, now? I don't want to get in trouble if you catch a chill."

"You won't. Now hand me that ratchet."

For Jake, the next two hours flew past. Frank did most of the work on the Beaver's engine, while he and Kelly functioned as assistants—fetching, handing, lubing, steadying the vintage parts. Rain misted down on them, pooling on their waterproof coats and dripping off their hair. Grease smudged their fingers and faces. They talked and laughed.

Raindrops drizzled down the back of Jake's collar. He was cold and dirty, but the contentment that had crept over him made him feel like he'd just walked into a cozy room. His gaze followed the sure movements of Kelly's delicate, grease-stained hands. His ears echoed with the rain-light sound of her laughter.

Now and again they touched—accidental brushes that shot prickles of heat through Jake's body. When it happened, she did not look away as she'd done so often before. The shyness was still there, he realized, but this time Kelly was fighting it. She almost seemed to be reaching out to him.

Jake could only guess at her reasons. But whatever they might be, he was not going to complain.

Bolt by bolt, wire by wire, the engine was rejoined to the sturdy old plane. At last Frank stepped back, wiped his hands on a rag and pronounced the job finished. While he rested, Jake and Kelly gathered up the scattered tools and stowed them in the cockpit.

"I'll be a while testing her out," he said. "You two youngsters go on back to the house and get warm. I'll be along as soon as I've done the fine-tuning."

"You're sure you won't need somebody here?" Jake asked. "Kelly should probably go back and thaw out, but I could stick around and help you."

Frank shook his head. "This old engine's like a shy girl-friend. She only talks to me when we're alone together. You two go on now. You've done enough."

Kelly gave Jake a discreet nudge. "He means it," she whispered. "Tuning the engine is something Grandpa likes to do by himself."

"Go! Get out of here!" Frank shooed them away with a grin and a wave of his hand. "I'll see you inside!"

Kelly slipped her hand through the crook of Jake's arm as they mounted the walkway. There was a lightness to her step, as if she had to hold on to him to keep from floating away. "Do you feel like a stroll?" she asked. "Unless you want to go right back to the house, there's something I'd enjoy showing you."

"Lead the way." Jake slowed his pace, savoring the pressure of her touch through his sleeve. "But your grandmother will probably give me one of those looks when we get back. I get the feeling she doesn't trust me."

"Oh, that's not true! Grandma likes you. She even told me she did." Kelly lapsed into silence for the space of a few heartbeats. "It's not you she doesn't trust, Jake. It's me."

"You?" Disbelieving, he quirked an eyebrow at her, then chuckled. "To tell you the truth, Kelly, I find that idea very intriguing."

Her color deepened becomingly. "It's not what you think, Jake Drummond."

"You mean my virtue isn't in danger? Dang it!"

"Oh, stop that!" She gave him a playful shove, then swung onto a rocky path that led off the walkway and wound uphill, on a course that paralleled the beach.

"What was it you wanted to show me?"

"You'll see." She let go of his arm and slipped in front of him on the narrow trail. By now they were in the trees, screened from both the house and the dock. Kelly's damp curls bounced as she wound her way among the boulders.

"Don't overdo it on that ankle," Jake cautioned, catching her elbow again. "It may feel all right now, but if you twist it—"

"I'll be careful. But please stop fussing over me, Jake. You sound like my grandma!"

Jake chuckled. "Your grandma, huh? I'll remember that. By the way, you never finished telling me. Why doesn't that dear lady trust you?"

Kelly froze. Jake felt her arm muscles clench beneath his fingers. He had meant the question to sound casual, but it hung like a red flag in the sudden silence.

Realizing he'd overstepped safe bounds, he attempted a swift retreat. "Sorry. I shouldn't expect you to answer a question like that. In fact, it really isn't any of my business. Forget I asked."

She glanced up at him, her expression still guarded. Then, deliberately turning away, she began to walk away. "No, it's all right. I... tend to get emotionally involved, that's all. Grandma's seen me hurt, and she's very protective. She's afraid it might happen again."

"And what about you?"

She stiffened, then moved ahead as if she hadn't heard.

Seized by an impulse he could neither control nor understand, Jake gripped her arm and spun her back to face him. Her startled eyes met his, still elusive in their gold-flecked depths.

"What about you, Kelly?" he grated. "Are you afraid of being hurt? Are you afraid of *me?*"

Her jaw tightened. Her eyes focused on his chin. "I don't know what you're talking about," she muttered.

"The devil you don't." His grip tightened on her arm. "Is that why we've been playing these cat-and-mouse games, because you're afraid I'll hurt you?"

"It's not you, Jake, it's—"

"Damn it, will you just answer my question?" His hand cupped her jaw, forcing her to look straight into his eyes. She trembled like a fawn.

"Kelly—"

A shudder passed through her body. She closed her eyes. When she opened them, her gaze was direct and unflinching. "It's all right," she said softly. "The answer is yes, Jake. I *was* afraid. But not anymore. I've made up my mind. Where you and I are concerned, I've grown up. I'm ready to be a big girl now."

Jake's breath burst out as if he'd been gut-punched. Kelly's answer was more than he'd asked for, more than he'd expected—and a hell of a lot more than he deserved. If he had any sense, he told himself, he'd turn right around and march her back to the house. Miss Kelly Ryan was definitely not safe with him.

But that was not to be. His arms were already drawing her close. "If this were a movie, I think the script would call for a kiss about now," he muttered.

Kelly did not speak. Did not move. Did not breathe.

Aching with tenderness, Jake lowered his face to hers. She stirred to life as their lips met. Her lovely, warm mouth opened like a flower. He tasted its honey in tiny, restrained nibbles, his tongue brushing the soft inside of her lower lip, then probing for deeper sweetness, thrusting into the moist, silky darkness.

Kelly whimpered. Her arms slid around his neck. She strained against him, all eager warmth now, open and trusting. Emotions tore Jake one way, then another. Doris was right to be worried, he realized. He *could* hurt Kelly. For all her brave talk, he knew he could crush her. She had given him the power. If he cared for her at all, he would put a stop to this madness right now.

But telling himself what to do was one thing. Doing it was another. Kelly was sweet heaven in his arms. His own need cried out for her warmth, her tenderness. His body responded to her nearness with surges of aching heat. Given another time, another place, he would have been hard-pressed to stop himself from—

No, this wouldn't do. It wouldn't do at all.

He kissed her one last, lingering time. Then, marshaling what was left of his strength, he eased her away from him.

"Kelly, sweet," he murmured, his mouth thick with desire. "Your grandmother is a very wise woman."

She stood facing him in the misty rain. Water beaded on her black lashes and formed tiny, opalescent jewels where her cheek was smudged with oil.

"I know," she whispered. "But it's all right, Jake. I realize you have your life, and I have mine. You'll be leaving tomorrow, and that will be the end. We won't be seeing each other again. But as long as we can accept that, why not make the most of the time we—"

With a muffled groan, Jake caught her close. His lips stirred her damp curls as he swore under his breath. Maybe Kelly could accept tomorrow's parting as the end of the relationship. But, damn it, could he?

Right now, Jake had no answer to that question. It was too soon. The memory of Ann was too sharp in his mind, too painful. Maybe someday... But no, he couldn't trifle with Kelly's feelings while he made up his mind about the future. That would be unfair, even cruel.

Under the circumstances, there was only one thing he could do.

He released her with a quick hug. "Hey." He cleared the huskiness out of his throat. "Didn't I hear you say you had something to show me?"

She returned his gaze with an understanding that needed no words. The smile she flashed him was as brilliant as it was brave. "Come on," she said, tugging at his hand. "But be very quiet. This is something you won't see in Seattle!"

Chapter Ten

The path zigzagged upward for three-quarters of a mile, winding through spruce clumps and outcrops of weathered gray rock. Kelly's ankle was beginning to feel the strain, but she kept her pace steady, her eyes focused straight ahead.

Behind her, she could hear the crunch of Jake's boots on the gravelly trail. She was glad she'd told him to keep quiet. Now that she'd made a complete fool of herself, she really didn't care to hear what he was thinking.

Hot color flooded her face as she remembered her response to Jake's kisses. Oh, she'd thought she was being so modern. She'd told herself she was being detached and nonchalant. She'd told herself—and him—that she could take their relationship as it was, with no expectations, no strings attached. Then he had taken her in his arms. His lips had seared hers with the heat of summer lightning. And dumb little Kelly Ryan had blown it all.

Jake, to his credit, had sidestepped her ardor with grace and skill. But what was he thinking now? What if he was laughing at her? She couldn't bear the thought of—

No!

Kelly battled the wall of self-protectiveness that was closing in around her. She had to break free. She had to trust her feelings and risk the hurt that would come when Jake was gone.

Otherwise her shell would harden for good. Trapped inside, she would shrivel into a cold, lonely old woman.

They were coming up on the crest of the bluff. Kelly motioned for Jake to keep still as the forest opened into a boulder-strewn clearing that overlooked Frederick Sound. There was no shelter here. Wind whistled over the bare rocks and sighed mournfully in the trees. Far across the water, storm-veiled mountains jutted into the sky. It was a wild, bleak spot, but Kelly had loved it all her life.

Her grandparents knew the place, of course. But Jake, she suddenly realized, was the first outsider she had ever brought here.

What if she had made a mistake? What if he didn't understand how special it was?

A massive dead spruce towered above the clearing, its ancient trunk bare of limbs except for a gnarled tangle at the crown. Its center was piled high with the twigs and litter of a huge nest. Turning, Kelly touched Jake's arm. Her hand pointed upward, guiding his eyes.

Something moved in the top of the tree. She heard Jake's breath catch as a fledgling eagle flapped from the nest to the end of a long, thick branch. It perched there, dancing impatiently, spreading its young wings for balance.

As they watched, a second eaglet joined the first. The two of them teetered there together on the limb, their wild cries mingling with the whistle of the wind.

Jake's arm tightened around Kelly's waist. "I can't believe this!" he whispered. "It's—"

"Shhh! Watch!"

A parent bird had dropped out of the sky, its dark wings wider than a man's outstretched arms. Its fierce, snowy head gleamed silver against the storm clouds. Its talons clutched a fifteen-pound salmon.

As the fledglings tore into the fish, another set of wings shadowed the ground. A second eagle, even larger than the first, settled onto the tree. This one brought no food, but it kept vigil while the family ate, its massive white head shifting warily, from side to side.

Jake's hand closed around Kelly's and tightened hard. His free arm drew her back against his chest, to cradle her as they watched. His lips brushed her temple.

"Jake, look," she whispered.

The bolder of the two fledglings had hopped back onto the long limb with a choice morsel of salmon in its beak. Backing away from its hungry nest-mate it edged farther and farther toward the limb's end until, suddenly, there was nothing beneath it but air. It dropped through space, the salmon falling unnoticed from its startled beak.

Then, instinctively, its powerful wings opened and began to pump. The young eagle flapped, rose and soared, its cries echoing its own astonishment.

"It could fly," Kelly whispered, delighted. "Jake, it could fly. It just had to discover its own wings."

Jake did not answer, but his arm tightened around her, and his throat moved against her hair.

Black clouds were moving in across the Sound. Wind dotted the water with whitecaps and ruffled Kelly's curls against Jake's chin. She closed her eyes, savoring the moment, memorizing each detail so that later, when he was gone she would have it for keeps, like a photograph of sweet-remembered time.

At last, when she could not bear it any longer, she stirr against him. "It's getting cold," she whispered. "We can g if you want."

"Not yet. I want to hang on to this a little longer, Kell It's beautiful. Thank you."

Kelly blinked back a freshet of emotion. Yes, he unde stood. Things would be all right. *She* would be all right.

She stood in the circle of his arm, surrounded by l warmth as they watched the eagles. She had no illusion Kelly told herself. This moment would pass. They would g back to the house and spend a proper evening with h grandparents. They would not be alone again until tomo row morning when they climbed into the plane for the sho flight to Juneau. Even then, there would be no chance f conversation in the Beaver's noisy cockpit—and in any cas Jake would be too preoccupied with his upcoming confe ence to do much talking.

They would say a public goodbye on the floatplane doc or in the crowded, noisy air terminal, and he would be gon

Here and now was the one perfect memory she wou keep—the warmth of his arms, the wind, the eagles and t storm sliding in like night over the wild gray water.

Engine roaring, the repaired Beaver skimmed the wat and rose into the midmorning sky. On the dock, Frank a Doris were waving. They stood arm in arm, watching un the plane was safely airborne. Then they turned and walk slowly back to the house.

As the doddering little craft banked and headed for J neau, the memory of the crash, in all its terror, tumbl back into Jake's mind. He took long, slow breaths a willed himself to relax. He was in capable hands, he reminded himself. More than capable. Kelly was the best.

His eyes traced the outline of her profile, memorizing each delicate detail—the tumble of dark hair over her forehead, the pert nose, the generous, childlike mouth, the determined chin. She had saved his life, he reflected. Perhaps in more ways than one.

He was just beginning to realize how much he would miss her.

Leaning back in his seat, he forced his mind to move ahead, to the two o'clock conference. His brain ticked through the figures—projections, expenses, returns, tariffs, liability insurance. He had everything down. It would go all right, Jake assured himself. He couldn't control the outcome, but at least the SEA-MAR board would know what his company could offer them.

Kelly... He glanced at her again, at her hands, relaxed and confident on the wheel. He wondered if she realized what an incredible woman she was. Maybe he should have told her. Up there on the bluff, with the eagles, maybe he should have let her know how he felt.

But no, it was too late. Minutes from now they would be landing. He would squeeze her hand, they would say goodbye and that would be the end of it. He would not even risk embarrassing her with a public kiss.

The flight was so short that the plane had scarcely leveled off before it was descending into Juneau. Over the crest of Douglas Island, Jake could see the city, sprawled picturesquely along the thin strip of land between the Gastineau Channel and the towering coastal mountains. The radio crackled as Kelly cleared for landing and eased the Beaver into a long glide. Jake felt the floats skim the water, and the slight jar as they settled into position. She did not look at

him as she taxied expertly up to the dock and switched o
the engine.

It was over.

Jake cleared his throat in the silence. "Not that I'm a
expert, but I'd say your landing was a little smoother tha
last time," he quipped inanely.

"Yes. Practice makes perfect, you know." Kelly fiddl
with the controls, avoiding his eyes.

He glanced at his watch. "Can I buy you a cup of co
fee?"

"Thanks. But you'd better not take the time. Dow
town's quite a distance from here. You'll need to get back
your hotel and get ready for your meeting."

Jake fumbled behind the seat for his jacket and paper
feeling like hell. He'd known all along that parting fro
Kelly would be hard. Now that the time was here—no,
wasn't just hard. It was damn near gut-wrenching.

"Are you going right back to Admiralty?" he asked.

She shook her head. "I've got some errands to run. I ne
to stop by the charter agency, see a friend or two and pi
up some odds and ends for my grandma." She hesitated,
if weighing emotional risks. "I keep an old car at the agen
for getting around town. If you'd like a lift—"

"That's all right. They're holding a car for me at t
rental office. If you need—"

"No. The agency's only a couple of blocks from here."

They gazed at each other in awkward, silent desperatio

"Well, then, I guess that's it." Jake opened the door
the Beaver and scrambled out onto the dock. The outsi
world swirled in on him as he waited for Kelly to climb o
of the plane. He felt as if he were going down on the *
tanic.*

She stood facing him now, her hand extended—a pil
saying a polite goodbye to her passenger. Her Coca-C

eyes were dry and bright, her brave little chin adorably squared.

"Good luck, Jake," she said.

He squeezed her fingers, forcing words past the rawness in his throat. "I owe you, Kelly Ryan," he muttered.

"Maybe we owe each other...." She bent down and caught up her duffel bag. Hoisting it to her shoulder, she swung away from him and strode breezily up the dock. "Send us a Christmas card from Seattle," she called back over her shoulder.

Jake stood glued to the spot, watching her figure grow smaller with distance until her flannel shirt became a red dot in the crowd that milled on the landing. The coldness that had settled around him was like a gray winter fog. He felt it creeping into his heart, freezing emotions that had warmed only when Kelly was with him.

When Kelly was with him.

Suddenly he was running, pounding up the dock, jostling people aside in his headlong rush to reach her. Glimpsing a flash of red, he sprinted forward. Yes, it was Kelly. She was rounding a corner of the terminal, on a beeline for the women's rest room.

He caught her sleeve. His fingers closed on the solidness of her elbow as he jerked her around to face him.

Her eyes were swimming with tears.

Jake struggled for something to say, but words had deserted him. He only knew that he couldn't let this feisty, vulnerable little woman walk out of his life. Not yet, at least.

It was Kelly who found her tongue first. "Did you forget something?" she asked tremulously.

"Have dinner with me tonight," Jake blurted.

"Why?" She blinked back furious tears.

"Call it a farewell party. I'd just like to say goodbye in a little grander style than the way we did back there."

"I . . . didn't bring any decent clothes."

"You're fine the way you are. I'm staying at the Water front. We could eat there, unless you've got a better idea. there someplace I could pick you up?"

Kelly hesitated. Jake held his breath, afraid she'd find a excuse to say no. When she finally sighed her acquiescence his relief was like the lifting of a leaden weight.

"The charter agency has a couple of empty rooms up stairs. That's where I usually crash when I'm in town. Bu as long as you're at the Waterfront, and I've got a car, wh don't I just meet you there? That'll save trouble for both o us."

"Fine," Jake agreed, although, where Kelly was con cerned, saving trouble was not a priority. "Time?"

"Is eight o'clock all right?"

"Fine. I'll make sure we have a table."

"Then we're all set." Her smile was tinsel-thin. "I'll b anxious to know how your meeting went."

"There probably won't be much to tell you. These thing usually take time. The board may not come to a final deci sion for weeks."

"I understand." Kelly adjusted the strap of her duffel then turned to go. "Good luck with your presentation, Jake I mean it. Break a leg, or whatever it is they say."

"Thanks." He drank her in with his eyes. "See you to night, then?"

"Uh-huh. See you." She broke away and veered towar the ladies' room again. Jake headed for the car rent counter in the main terminal, his boots moving double-tim He was already looking ahead to tonight. But first, he ha a shipping contract to win. Until the meeting was over, th presentation would require his full focus, his full energy People were depending on him—people he couldn't le down. He could not afford to be anything less than his best

* * *

Kelly sank against the wall of the rest room, her emotions ricocheting between elation and dismay. Oh, she had almost pulled it off. She had actually managed to walk away from Jake Drummond without losing control. Then he had come running after her—and caught her with her guard down.

She must have looked like a fool, with tears streaming down her face. Maybe Jake had felt sorry for her. Maybe that was why he'd asked her to dinner.

She snatched a tissue out of the dispenser and blew her nose hard. Whatever Jake's reason, she was going to see him again. Part of her wanted to dance. Part of her wanted to jump up and down and hug herself like an excited little girl.

But the other part—her wise, sensible side—was already urging her to call the hotel, leave Jake a message canceling dinner and be gone by the time he finished his meeting. She was getting off easy as it was. They'd had a few laughs and shared some tender moments, without anybody getting hurt. Why not leave it at that? Why not cut the risks and make a clean getaway right now?

But even as she argued with herself, Kelly knew it was useless. She would be at the Waterfront Inn at eight o'clock, ready to meet Jake. She would hold on to every minute of their time together, like a squirrel hoarding nuts for a long, cold winter. And when they said goodbye—yes, then she would give in to the pain, and learn from it.

As she turned to leave the rest room, she caught a glimpse of herself in the mirror. She paused for a longer look, heart sinking as she took in her windblown hair, her unadorned face and red eyes, her baggy flannel shirt and khakis. It had been a long time since she'd paid much attention to mirrors. Maybe too long.

In any case, she couldn't go to dinner looking like a refugee from a moose hunt. She would need a dress, at least. And it wouldn't hurt to do something with her hair.

Kelly glanced at her watch. The errands she'd planned would take a couple of hours, at most. That would leave the rest of the afternoon free.

Bending closer to the mirror, she scowled at her reflection. She'd never taken pains with her appearance. Somehow it had never seemed important.

But it was suddenly important now. She wanted to look good, not just for Jake, but for herself. She wanted to walk into that restaurant with her head held high. And—Kelly swiftly reminded herself—she wanted to leave the same way.

An old high school chum of hers was a beautician here in Juneau. Kelly strode to a phone booth and ruffled through the directory until she found the number. Heart skipping with unaccustomed giddiness, she dialed, heard the ring, heard her friend's answering voice.

She took a deep breath. "Margo, I need a fairy godmother," she said. "...Uh-huh. That's right, you heard me. I want the works."

Jake had reserved a quiet table with a view of the harbor. At ten minutes to eight, he ordered coffee and sat down to wait. He knew it was early, but he wanted to be there when Kelly showed up. He didn't want anything to go wrong tonight.

He had made a point of dressing casually, in a dark blue cashmere pullover, gray slacks and a light blue oxford shirt with no tie. He wasn't sure what Kelly would be wearing, but from what he knew of her, she wouldn't be overdressed. He wanted to make sure she felt comfortable.

He leaned back in his chair and sipped the hot black coffee, his mind running through the things he wanted to say to her. *Lord,* this was tougher than the SEA-MAR presentation! He felt confident when it came to spreadsheets, projections, profits and losses. In fact, he'd handled this afternoon's board meeting pretty well. But he had never known a woman like Kelly. And he had never told any woman the things he planned to tell her.

Let's see, how would he begin?

Kelly, I know this sounds crazy, with you in Alaska and me in Seattle, but I'm just not ready to walk away from what we've found. You're the first woman since my wife who's made me feel alive, and I want to...

No. Bringing up Ann wouldn't do at all. He would have to phrase it some other way.

Kelly, I want to see you again. I know it's too soon for any kind of commitment, but I think we just might have something here. Something rare and precious and fine. I'd like some time to explore it....

No.

Damn it, Kelly, I think I'm falling in love with you, and I need to know if—

All words evaporated from his mind as Kelly appeared in the doorway.

He could see her through the blur of crowded tables. She was standing just inside the entrance, glancing hesitantly around as if afraid he might have stood her up. She looked... absolutely perfect.

Jake swung out of his chair and strode across the dining room to meet her. He could see she'd had her hair cut. It was trimmed to curl softly around her elfin face, with a fringe of bangs setting off her eyes. And she was wearing an understated little black silk dress—cut like a man's shirt and cinched to her minuscule waist with a silver belt that matched her dangling hoop earrings. The skirt was short

enough to reveal shapely legs, clad in sheer, black silk
stockings. One hand clutched a tiny beaded evening bag.

Her anxious face softened as he reached her and offered
his arm. She teetered slightly in her high-heeled pumps, like
a coltish fifteen-year-old at her first formal party.

"Kelly, you look lovely," he said, meaning it.

"Thank you." She flushed self-consciously as she walked
beside him, the silk fabric whispering over her curves.

"Coffee?" He held her chair.

"No, thanks. Let's just order. I'm starved."

Jake took his seat across the candlelit table and passed her
one of the menus the waiter had left. As she studied it, he
devoured her with his eyes. Kelly had looked beautiful with
wind-tousled hair and a grease-smudged face. She had
looked beautiful in white terry toweling, her skin glowing
from the hot bath.

And now... Jake leaned back in his chair to take in the
full effect. Yes, Kelly Ryan was a stunner. On her, that
modest little black dress packed more wallop than skintight
décolletage on any Seattle postdebutante he could name.

Kelly looked hip. She looked meltingly, damnably sexy.

And part of her charm, Jake realized, was that she didn't
know it. She'd clearly gone to a lot of trouble to look good.
But even now she was hiding behind the menu, as if she were
afraid he might look at her too closely and discover some
flaw.

Didn't she know how desirable she was? Didn't she realize that he ached every time he looked at her? Couldn't she
feel it?

Jake sipped his coffee, frustration smoldering inside him
like a fire too long banked. She would know it before the
night was over, he resolved. Whatever it took, Kelly Ryan
would know exactly how he felt about her.

She would know exactly where he stood.

* * *

"I'll have the king crab," Kelly said. The waiter nodded and whisked away her menu. Suddenly she felt exposed and vulnerable. She'd been a fool to accept Jake's invitation, she told herself. The evening was going to be one big disaster. She could feel it in her bones.

Jake ordered salmon, with a bottle of vintage chardonnay. She sat facing him across the table now, taking tiny sips of the sparkling white wine and gazing across the candle flame into Jake's marvelous azure eyes. She'd never had much practice at being worldy and nonchalant. But she would pull it off tonight if it killed her. Whatever it took, she would at least walk away with her dignity intact.

"So tell me about your conference," she said, smiling at him over the rim of the glass. "Do you think it went well?"

Jake nodded slowly, his eyes never leaving hers. "Well enough, I think. They won't be awarding the contract till some time next month. But they were very receptive. I think my company's got a shot at it."

"I'm glad," Kelly murmured. "Especially after what you went through to get to that meeting."

Jake chuckled warmly. "I guess I was pretty obnoxious. And I never really apologized for it. I'd like to do that now, if it's not too late."

"Forget it." She broke off the riveting eye contact and stared down at the bubbles in her glass. At least when Jake was being obnoxious, she'd had no trouble dealing with him. It was *nice* she couldn't handle so well.

"You were concerned about letting people down," she said. "I understand that now, and it's all right."

Jake put down his wineglass and leaned closer, his gaze so compelling that Kelly could not look away.

"If we do get the contract, I'll be coming to Juneau fairly often," he said. "I'd like to see you again."

"Why?" The word tumbled out before Kelly could stop it.

"Don't you know?"

The glass wobbled in her hand. "Are you saying you haven't seen enough of me already?" she asked, trying to sound casual.

"That's exactly what I'm saying."

Kelly's eyes lowered to fix on the texture of the damask tablecloth. "Then you've got the wrong notion, Jake. We've had some good times, but you don't know what you'd be getting into. You don't really know much about me."

He reached across the table and captured her hand. "That's the whole idea. I *don't* know you well enough. And I'd like to. We've gotten off to a pretty decent start, and I'd like to give this thing a chance. What do you say?"

Kelly's hand quivered in the warm prison of Jake's fingers. She battled the impulse to leap out of her chair, tear herself loose and run from the room.

"Kelly?" A note of worry had crept into his voice.

She shook her head, fighting back tears. "You wouldn't want to know me any better than you do," she said. "There are things about me you wouldn't like. Things you're better off not knowing."

His grip tightened on her hand. "What things?" he grated. "Damn it, Kelly, I care about you. There's nothing you could tell me that would change that."

Slowly, painfully, she withdrew her fingers from his clasp. Out of the corner of her eye, she could see the waiter bringing their meals. "Please," she said softly. "Can't we just have our dinner and part as friends?"

"Is that really what you want?" He exhaled tensely as the waiter bent over their table and whisked the covers from their plates. The orange chunks of crab blurred before Kelly's eyes as she forced all emotion from her voice.

"What I want doesn't make any difference. I like you a lot, Jake. I was thrilled when you asked me to dinner tonight. But some things can't be changed." She picked up her fork, then swiftly put it down again so he wouldn't notice how hard her hand was shaking. "I should have stayed away. Then there'd have been no need for this conversation."

"Kelly, you told me you'd been hurt once—"

"No more questions." She pushed her face into a determined smile. "We don't have enough time left to waste arguing. Now let's relax and enjoy our dinner. Then . . ."

"Then?" Jake's voice was a raw whisper. Kelly took a sharp, hard breath.

"Then, my dear friend, we can say a nice, civilized goodbye."

For Jake, the next half hour was torture. He picked at his meal, making polite conversation, while Kelly did the same. When they weren't talking, they stared at their plates, or out the window at the glowing lights of the harbor—anything to avoid meeting each other's eyes.

Kelly's gaiety was as brittle as Christmas glass. She toyed with the food on her plate and laughed at everything he said, whether it was funny or not. Jake played along, but it was all he could do to keep from grinding his teeth in frustration.

Kelly's secrets were her own business, he reminded himself. If she didn't want to see him again, that was her choice. But reason was one thing, emotions were another. And with every passing minute, Jake's desperation grew. How could he simply let her walk away? How could he lose her now, just when he was beginning to realize how much he needed her?

He studied her over his wineglass, his eyes tracing every detail of her face. She was leaning forward now, making an effort to smile. Her perfume—new and provocative—teased his nostrils. Her silver earrings burned with reflected candlelight as she reminisced about the time after their crash.

"Remember how hungry we were out there?" she was saying. "Remember those wild blueberries, and how wonderful they tasted?"

Jake nodded obligingly, keeping up his part of the facade. "I remember. But we lost our appetites when we saw those bear tracks, didn't we? Admit it. You were as scared as I was."

"I'll never tell." Kelly's brave grin did not quite reach her eyes. She glanced at her wristwatch. "It's getting late. Maybe...maybe it's time we wrapped up this evening and said good-night."

Jake's heart plummeted. He groped for an excuse to delay her. Maybe some miracle would happen in the next few minutes. Maybe something would change her mind.

"We were talking about blueberries," he said. "For what it's worth, I noticed that one of the dessert choices is blueberry pie. Would you like some...for old times' sake?"

"Dessert?" She glanced down at the shambles of her dinner, then back to Jake. A spark of mystery flickered in the depths of her eyes.

"Yes, I was thinking dessert would be nice. But not blueberry pie. I...brought something special."

"Brought?" Jake blinked. "You *brought* dessert to a restaurant?"

Kelly was fumbling in her evening bag, her face in shadow. "You'll remember this, I think. I found it in my jacket...."

Reaching across the table, she handed him a half-crushed Hershey's bar in a tattered wrapper.

Jake stared at the candy bar. Kelly watched the emotions flash across his face—first disbelief, then laughter, a flicker of tenderness and finally, sliding into place like a mask, a hard-edged smile.

"Here," he said, tearing off the paper and breaking the bar along the center line. "Half for you, and half for me. Cheers." He raised his half of the bar in a mock toast.

Kelly accepted her piece and bit into the stale, crumbly chocolate. Her eyes welled with tears. She tried to laugh, but the sound came out as an odd little half sob. "This would have tasted like heaven in the bush. It's not quite the same here, is it? But then, maybe nothing is."

Jake's eyes glittered like a wolf's. "Stop analyzing and eat your blasted Hershey's bar," he growled. "Then we'll say— as you so aptly put it—a civilized goodbye."

He took slow nibbles of chocolate, his eyes never leaving hers. Kelly watched him through the sputtering candle flame, memorizing his face as their time together dwindled to seconds. If only things could be different. If only she could be a different woman, bright and perfect, with no secrets to hide—the kind of woman who would fit into Jake Drummond's life.

If only...

But it was no use dreaming. Some things couldn't be changed. Not ever. And the sooner she said goodbye to Jake, the less it would hurt.

They finished the chocolate, prolonging the last bites like a ritual. Jake leaned back in his chair, waiting for her to make the next move. His eyes were hard and narrow, his defenses already in place. Kelly knew he would not try to stop her from leaving.

She gathered up the napkin from her lap and crumpled it resolutely beside her plate. "Well, I guess it's time," she announced.

He stirred then, and rose to his feet, moving silently around the table to help her with her chair. His eyes burned into her back as she stood up. She could almost feel them through the thin black silk.

With the last of her strength, Kelly forced herself to turn around. His face was a mask in the candlelight as she caught his hand and gave his fingers a quick, hard squeeze.

"I'll walk you to your car," he said.

"No, it's not far. Goodbye, Jake." She tore herself away before he could see her tears. Then, with all the dignity she could muster, she hurried out of the restaurant, her spike heels clicking a frantic staccato across the floor.

The harbor wind was cool on her hot face. She strode through the blue twilight, willing herself not to break and run. It was all right, she told herself. Soon she would be in her car, driving away. She would sleep above the agency and fly home at dawn. And she would never see Jake again.

The battered brown Chevy wagon was waiting at the rear of the parking lot. Kelly was fumbling for the door latch when she remembered her keys. She had zipped them into her evening bag, along with the chocolate bar.

Her heart dropped as she realized she had left the bag on the table in the restaurant.

Chapter Eleven

Kelly hesitated outside her locked car. The heels of her black patent pumps clicked one way, then the other as she agonized over what to do next.

March back in and get her bag—that would be the sensible action. But it would mean one more encounter with Jake. Walking away the first time had drained her emotional reserves. Now, even the thought of going back to face those cold, bitter eyes was more than she could stand.

She could try to wait him out, she reasoned frantically. Maybe if she went for a walk, he would turn in her bag at the host desk and leave. Maybe he'd already done it, and she was being a fool.

Clouds, night-dark in the indigo twilight, rolled in across the harbor. A fresh breeze whipped Kelly's dress against her body, chilling her skin through the wispy silk. A storm was moving in, and her coat was locked in the car. She couldn't stay out here much longer.

Her mind scrambled for solutions, however silly. She could sneak back inside and hide out somewhere, like the ladies' room. She could—

Kelly's thoughts scattered as she glanced back toward the restaurant and saw Jake striding down the stairs, one hand holding her bag. Steeling herself for another wrenching encounter, she stood still and watched him approach. He moved like a tiger, she thought, each step a study in restrained fury.

His pace slowed purposefully as he came within speaking distance. The evening wind ruffled his dark blond hair. His eyes were cloaked in shadow, but something electric, something dangerous, flashed in their depths.

"You forgot this," he said.

"Yes, I know." The words emerged half-strangled from Kelly's throat. "I was about to go back inside for it. If you' just—"

She reached for the bag. As she snatched it away, his fingers closed around her wrist. A hard jerk spun her against his chest. Kelly stood rigid and trembling, staring up into volcanic blue eyes that were inches from her own.

"If you never want to see me again, that's your privilege," he grated. "But after what we've been through together, I'll be damned if I'm letting you go without a proper goodbye!"

He caught her to his mouth, not gently this time, but with the unleashed force of his passion. His arms crushed her hard against him, fingers almost bruising her flesh through the thin black silk.

Kelly struggled, but her resistance was no more than a flutter as desire exploded in her like a Roman candle. This, she realized, was what she had wanted all along tonight—Jake's arms around her, his mouth searing hers. She had wanted his hands—oh, yes, his hands—melting her body through her dress, molding her curves to his touch. It was the reason she had come here, the reason for the dress, the reason she had forgotten her keys. . . .

And suddenly nothing else mattered.

Her arms were around him now. Her fingers tunneled his hair and gripped the soft cashmere of his sweater, clasping and seizing in frenzied abandon. Her swelling mouth opened to the rough coaxing of his lips, opened to the velvet thrust of his tongue. Through the web-thin silk of her dress, she could feel every contour of him—buttons, buckles and the compelling hardness of his male body underneath.

His mouth grazed her cheek, nibbled her ear, skimmed her closed eyelids. "So help me, Kelly, I couldn't let you go," he murmured between kisses. "I couldn't just let you walk out of my life like that."

Kelly arched into the exquisite contact, her whole body alive and singing. "Shhh . . ." she whispered. "Don't talk. Just hold me, Jake. That's enough. That's all I'm asking."

Lightning ripped the storm-roiled sky. Dark sheets of rain burst down, soaking them both. They clung desperately, ignoring the downpour until they were both wet to the skin. Only then did Kelly break away to fumble for the car keys in her bag.

"I'd better—"

"No—" Jake's fingers touched her wrist, stopping her in midmotion. She met the hunger in his eyes. Even before he spoke, she knew.

Without a word, she dropped the keys back into her bag and closed the clasp. His arm slid around her shoulders. He gathered her against him, protecting her a little from the rain. "Come on," he whispered, his voice raw with need. "There's a rear entrance."

Soaked and out of breath, they reached the shelter of the hotel. In the elevator, they stood apart, water puddling

around their shoes. Kelly's skin was goose bumpy under th
clinging, wet silk. Her teeth were chattering, but she scarce
felt the cold. She was aware of nothing except Jake's pres
ence beside her and her own aching need for him.

She glanced at him furtively now, through the drippin
veil of her hair. Her heart contracted as she saw how co
and wet he was. Her face burned as she thought of how sh
would warm him. It was all right, she told herself. This wa
meant to happen. Here. Now. With this wonderful, giving
passionate man.

From the day she'd met Jake Drummond, she had sense
in her heart how things would develop between them. Sh
had tried to run away. But now...yes, she was throug
running. She was ready to give herself again, accepting h
own share of responsibility for what happened. And th
time she had no illusions, no naive, girlish hopes for the f
ture.

Tomorrow was tomorrow. And she would never be se
enteen again.

They left a wet trail from the hotel elevator to Jake
room. Kelly hugged herself to keep warm while he u
locked the door and closed it safely behind them. Then the
were alone in the darkness, standing a scant two paces fro
the king-size bed.

Jake turned and caught her in his arms again, his mout
crushing hers, his tongue hot and seeking. This time the
was no storm to stop him, no one to see as his hands move
down her wet back to cup her taut buttocks, pulling her hi
in hard along the firm ridge of his own desire.

"Jake...yes...oh, dear heaven, *yes*..." Wild with nee
she butted against him, touching off explosive quivers th
forked like lightning through her body. Nothing could ha
stopped Kelly now. She had to have him—to feel him,

taste him, to smell him, to know his touch on every part of her.

Her head fell back as the fingers of his right hand worked down the front of her dress, loosening each tiny black-pearl button. Her eyes closed as the rough, warm silk of his mouth nibbled down her throat to settle into the damp cleft between her breasts.

"You're cold," he murmured against her tingling skin.

"Warm me," she whispered, her fingers taloning his hair. "Warm me, Jake Drummond."

"So cold..." His hands glided up her legs, beneath her black satin slip. She heard him gasp as he discovered the garter belt and stockings she'd worn instead of panty hose—which she'd always found uncomfortable. "Kelly, you're going to be the death of me—" he rasped.

"No." She struggled to keep her senses as his fingers fumbled for the wispy black lace panties she'd bought that afternoon. "But if we don't get out of these wet clothes, we'll both end up with pneumonia—"

"Right." He pulled reluctantly away from her. His cashmere sweater disappeared with a wet slap against the floor. The shirt—Kelly might have torn it off him herself if his own hands had not been so eager. She heard his belt fall with his wool trousers in the darkness, heard the subtle thud of his shoes.

"Jake, I want to see you," she whispered, seized by a wild impulse.

"And I want to see you, my lovely Kelly." He bent to a side lamp and switched it on low. In the soft light that flooded the room, he stood gloriously naked, as beautiful as a sunrise and absolutely perfect, from his broad, muscular shoulders and gold-frosted chest to his tapering hips, and in the very center—Kelly lowered her eyes, suddenly afraid. Not of Jake. Never of Jake. But she was afraid of

what he would see when he removed the rest of her clothes—
the smallish, ordinary breasts, the body that was as trim as
a boy's, the sturdy legs she'd always thought were too short
for her long torso.

"Come here, Kelly." He held out his arms.

Kelly's lips trembled. She took a hesitant step toward him

"I think it's time we evened things up a bit," he murmured, catching the clasp of her silver belt so that it slith-
ered to the floor. Her dress was already unbuttoned to the
waist. Now he finished the job, fingers moving deftly until
the wet silk swished to the floor, leaving Kelly shivering in
her black slip.

His arms went around her again, drawing her close to
warm her against his golden flesh. Cupping her chin, he
tasted her lips again, his caresses growing rougher, wilder
Kelly whimpered as his hand tugged the straps from her
shoulders, his mouth moving lower to explore each breast—
lips grazing the soft swell of flesh, tongue tracing the exquisitely sensitive circle of areola and puckered nipple. "You're
beautiful, Kelly," he whispered against her skin. "You're so
beautiful...."

No, something inside her protested, *I'm not beautiful at
all. Look at me, Jake. See how plain I am, how ordinary...* But even the thought was lost in the rush of sensation that flashed through her as he tugged down the cover
and arched her back onto the bed. She lay across the sheet
her breath coming in tiny gasps as her slip, her bra and her
panties seemed to melt under his fingers, leaving her in
nothing but her black stockings and garter belt.

He leaned above her now, braced on his arms, his blue
eyes as dark as midnight. "I want you, Kelly Ryan," he
rasped. "I want to make love to you, as much as I've ever
wanted anything in my whole life. And damn it, unless you
want to stop me right now—"

Kelly's mouth blocked his words as she pulled his head down to hers. She was frantic with need for him. Her palms ranged hungrily down the hard curve of his splendid back to cup the firm golden moons of his buttocks, drawing him down to her. A long, deep quiver went through his body. Easing backward, he lowered himself to kiss her breasts, to brush her ribs, to press his face to the trembling flat of her belly.

"My sweet, sweet love..." he murmured.

At the word *love*, Kelly's breath caught. Her pulse surged in sudden panic. Even now, she could not put herself in a position to be hurt. "Jake," she whispered, "I don't want you to worry about me after—after it's over. I know this is only for tonight, and I don't intend to—"

His finger brushed her lips. "No more talk, my beautiful Kelly," he whispered. "We've done too much talking as it is. Hush, now..."

His wonderful, tormenting mouth moved lower, then lower still, until suddenly—

"Oh!" Kelly gasped in wonder as a sensation more exquisite than the opening of a hundred flowers rippled through her body. Her hips arched toward the source of incredible pleasure, wanting more, and still more. Her eyes closed. Her lips parted in silent ecstasy.

"Do you want me, sweet Kelly?" The breath of his whisper ignited rockets inside her. "Do you want me as much as I want you?"

Her only reply was a low, whimpering moan as he paused to protect her, then shifted his weight above her and eased between her thighs. He entered her very tenderly, almost as if he'd thought— But, no. The idea blurred in Kelly's mind. He would realize that she wasn't a virgin, and there was nothing to be done about it. Not now. She could only close her eyes and give herself up to the heaven of his closeness, his arms, his mouth, his hard, thrusting heat. She could only love him, for now, for this moment, for as long as it would last.

Unable to hold back any of herself, Kelly began moving with him, meeting each stroke with her own. His strong heart pounded his ribs beneath her hands. The raw, labored rasp of his breathing filled her ears. She buried her face against his shoulder, savoring the sweet man-musk of his beautiful body. For now, she told herself, Jake was hers. And now was all that mattered.

She could feel his desire mounting with her own, lifting, then soaring. At last, when they burst together in a shattering climax, she heard him cry out. His head dropped to the cleft between her breasts, and he lay there holding her murmuring soft little endearments that would be forgotten tomorrow. But it was all right. This was now. This was here.

Kelly's eyes moistened with tears of love.

The rain had stopped. Thin gray streaks of morning fingered the curtains, probing the darkness of the room. The neon red numerals on the bedside clock said 6:43.

Jake stirred sleepily. For a long moment he lay still, listening to the morning boat whistles from the harbor, the faint mewl of sea gulls and the sound of water dripping off the eaves. His body ached deliciously from last night's lovemaking.

He kept his eyelids deliberately closed, savoring the delay as he pictured Kelly, slumbering pink and fragrant beside him. He would open his eyes slowly, he resolved. For the first few seconds he would simply look at her, watching the play of light on her face. Then, little by little, he would awaken her with teasing kisses until she came to life in his arms. If she was willing, they could even take up where they'd left off last night, and—

But he was getting ahead of himself. Before he made love to Kelly again, Jake vowed, she would know exactly where he stood. Maybe it was too soon to talk about commitment, let alone marriage. But he could tell her, at least, what the past few days had meant to him. He could let her know that she was more than a fleeting episode in his life. He could make it clear that he wanted to explore their relationship, to nurture it, to give it a chance to grow.

Realizing how good he felt, Jake grinned. Hell, what he really wanted was ten thousand nights like the last one. And ten thousand mornings just like this—waking up sore and salty and happy as a clam, with Kelly no more than half a bed away.

What would she say if he told her that?

Overcome by an urge to hold her, Jake turned on his side and reached across the mattress. His arm fell on the cool, empty sheet.

He was instantly awake, sitting bolt upright and throwing the covers aside. The room lay in silent shadow, its adjoining bath dark. There was no sign of Kelly or her clothes.

With a muffled curse, Jake swung his legs off the side of the bed. He remembered what she'd said—her crazy disclaimer about not expecting anything beyond that night. Lord, he hadn't even taken her seriously. How the devil could she go, after what they'd shared? How could she believe she was no more to him than a one-night stand?

Switching on the table lamp, he prowled the room like a naked savage, gathering up his scattered things. His shoes lay a half-dozen paces apart, the socks hanging out of them like limp, wet tongues. His shirt, nearly dry, was flung over the back of a chair. His wool trousers sprawled damp and rumpled alongside the dresser. His wallet had fallen out of the back pocket. It lay open on the carpet, where a streak of morning light fell across Ann's picture.

Ann's picture.

Jake picked up the wallet and sank down on the bed with a muffled groan. Was that where Kelly was coming from? Had she slipped out of bed this morning, noticed the picture and concluded she could never compete with another woman's memory?

Jake stared down at the elegant snapshot. Ann's perfect features gazed back at him, as serene and loving as ever. But it wasn't enough. Ann was gone, and he was here. He was alone, and so damnably lonesome that the pain was more than he could stand.

With Kelly, the pain had almost gone away. Now it was back, like an ice splinter in his soul.

He hunched over the picture, his eyes tracing the familiar contours of Ann's face. What if he had been the one to die? Jake asked himself. Would he want to leave Ann like this, lonely and hurting for the rest of her life? Or would he set her free, to find happiness with someone else?

Numb and confused, he tossed the wallet on the pillow, headed for the shower and turned the tap on full force. The hot beads of water peppered his skin, shocking him to full wakefulness.

One thing was certain. If Kelly Ryan wanted to leave, he had no right to stop her. But he'd be damned if he would let her go without giving him some answers. He had to know what kept pulling her away from him. If there was a way to make things right, he had to try.

Wherever she had gone, Jake vowed, he would find her. Whatever it took, he would learn the truth.

Kelly eased the floatplane down through the morning clouds. She could see the inlet below, and her grandparents' house, with smoke curling from the big rock chimney. In a few minutes she would be home.

Her hands trembled on the wheel as she started the long, descending glide. She was coming back to the island, the house and the people she had known all her life. But she was returning a different person. For her, nothing would ever be the same as before.

Wind gusts buffeted the wings of the Beaver and streaked whitecaps across the dark gray water. The dock was empty this morning. Kelly was relieved. She would need some time to compose herself before she saw her grandparents.

Escaping from Jake's room before dawn had been easy enough in principle, since he was sleeping soundly and she'd lain awake all night. But leaving him had torn her apart. She had cursed her own cowardice as she fumbled for her clothes, dressed in darkness and slipped out the door. To stay and confront this thing honestly—that would have been the decent thing to do. But she had known, even then, that if she so much as looked at Jake's sleeping face, she would be lost. This was the only way out. She could only hope Jake would understand.

She had showered and changed at the agency, jamming the dress, shoes and black underthings into her duffel. She would be all right, she'd assured herself. She was a sophisticated woman now, not a seventeen-year-old child. She would simply put the hurt behind her, remember the good things and go on with her life.

Sophisticated woman? Put it behind her? What a joke! By the time the Beaver was airborne, Kelly had known she was in trouble. Over Douglas Island, she'd begun to sniffle. Crossing Stephens Passage, she'd bawled like a baby.

Damn. Damn. Damn.

She felt the familiar bump as the floats grazed the water and settled. Red-eyed and exhausted, she taxied up the inlet and cut the engine at the dock. Her head sank wearily onto her arms.

Her grandparents would know she was here, and they'd be waiting. Grandpa would want to know how the Beaver's engine had performed. That part would be easy. But her grandmother, and those all-knowing green eyes... Kelly shivered, dreading the moment of truth. Oh, it wasn't that Grandma would pry, or demand to be told where her grandchild had spent the night. Grandma didn't need to go that far. She just had a way of looking right through a person's skin to whatever was going on inside. Nothing got past Doris Ryan.

Shouldering her duffel, Kelly climbed out of the plane, secured the lines and walked slowly up the dock. A gust of wind rumpled her uncombed hair and stung her tear-reddened eyes. What did it matter, how she looked or what she'd done? What did anything matter?

She reached the base of the path that wound up through the rocks toward the house. There she paused, suddenly cold with fear.

Was it happening again?

No, it couldn't be. She couldn't let it.

Abruptly she veered off the walkway and headed for the bluff. Her booted legs moved in long strides, carrying her swiftly up the rocky slope and into the trees. She needed to think things out, to get her bearings before she went back to the house. She needed to make some tough, hard decisions and stick with them. Otherwise, she could open the door to the one thing she dreaded most.

Just as before, she could begin to drift, aimless and uncaring, from one day to the next.

She could drift until she crashed.

The chartered floatplane skimmed the whitecapped sound and taxied into the inlet. Jake strained to see through the salt-sprayed windshield. Yes, there it was—Kelly's Beaver, tied up at the dock. He had found her.

Frank and Doris had come out of the house and were hurrying down the walkway. But there was no sign of Kelly—but then, why should there be? She had just run away from him. He could hardly expect her to be part of the welcoming committee.

The plane sputtered to a stop on the near side of the dock. The middle-aged pilot, who worked for the same charter agency as Kelly, seemed to know the Ryans well. He waved as he swung out the door of the plane. Returning the wave, Frank came bounding down the dock. Doris hung back, her gaze riveted on Jake.

Frank was talking to the pilot. Seeing his chance, Jake broke away from them and hurried up the walk to where Doris stood waiting, her face shadowed with concern.

"I've got to talk to Kelly," he said softly. "Would you let her know I'm here?"

Doris's eyes narrowed. Did she dislike him? Jake wondered, or was she just being protective?

"I haven't seen Kelly," she said.

"The plane—"

"Oh, she came back. But not to the house. I'd guess she went for a walk. She does that sometimes, when she wants to be alone and think."

"Where would I find her?"

"I think you know the answer to that question as well as I do." Doris's voice was taut with worry. "Don't hurt her, Jake. Kelly's more fragile than you know. It would be a kindness for you to climb back into that plane and leave right now."

Jake hesitated, then shook his head. "No, I'm sorry," he said gently. "I don't want to cause Kelly any pain, but there are things I need to understand. I have to talk with her."

Doris did not reply at first, but a flicker of resignation passed across her mobile face. In a gesture that caught Jake off guard, she reached for his arm and gave it a warm, hard squeeze. "Be careful," she murmured. Then, before he could respond, she released him and turned away. In the next instant she was bustling down the dock, cheerfully inviting the pilot inside for coffee.

Jake mounted the trail, remembering how Kelly had taken him that way to show him the eagles. She had seemed so happy that day, so strong and confident. In fact, he had never thought of her as *fragile*. Now, as he walked, he turned the word over in his mind, wondering what Doris had meant.

He saw Kelly before she saw him. She was standing a few paces from the edge of the bluff, gazing out at the water, looking small and lonely.

Fragile.

She turned at the sound of his footsteps, as if she had been expecting him. Wind buffeted her hair around her face. Her eyes were red, her skin blotched with pink.

"I saw the plane come in," she said softly. "You shouldn't have followed me, Jake."

"You shouldn't have run off." He came up beside her. They stood side by side, staring out at the leaden waves, not quite touching. "I need some answers," he said.

"Do you?"

"Damn it, stop evading me," he growled. "I don't understand any of this. I thought we had something good. I was happier than I'd been since—"

"Since Ann?" Pain threaded her voice.

"Was that why you left? Because of Ann?"

She was silent for the space of a long breath. "Not really. It helped, knowing what I'd be up against if I stayed. But no, Jake, it wasn't Ann. It was me."

"Look, I can't take much more of these riddles."

"I'm sorry," she whispered. "I didn't mean to do this to either of us. I thought I could be modern and sophisticated. But I . . . didn't count on falling in love with you."

"Kelly—" Stunned by her honesty, Jake made a move toward her, but her eyes stopped him.

"You don't understand," she said. "This has to end. It has to end here and now."

Jake forced his eyes away from her. Frustrated, he glared at the ground. His toe kicked impotently at a rock. "Well, you're right about one thing," he said. "I *don't* understand. I wish I did. Then maybe I could make some sense of all this."

"Jake, it's so complicated—"

"I've got time to listen. I've got as long as it takes."

"I wouldn't even know where to begin."

Jake thrust his hands into his pockets. He wanted to explode. He wanted to grab her in his arms and hold her by force until she saw things his way. But it wouldn't work, he knew. Kelly had a mind of her own. He couldn't change it for her.

Jake exhaled slowly, trying to be patient. "You said you'd been hurt once. You could start by telling me about it."

"You don't know how hard it is." She turned and walked away from him in an agony of hesitation. Behind her, the ancient tree with the eagle's nest in its crown towered against the gloomy sky. Jake glimpsed a movement in the maze of twigs, but that was all.

Trembling now, Kelly swung back to face him. "You said you wanted some answers. If I tell you everything, will you promise to leave as soon as I've finished?"

"Kelly, I can't force myself on you. I'll leave anytime you insist. But yes, damn it, I'd like to take some answers with me when I go. If you'll tell me—"

"You promise, then."

Jake felt as if the life were being sucked out of him. He swallowed hard. "All right. I promise."

Kelly slumped into her jacket. For a long moment she stared out at the water. Then, on weighted feet, she moved across the clearing to a fallen tree trunk. "Come and sit down," she muttered. "This could take a while."

Jake joined her on the mossy log, settling at a comfortable distance. He didn't understand why Kelly would feel threatened by his closeness, but he sensed that she was.

"Take your time," he said.

She sank into a silence that was broken only by the wind. The strain tugged at Jake's nerves as he waited. He had to be patient, he told himself. He had to let her know she could trust him. But, Lord, it wasn't easy. Waiting had never been his style. It was all he could do to keep from seizing her in his arms and trying to make everything right that instant.

And that wouldn't work, he knew. Not for either of them.

"Jake, what do you think of me?" she asked.

"I think you're beautiful," he answered without hesitation. "I think you're warm and sweet and sexy—and all that aside, you're also one of the finest, bravest, most competent people I've ever known."

She sighed, and the sound was as dismal as the wind. "You're very kind," she murmured. "But you're wrong on all counts."

"I'm never wrong." Jake tried to smile, but the joke had already fallen flat.

"You don't know me, Jake. When I look in the mirror, I see a woman who couldn't hold a man's love. I see a coward. I see a weakling—"

"Whoa," he said gently. "Maybe you'd better start at the beginning."

Kelly stared at the clouds. Her fingers stroked a clump of thick, green moss that sprouted from a knob in the wood. "This island is the only home I remember," she began in a hushed voice. "I love it now. But when I was in my teens, it seemed more like a prison. I could hardly wait to get away and experience the world."

"That's not so unusual." Jake checked an impulse to reach out, catch her shoulder and pull her against him.

"I guess I was pretty wild," she continued. "Grandma and Grandpa were good to me, but they were strict, and I didn't appreciate them the way I do now. Looking back, I don't know how they stood me."

"They love you, Kelly. Anyone can see that."

"I know," she said softly. "I understand it now. But I didn't then."

Jake shifted on the hard log. "So you were a bratty kid. Join the club, Kelly Ryan."

"Bratty? You don't know the half of it." Kelly zipped her jacket to her chin, took a deep breath and stumbled on. "When Grandpa took me up in the Beaver—that was the only time I felt free, the only time I was really happy. Back on the ground, I was miserable, and I did a pretty good job of spreading the misery around. When I went to Juneau for my last two years of high school, I told myself they were glad to be rid of me—as glad as I was to be gone."

"So you did get away from the island."

She nodded. "I'd taken my schooling with the kids in Angoon, or by correspondence. But to be ready for college, I needed something more structured. There was a lady in Juneau who ran a sort of boarding house for high school kids. The rooms were clean, and the food was all right, but there was no supervision. I was on my own. I could go anywhere, do anything I wanted.... And when I came back, there was nobody to ask me where I'd been."

Kelly stared down at her boots. Jake sensed the pain moving in, surrounding her like a dark aura. He could imagine the kind of things she'd done—dumb, wild kid things that were far behind her now. He wanted to take her in his arms, to hold her, to cover her sweet, pink face with kisses and tell her how little it mattered to him.

But he held back. Kelly needed to talk, and he needed to listen. Otherwise, there'd be no chance of ever resolving this mess.

"I met a young man in a club." She spoke from a well of anguish. "I'd lied about my age to get in, and I told him I was twenty-two. The truth was, I'd just turned seventeen. His name was Cody. He was from Arkansas, and he worked on an oil rig."

She paused to gulp back her emotions. "Jake, I'd never been in love before. For all the wild things I'd done, I'd never given myself to...to a man. But I did. Oh, I did. Every chance I got, I'd run to him. He said he'd take me back to Arkansas when his job was done. He said we'd be married. And I believed him. I believed every word."

"Kelly—" This time Jake did reach out to her. His knuckles grazed her cheek before she pulled away.

"Don't," she said in a dull voice. "There's more. A lot more."

"Kelly, you were young and innocent. You made a mistake—"

"No." Her voice was leaden. "You wanted to hear this. You can hear it all." She fished a wadded-up tissue out of her jacket and dabbed at her tear-reddened nose. "You can guess what happened next. Two months after I met him, I found out I was pregnant. At first it seemed all right. I was in love. I was planning to be married. And the idea of having a baby, someone tiny and sweet and totally mine..."

Kelly's hands clenched and unclenched in her lap. "I told Cody," she said. "He agreed we should be married right away. He promised to meet me at city hall the next afternoon to get the license. . . ."

Jake watched her, his throat aching as he anticipated the outcome of her story, the disappointment, the humiliation. He saw how she huddled into herself as she spoke, as if she were trying to hide from him. "It's all right, Kelly," he said gently. "Being hurt by someone is nothing to be ashamed of."

But Kelly paid him no attention. Jake could feel her agitation growing as the memories unfolded. "He didn't show up, of course. I sat there all afternoon, on a bench outside the clerk's office, wearing my best dress. I felt as if everyone who walked past knew why I was there, and what had happened. I could imagine the snickers, the gossip."

She was on her feet now, the wind whipping her hair into tiny corkscrews around her face. "At first I was afraid he'd been in an accident. I finally called his company. Somebody there told me he'd quit his job and left town that morning." She attempted a feeble laugh. " 'Shipped out on a freighter,' they said. It sounded like a line out of some B-grade movie."

"And you never saw him again? Never heard from him?" Jake gulped back a surge of anger. How could any man walk out on a girl like Kelly, leaving her alone and in trouble?

"No." She sank back onto the log. "Not that I tried to find him. What was the point? He didn't want me."

"But he should have helped you financially, at least—"

"No. It wouldn't have been worth it, Jake. Facing him again would have been more than my pride could stand. But at least I had Grandma and Grandpa. Once they got over the shock, they were wonderful. They said I could stay with them, and they'd help me raise my baby. Grandpa fixed up the spare room and repainted my old crib. And Grandma sewed me a whole layette of little clothes and blankets. I...still...have them tucked away in—in the cedar chest.''

She was battling tears now, and losing. Jake was frantic to gather her in his arms and comfort her. But there was one more question. It hung between them like a dark weight, demanding to be voiced.

He forced the words out of his tight throat. "Kelly, what happened? Why didn't you keep your baby?''

Kelly met his gaze with haunted, red eyes. "He died, Jake. My beautiful little dark-haired boy. He came early, and there was a problem with his lungs. For two days, they kept him alive in an incubator, and then he was gone. I...didn't even get a chance to hold him.''

"Oh, God, Kelly—''

"I sort of fell apart after that. Acute clinical depression, the doctors said. I stopped eating. I almost stopped living. Wound up in the hospital, with tubes in my arms...''

Kelly stood up, wiped her eyes and forced her face into a strained smile. "So now you know. You know everything.''

"Yes...I guess I do.'' Jake gazed at her, heartsick, as the answers fell into place. Things were beginning to make sense now. Kelly's fears, her inability to trust him, her grandmother's protective concern. Still holding her with his eyes, he eased himself off the log. How could anyone survive so much hurt? he wondered. Where had Kelly found the strength to pick up her life again? He was awed by her resiliency.

"You made me a promise,'' she said in a voice drained of emotion. "You said you'd leave if I told you the truth. It's time for you to keep that promise.''

"Damn it, Kelly.'' He took a step toward her, frustration seething inside him. What did she think he was, a spineless jerk like the first man she'd loved? Did she think her past made any difference to him? Lord, if anything, what she'd told him made her all the more human, all the more precious.

"Damn it, Kelly, I'm in love with you!" he exploded.

She stood her ground, rigid as an icicle.

"Goodbye, Jake," she said softly.

Chapter Twelve

Jake was grabbing a quick lunch at Seattle's Pike Place Market. The restaurant he'd chosen was little more than a cubbyhole, with dingy windows and worn green oilcloth on the tables. But service was fast, and the ex-merchant marine chef made the best clam chowder in the known universe. Over the years, Jake had become a regular.

Absentmindedly, he took the tissue-wrapped roses he'd just bought and laid them on the seat of the booth, next to his briefcase. The roses were for Vanessa, a woman he'd met while playing tennis at the club. Tonight she'd invited him to her condo for home-cooked paella, but he planned on working right up to dinnertime, so the lunch hour had been his only chance to get flowers. He hoped the long-stemmed yellow roses wouldn't wilt before tonight. Maybe if he stuck them in the office fridge—

"Here y'are, Cap'n." The waiter, who was also the cook, plunked the piping hot chowder, in its thick, white bowl, onto the table. "Eat hearty now. It's chilly outside."

Jake dipped into the chunky soup, blowing on each steaming spoonful to keep from scalding his mouth. As he ate, he forced himself to think about tonight's dinner. Yes, he reflected, it would be nice if he could work up some enthusiasm. Vanessa was anxious to show off her cooking skills—and a few other skills as well, he gathered. Her invitation had carried an unspoken innuendo that no man could have missed.

Deliberating, Jake stared out the window at the mist-enshrouded Sound. A lumbering ore freighter, belching smoke, chugged across his vision and vanished into the fog.

Shipped out on a freighter... like a line from a B-grade movie...

Jake tore the words from his mind.

Why the hell shouldn't he go to bed with Vanessa? He'd taken her out a half-dozen times, and she'd made it clear enough that she was willing. He even liked her. She was tall and redheaded, with sexy, long legs and an easy laugh. Any sane male would be happy to—

Damn!

What the devil was the matter with him? He'd been back from Alaska for nearly two months, and he still had trouble getting his bearings. Everywhere he looked, he seemed to see Kelly. He had glimpsed her walking ahead of him on the street, half-hidden by a black umbrella. He'd seen her flashing past in the window of a bus, and crossing the street in a crowd, in front of his car. Reason told him he was not seeing her at all, but his mind kept playing the same old tricks. He'd tried everything, short of sleeping with Vanessa, to get Kelly Ryan out of his system. So far, nothing had worked.

His memory had replayed their last conversation a hundred times, and he had yet to make any sense of it. Kelly had confessed to falling in love with him. He'd blurted out that he loved her, too. And in the end, even that hadn't been enough. They'd said goodbye, and he had walked away. He'd flown back to Seattle that very afternoon, and tried to pick up his life where he'd left off.

But it wasn't working. Those few days he'd spent with Kelly only underscored the emptiness of his existence and the need for a warm, lasting relationship.

To put it simply, he was tired of living alone. He was tired of the social whirl, tired of the guessing games. He needed a partner, someone to share his victories and cushion his disappointments—someone to care for and build a life with. It was a need that even Ann would have understood.

He had put the house up for sale. He had packed Ann's belongings and tenderly consigned them to her parents' attic. It was time to move on. But where? And with whom?

Kelly's pert face floated in his mind, the vision so clear that he could almost count the freckles across her nose. He pictured her across the breakfast table, curled in her white terry robe, laughing over morning coffee. He pictured her floating on his arm at the company Christmas dance, charming everyone in sight. He pictured her on his boat, with the wind ruffling her hair, and on the tennis court, whacking balls at him from across the net. Of course, he would likely have to teach her to play....

But he was only daydreaming now. Kelly's distrust of men made things damn near impossible. She had been hurt so deeply, he realized, that she might not ever marry. And even if she did, her insecurity would drive most husbands crazy. If he had any sense, he would put her behind him and move on—maybe to a woman like Vanessa.

Again he thought about tonight. He pictured Vanessa's tasteful apartment, the candle-lit table, the soft music, the seductive perfume—everything calculated to lure him into her bed. So why the hell not take her up on it? Maybe the distraction would purge him of Kelly, once and for all.

He was fishing in his wallet to pay for the soup when the pager on his belt went off. Switching off the beeper, he glanced around for the nearest phone.

"Here." The grizzled chef shoved a greasy, black desk model across the counter. "Be my guest, Cap'n."

Jake dialed the office, wondering what was afoot. It had to be something urgent, or he wouldn't have been paged at lunch.

"What's up, Marlene?" he greeted the receptionist who answered.

"You'll soon know. Hang on, I'll put you through to Shamus. He's in there making like Fred Astaire on top of his credenza."

The line clicked through to Shamus O'Toole, Jake's senior partner in the shipping company. "Hey! You did it, old man!" Shamus's voice blasted Jake's ear. "Rog just got off the phone with the SEA-MAR folks. We got 'em, boy! We got the contract!"

"We...got it." Jake felt himself go limp with relief. He'd tried to put SEA-MAR out of his mind while the board delayed its decision, week after week. Only now did he realize how worried he'd been, and how responsible he felt.

"Jake...? You still there?" Shamus's voice broke into his thoughts. "Listen, they want you up there bright and early tomorrow morning to wrap up the paperwork. That's right. They requested you by name. Marlene's already booked you on the five-oh-five for Juneau tonight. You'll have a car waiting and a room at the Waterfront. I won't even ask if you can make it."

Visions of a peeved Vanessa flashed through Jake's mind. "Of course I can make it," he said.

"See you in a few minutes, then," Shamus boomed. "I'll get Marlene started copying those contracts right now."

"Right. I'll be there." Jake hung up the phone in a happy daze. He wanted to dance. He wanted to shout. He wanted to pick up the phone and call somebody, anybody, and share the good news.

But who would he call? His own mother had died years ago. Ann's parents wouldn't care that much anymore. Vanessa would need to be told soon, but she'd only be sour about his missing their date tonight.

Right now, Jake realized to his dismay, there was only one person he truly wanted to talk to. And she would be far out of reach—in a house with no phone, or somewhere in the air. Even if he could call Kelly, it wouldn't be a good idea. It would only start the wheels in motion once more—the wheels of mistrust and frustration that kept them apart.

If only he could convince her once and for all . . . But no, it was useless even to think about it. Kelly would never give a man her full trust again. She would spend her life running away, and there was nothing he could do to stop her.

He finished paying for the chowder, caught up his briefcase and headed for the restaurant door. "Hey, Cap'n!" the cook called after him. "You forgot your posies!"

With a sigh, Jake walked back and retrieved the tissue-swathed bouquet from the seat of the booth. "Here," he said, thrusting the flowers into the hands of the unshaven, tattooed ex-seaman. "Enjoy."

The Alaska Airlines jet banked over Juneau and glided downward through the October twilight. Through the double panes, Jake could see the harbor lights, their long, gold fingers stabbing the rippled water. He could see the city, ly-

ng like a jeweled pin at the foot of the black velvet moun-
ains. For perhaps the hundredth time, he tried not to think
bout Kelly, or to remember that she would be down there
omewhere below him in the darkness.

It was over with Vanessa. She'd put up such a snit about
iis missing their date that Jake had said a polite goodbye
nd written off the relationship. It was just as well, he told
imself. Better to break it off now than to become physi-
ally involved and let things die a slow, messy death. All the
ame, he felt like a heel. Vanessa had done her best. It wasn't
ier fault he was in love with somebody else.

The wheels touched the tarmac with a bump, the runway
ights blurring as the taxiing plane sped past. Maybe Kelly
vas spending the night at the agency again. He had the
hone number. He could call. . . .

Forget it, he admonished himself. Even if Kelly would see
iim, it wouldn't work. He'd only end up frustrated by that
naddening distrust of hers.

All the same, after he'd picked up his rental car, Jake
ound himself driving the longer route to the hotel—a route
hat took him past the charter agency.

He needn't have bothered. The place was closed for the
iight, and there were no lights on upstairs. Behind the
uilding, Kelly's old Chevy wagon was parked in its usual
lace. One tire had gone flat. The hood and windshield were
overed with moldering leaves.

Worry formed a knot in Jake's chest. It was clear that the
ar hadn't been driven in weeks. What if something had
iappened to Kelly? An accident—a crash? She could have
iied, and no one would have thought to tell him.

Jake forced himself to get back behind the wheel of the
ented car and drive to the hotel. There was nothing more he
ould do tonight. Besides, Kelly was probably fine. She was
usy, that was all. Or maybe the fool car had stopped run-

ning, and she hadn't bothered to fix it. Any one of a dozen explanations could fit.

All the same, Jake could not shake the gray weight of worry from his mind. It stayed with him all the way to the hotel, leaving him too agitated to eat dinner. Even later, as he hunched over the table in his room, going over every line of the shipping contracts, the unspoken fear returned to gnaw at his guts. He imagined Kelly out in the frozen bush, lost, hurt, even dead. It was all he could do to keep from leaping up and pacing the floor.

At eleven-thirty, he gave up on the contract and switched on the late-night movie. The film was an old John Wayne Western he'd seen three times as a kid, but he sat through the full two hours, commercials and all, sprawled glassy-eyed on the bed. Even when it ended, he could not fall asleep.

Where was Kelly? What could have happened to her?

It was a relief when the six-thirty alarm went off. Jake showered, shaved and laced his bloodshot eyes with drops. At seven o'clock he dialed Kelly's charter agency. He knew it was early, but just on the off chance...

A recorded message answered the call. The agency would be open for business at nine o'clock. He could leave a message at the tone.

The conference with the SEA-MAR board was scheduled for eight-thirty. Jake gave his name and room number to the machine and said he needed to get in touch with Kelly Ryan. The agency people could leave word.

Damn.

Jake ordered toast, fruit and oatmeal from room service. While he waited for breakfast, he dressed and went over the contracts one more time. He owed his company and their new clients his full attention. For the duration of the meetings, even his concern for Kelly would have to be put aside.

He did his best—and the first session with SEA-MAR went well enough. Even so, at the ten-thirty break he dashed for the nearest phone to check his messages.

Nothing.

Seething with frustration, he dialed the agency again. "I'm trying to get in touch with a pilot named Kelly Ryan," he growled at the young man who answered.

"You're Mr. Drummond, right?"

"That's right. And I was hoping you'd answer my message."

"I'm sorry," the young man said. "But I didn't know what to tell you. There's no Kelly Ryan working with us now."

"But she was—"

"Hang on, bud. I know you're not crazy. There's a Kelly Ryan in the files, all right. But I've been working here since September, and I've never even seen her."

"Look, her car's still parked out back. That brown Chevy wagon—"

The voice chortled annoyingly. "So that's who that old junker belongs to! Boss has been after me to have it towed! If you catch up with her—"

Jake ground his teeth. "Maybe your boss knows what happened to her. Could you ask him for me?"

"I could. But he wouldn't likely know. He bought this business from the old owners last month. Most of the pilots stayed on with us. But not Kelly Ryan. Fact is, till you called this morning, I'd never heard of her."

"If you could check around—"

"Oh, I'll do some asking. But if you don't hear, just figure I never learned anything. Bush pilots are a strange breed anyway. Kind of wild—even the chicks. Wouldn't be the first time one has dropped out of sight without a word."

"I see. Well, you have my number here in Juneau. If you don't mind taking my Seattle number, too, I'd be happy to pay for a collect call anytime."

"Sure thing. Hang on, I'll grab a pen."

Jake left the number and hung on, churning. How could Kelly just vanish like that? Despite what the brash young clerk had said, it wasn't like her. She could be in some kind of trouble. She could be sick. Or hurt. Or—

Damn it, he was going to find her. And once he did, he was never going to let her—

"There you are, Mr. Drummond." It was the board chairman's secretary, scurrying past with her notes. "Everyone's headed back into the conference area. We'll be starting again in a couple of minutes."

"Right. Thanks." Jake forced himself to shift mental gears as he strode back to the boardroom. Maybe tonight he could find a radio operator to contact Frank and Doris. But no, that wouldn't do. Kelly could be avoiding him. They could be protecting her. There was only one sure way to learn the truth.

The board members were taking their seats. Wrenching his mind away from Kelly, Jake settled into his chair, reshuffled his papers and took a sip of ice water. "If there are no questions," he began, "we'll start at the top of page six."

October's pale sun lay low in the southern sky. The inlet reflected tones of pewter and amethyst as the floatplane skimmed onto the water. It was nearly ten in the morning, but the day still wore dawn's muted tones, a portent of the winter darkness to come.

Jake strained against his seat belt as the plane whirred up to the dock. His heart leapt as he noticed the Beaver—the one he'd helped repair—pulled into an open-fronted shed on the beach. But the house was quiet. A curl of smoke from the chimney was its only sign of life.

As he watched, the front door opened, and Frank came out on the porch, followed by Doris. There was no sign of Kelly anywhere. Jake's stomach clenched. She could be on her bluff, he told himself. She could be inside studying, or bathing or simply avoiding him. Or—

No, he wouldn't even let himself think it. Her plane hadn't crashed. She had to be safe.

He climbed slowly out of the plane, never taking his eyes off the two approaching figures. Frank and Doris looked all right. They were exchanging waves with the pilot now, as they jogged down the dock. Jake stood half-hidden by the wing, wondering whether it had been a good idea to come. After what had happened with Kelly, he could hardly expect to be welcomed with open arms.

It was Doris who noticed him first. "Jake?" She hurried toward him, leaving Frank to visit with the pilot. Her face was a carefully composed mask, but her green eyes burned with unspoken questions. "What a surprise! We didn't expect to see you so soon. What brings you here?"

"The SEA-MAR contract." Jake kept his tone polite and neutral as he geared up his courage. "I've been in Juneau for the past two days, wrapping things up."

"Your hard work paid off, then. Congratulations."

"Thank you." He swallowed hard and plunged ahead. "I came to see Kelly. When the new agency people said she wasn't working with them..." He tried to shrug, but the gesture came off awkwardly, like something out of a high school play. "I guess I got worried, especially when I saw that her car hadn't been driven."

"And you were hoping she'd be here."

"Is she?" Jake found himself stumbling over his own tongue, like an anxious schoolboy. "Is she all right?"

"Yes, Kelly's all right. She's fine."

The words set Jake free. The awful weight of the past three days evaporated, leaving him dizzy with relief. Doris watched him, measuring his emotions.

"I'd like very much to see her," he said.

"Why?"

"I . . . It's hard to explain. I left a lot of things unsaid the last time I was here. I need to talk to her again. I need to let her know how important she is to me."

"Important?" Doris's expression softened. "Do you love her, then, Jake?"

"I do." Jake spoke with absolute conviction, knowing it was true. "I tried to tell her the last time we were together. But it wasn't enough. I couldn't make her believe me."

"She's afraid to believe you." Doris took Jake's arm and began to walk, steering him gently toward the house. "Can you blame her? Look what happened the last time she took a man's words to heart."

"I'm not like that."

"Aren't you?" Doris sighed worriedly. "You're an outsider, Jake. Your world is in Seattle, not here. Sooner or later you'll leave. Kelly knows that."

"So why couldn't I take her with me?" Jake's mind was leaping ahead into plans he'd scarcely thought out himself. "I could give Kelly a wonderful life in Seattle. She'd have everything a woman could want—"

"Oh, Jake!" The dismay in Doris's voice was like a dash of ice water in his face.

"What?"

"My dear Jake, I know you care for Kelly. But if you think she'd be happy in a place like Seattle, you don't know her. You don't understand what truly matters to her."

"Maybe not." Jake strove to keep up his bravado. "But that should be Kelly's decision. I'd like the chance to ask her in person. And I'd like to hear her answer. If it's no..." He shrugged, feigning a resignation he did not feel. "I'd like to talk to Kelly right now, if she'll see me."

"You can't." Doris shook her head. "Kelly isn't here."

Jake glanced back at the Beaver. "But I thought—"

"I'm sorry. I should have made that clear right away. Kelly's gone. She's in Fairbanks."

"Fairbanks? What the devil—?"

"She's gone back to college, Jake. She's living on campus at the university while she finishes the work on her teaching certificate."

"But Fairbanks—"

"I know. There's a perfectly good branch of the university in Juneau. But that wasn't what Kelly wanted. She said it would be too easy to get distracted and come home. As it is, she doesn't plan to be back here until Christmas break."

Fairbanks. Visions of northern lights and dogsleds and eleven-foot snowdrifts paraded through Jake's mind. "What do you hear from her?" he asked, still stunned. "Is she happy?"

"She's doing all right." Doris mounted the front porch and turned to gaze out over the inlet. "It took a lot of courage for her to go, Jake. If you really care about her, you won't throw her off track again. You'll leave her alone and let her get through this."

"Are you saying you won't give me her address and phone number?"

"Of course I'll give them to you. I may be a meddling, overprotective old woman, but I can't run other people's lives. What happens next is your choice, and Kelly's."

Doris's sun-freckled hands gripped the porch railing. When she turned back to face Jake, he caught the glimmer of a tear in her eye. "I'm only asking one thing. Don't trifle with her, Jake. Kelly is doing her best to heal, but even after all this time, she's so tender, so vulnerable. I know you think you love her, but unless it's for always—"

"I understand," Jake whispered through the tightness in his own throat. "And I promise you, I'll think this out in terms of what's best for Kelly. I won't risk hurting her."

"Thank you." Doris's arm darted around Jake's ribs in a motherly squeeze. "Now come on inside. I just took some bread out of the oven. We've got homemade salmonberry preserves and real butter to go with it. Now, I know what you hear about cholesterol these days, but I always say that butter on fresh, hot bread shouldn't count. There are times when low-fat margarine just won't do...."

She swung in through the screen door, still chatting. Jake glanced back over his shoulder to see Frank and the pilot coming up the walkway together. He knew how the rest of the visit would go. The four of them would sit around the table making small talk, drinking coffee and stuffing on Doris's wonderful bread. Doris would not speak with him privately again, but in her bustling around the table, she would manage to slip him a critical piece of paper.

The rest would be up to him. And to Kelly.

Snow, blasted by icy wind, swirled in dizzying circles against the violent sky. Bundled into her thick down parka, Kelly staggered through the storm. She counted her steps, willing her numb feet to keep moving. Another fifty yards and she would reach the blissful warmth of her dormitory. Then it would be time for flannels, toasty sheepskin slippers, hot chocolate and homework. Especially homework. With two midterms tomorrow, she planned to be up most of the night cramming. In fact, she'd be lucky to get any sleep at all.

But that was all right, she swiftly reminded herself. Coming here had been the wisest decision of her life. Every class she sat through, every book she read, every exam she took brought her a small step closer to her dream. By the time the snow melted and the birches leafed out again, she would be a teacher—a teacher who could fly to her students.

Oh, it got lonely here sometimes. Kelly got along with everyone, but she hadn't gone out of her way to make friends. As for dating, it was the farthest thing from her mind. Most of the men on campus were so young, they seemed more like boys. And after Jake—

But no, thinking about Jake was against the rules. She couldn't afford to get bogged down in memories—not when she had so much to learn, not when her dream was just out of reach. She would always love Jake, but he was part of the past now, and she was moving ahead on her own. That was how things had to stay.

By the time she reached the front porch, Kelly's face had lost all feeling. She stomped the snow off her boots, pushed into the lobby and peeled off her coat. The blast of heat that struck her icy skin was pure heaven.

"Hey, Ryan, who's the hunk?" Rachel, the red-haired girl at the front desk hailed her as she passed.

"Hunk?" Kelly stopped in her tracks, still half-dazed with cold.

"Hunk. Tall, blond and drop-dead gorgeous. He was here about an hour ago, asking for you. I tried to stall him, hoping he'd settle for me instead, but no luck. He said he'd get some coffee and check back later."

"Blond?" Kelly had begun to tremble. "And older, say, in his thirties?"

"Uh-huh. With blue eyes you could skinny-dip in. Come on, Ryan, don't break my heart. Tell me he's your cousin, and that he's looking for a redheaded woman who'll give him a lifetime of wild sex and unbridled passion!"

Kelly made a feeble effort to joke back. "Actually, he's from the IRS. It seems I haven't bothered to pay my income tax for the past six years, and they've finally caught up with—"

Her words froze as she heard the front door open and felt a sudden draft on the back of her neck. The expression on Rachel's face told her who had just come in, but Kelly stood frozen to the spot, afraid to turn around. The heat in the room had suddenly become oppressive. Beneath her thick Icelandic wool sweater, she was burning hot. Her parka dangled from one hand, dripping melted snow on the tiles. She wished passionately for the power to disappear in a puff of smoke.

"Kelly?"

The sound of his voice sent a thrill through her body. She battled the urge to spin around and fling herself into his arms. Oh, why had he come? Why now, just when she was doing so well? Just when she'd begun to hope she was getting over him?

Torn, she stood without moving. A tear trickled down her cheek. How could Jake have come here like this? Didn't he know what seeing him again would do to her?

She was dimly conscious of Rachel, watching goggle-eyed from behind the desk. Any confrontation that took place now would soon be gossip fodder all over the dorm. She and Jake needed to resolve some things, but certainly not here.

By slow degrees, Kelly forced herself to turn around and see him. He stood gazing at her, looking tired, strained and chilled, in a dark blue wool peacoat with the collar turned up around his ears. For him to travel all this way, in this weather—

But he would be waiting for her to say something, and so would Rachel. Kelly glued her face into an artificial smile. "Jake Drummond, of all people! What a surprise!" She sounded like a talking Barbie doll, Kelly thought. No wonder he looked pained.

"I...was hoping we could talk," he said, his voice hoarse, as if he were coming down with a sore throat.

"Uh—the lounge is in there." Kelly gestured toward an open room off the lobby, where a formation of worn sofas faced a crackling fire. On one of the sofas, a couple writhed in feverish embrace, paying no heed to other students who wandered past.

"I was thinking more of dinner," Jake said. "Unless you've eaten, of course—"

"No. That would be fine," Kelly conceded. "There are a couple of decent restaurants just off campus. If you'll give me time to drop these books in my room and put on some dry clothes—"

"Fine." He sagged against the wall to wait.

"I'll only be a minute!" Kelly dashed for the swinging doors that led to the elevator, her pulse bursting into a panic-stricken gallop. She and Jake had not been in touch since that wrenching afternoon on the bluff, when she'd sent him away for good. It was over, she'd told herself. Since he knew the whole, ugly truth about her past, he would never want to see her again.

Now, suddenly, here he was, back in her life, wanting to talk—and breaking her heart every time she looked at him. If he so much as crooked a finger, she would be in his arms. But no, she couldn't let it happen. She had come too far, at too high a cost. It was too late to go back.

Whatever happened, she had to let Jake know that.

Chapter Thirteen

The walk-down Italian restaurant was straight out of the 1960s, with red-checked tablecloths, fake ivy and candles that sputtered in wax-encrusted wine bottles. The atmosphere struck Jake as a little hokey—but never mind, it was warm, at least. And Kelly had said the lasagna wasn't bad.

She sat across from him now, in the intimacy of the booth, wearing jeans and a thick, black turtleneck sweater that set off the rose-pearl luster of her skin. She looked wonderful, he thought. But it wasn't just her appearance that struck him now. Kelly had always been beautiful. But some changes had taken place in her—a good change, Jake sensed. She seemed more confident, more resolute, more at peace with herself than he had ever known her to be.

"You had me worried half to death," he said. "When I found your old wagon at the agency, and the new people there didn't know what had happened to you... Damn it, Kelly, I wish you'd have let me know what you were up to!"

Her slim, strong hands cradled the mug of steaming black coffee. Jake had suggested ordering wine, but she'd declined, insisting she had to study most of the night. It didn't bode well for the romantic evening he'd had in mind.

Kelly fixed him with her effervescent Coca-Cola eyes. "Are you implying that I needed your permission?" Her tone was playful, but there was no missing its underlying steel.

"You know better than that." Jake ripped open a packet of sugar and dumped it into his own coffee, then remembered he'd already sugared it once. No, he reflected, this evening wasn't going well at all.

"Look," he began again, struggling to put things right. "Whether you know it or not, I care about you, Kelly Ryan. I care about what happens to you."

She glanced down at her cup, giving him a glimpse of the shy, unsure Kelly he remembered. Then she swiftly met his eyes again. "As you see," she said with a little smile, "what's happened to me is good. I'm doing well, Jake. I'm very happy here. And in a few months, I'll be a teacher."

"I'm glad," he said, not quite sure whether he meant it. "What finally gave you the courage to make the break?"

"You."

"Me?" Jake's heart somersaulted.

Kelly fiddled with her coffee cup, her shoulders rising and falling in a slow, painful sigh. "After you left—"

"After you sent me away," Jake corrected her gently.

"After I sent you away, I took a long, hard look at my life. I realized what a trap I'd woven for myself. I'd become so fearful of making a mistake and getting hurt again that I was afraid to live."

"So where do I fit into all that?"

She leaned toward him a little, her eyes warm and liquid in the candlelight. "Don't you see, Jake? Watching you walk away from me that day, knowing it was over, and that there was no way to make things work—I was hurting so badly, I wanted to die right there. And suddenly it dawned on me . . ."

"What?" Jake's hand moved across the table to surround hers. Her fingers were warm from the coffee mug. They curled in his, fitting as if they had been molded to his own clasp.

"I . . . realized that what we'd had was worth the pain. I finally understood that there were worse things than being hurt—and that the worst of all was being afraid to love."

"Kelly . . ." His hand tightened around hers. "It doesn't have to hurt. It doesn't have to be over."

"Please." The emotion was welling into her eyes, into her voice. "You don't understand. Let me explain the rest of—"

She broke off as the waiter bent over the table with steaming plates of lasagna. "Here you are," the young man murmured. "It's hot now. Don't touch the edges. More coffee, either of you?"

"I'll take a fresh cup," Jake growled, silently damning the interruption. He could sense Kelly retreating, regrouping her defenses. The chance to reach her was slipping away.

"Kelly, did you hear me?" Jake's voice rasped with urgency, when the waiter was out of earshot. "I'm saying it doesn't have to hurt. We owe ourselves a chance, and if you're not afraid—"

Reaching toward him, she brushed a finger across his lips. "Hear me out, Jake," she said softly. "Loving you was one of the best things that ever happened to me. But it's not enough."

"I could make it enough, if you'd give me a chance." Lord, didn't she know how hard this was for him—what it was costing his pride?

Kelly shook her head. "You don't understand. What I need is something you can't give me. It's something I have to give myself. Something that's mine. Something I earned."

"You're talking about this—this dream of yours? Damn it, Kelly, do you love me, or don't you?"

The surge of color in her cheeks told him what he needed to know.

"You could finish your schooling anywhere. You could teach *anywhere*—"

"Your lasagna's getting cold."

"Kelly—"

"Jake, our time together is so short and so precious. Let's enjoy what we have of it. Please."

"Will you stop evading me for once?" He recaptured her hand and held on tight.

"Jake—"

He caught the flash of cornered wildness in her eyes, and he realized he was pushing her too hard. "All right." He sighed, releasing her hand and picking up his fork. "But I would like to hear the rest of your story. What possessed you to pack up and head for a place that's straight out of *White Fang*? Your grandmother told me you could have finished your degree in Juneau—"

"Maybe I needed to run away."

"From me?"

Kelly stared down at her hands. When she met Jake's gaze again, some of the warmth had returned to her eyes.

"Not you," she said gently. "In fact, until an hour ago, I'd convinced myself that I was never going to see you again. But I was scared, Jake—scared that with you gone, I might fall apart, the way I did before—"

"Kelly, you didn't have to—"

"No, it's all right. I soon realized that wasn't going to happen. But I realized something else, too. If I didn't stand up and face my fears, one day I'd look in the mirror and see a sad, old woman, who'd never realized her dreams. I knew I had to get away, and not just to Juneau, or even Anchorage. I had to start over. I had to make a complete break with my past."

Including us? Jake bit back the question. At least Kelly was opening herself to him now. He'd be a fool to put her back on the defensive.

"Remember the eagle, that day on the bluff?" She was leaning toward him again, achingly beautiful where the candlelight warmed her cheeks. "Don't you see? I had to leave the nest, too. I had to let go and throw myself into the sky." Her voice dropped to a whisper. "I have wings, Jake. They work, and I'm not afraid anymore."

"Kelly." Jake fought back an avalanche of emotion. Damn it, he *loved* her—this stubborn, muleheaded, courageous little spitfire of a woman. And he wanted her with him. Now. He wanted her in his arms, in his bed, in his life. He wanted to protect her, provide for her, give her children, grow old with her. And suddenly the thought of not having her filled him with stark dread.

Hiding it as well as he could, he forced himself to start on the lasagna. "Mmmm ... you're right, this isn't half-bad," he said. "Now tell me about school. Judging from what I've seen and heard, it must be going well."

"It is." Jake sensed the relief in her voice at his move to safer ground. "But it's hard work. I have to study all the time. In fact, that's how I plan to spend the night, after you take me back to the dorm. Midterms, you know."

"Uh-huh," Jake muttered, feeling out of place, like a stodgy stranger in Kelly's exciting new world. "Do you date much, or is that something you'd rather not discuss?"

"There's nothing *to* discuss. I've been too busy with school to have much of a social life. How about you?"

"Me?"

"How's *your* social life, Jake? Or isn't that any of my business?" The eyes Kelly fixed on him now were as penetrating as her grandmother's.

Jake glanced up at the plastic greenery on the ceiling, grateful he'd done nothing to tempt a lie. "I dated a woman for a few weeks. It's . . . over."

"Was she beautiful?"

"Does it matter?"

Kelly toyed with her lasagna. Jake noticed that she'd eaten even less than he had. "No," she said slowly. "I don't suppose it should."

"Kelly, I'm here. I've come all this way to see you. Haven't you even asked yourself why?"

"Don't, Jake," she whispered. "You're only confusing me. And I can't afford to be confused right now. There's too much at stake."

"You're saying I should back off and go home."

A spark of desperation flickered in her eyes. "Don't you see, Jake? I'd be lying if I said I didn't care for you. But I've wanted this for so long—I've worked so hard. If I let my emotions get in the way now—"

"Okay, I may be a little dense, but I get the point." Jake forced a dejected smile. "Now finish your dinner like a good girl, and then I'll run you back to the dorm. You've got some heavy-duty studying to do, and I've got an early flight back to Seattle tomorrow morning."

Kelly did not answer right away, but her shoulders sagged, as if her nerves had suddenly come unraveled. She picked up her coffee mug and tried to take a sip. But her hands were shaking. The dark liquid sloshed on the tabletop before she could get it to her mouth.

"Are you all right?" Jake asked her gently.

"Fine. Just tired." Her smile was as forced as his had been. "Jake, I...just wish things could have been easier, for both of us."

"Uh-huh, I know what you mean. We should have grown up next door to each other and gone to the same schools. Then you could have been a cheerleader while I played football. I could have asked you to the prom. Then, after a few years, we could have found ourselves a little white cottage with two-point-five kids and a dog, and—"

"Oh, stop it!" Kelly's giggle was thread-thin and frenetic. "How would you like a faceful of lasagna, Jake Drummond?"

Jake forced his mouth into a grin. "That's the spirit. That's the Kelly I know and love. Now, come on. Let's finish our dinner and get out of here."

"I...think I've had enough. How about you?"

"Yeah. Same here." Jake signaled for the check. Inside, he felt as if he were sinking into a cold, black sea, with his last chance at a lifeboat drifting out of reach. Kelly was pulling on her parka, shrugging into the sleeves without waiting for him to help. Even for that, she didn't need him. The truth was, she didn't seem to need him at all.

But he needed her, that was the devil of it. He needed her softness, her laughter, her strength. He needed her love to fill those awful black nights that had haunted him since Ann's death. He needed her to share his dreams and his life.

Now he was about to lose her.

The desperation that welled up in Jake was like a drowning man's hunger for air. If there was one chance left, any chance at all, he had to take it.

Kelly's dormitory was only minutes away, and time was running out. As he paid the cashier, Jake steeled himself for what could turn out to be a crushing rejection. He was about to risk making a complete fool of himself—but that didn't matter anymore.

At this point, he had nothing to lose.

Kelly stepped outside, with Jake just behind her. Her breath caught as the arctic air struck her hot face. *Hang on, Ryan, you're doing fine,* she told herself. *Just a few more minutes and this crazy masquerade will be over. You'll be free to go back to your room and bawl your silly eyes out. And after that's done, you'll have the rest of your life to get over him.*

Jake's hand pressed the small of her back, the contact electrifying, even through her clothes. Had she hurt him tonight? Maybe a little. But tonight was nothing, compared to the pain of what would happen if she didn't break this off now.

Oh, Jake thought he wanted her. Maybe he even thought he loved her. But he would change his mind once he got her back to Seattle—a shy, clumsy little hick who didn't know how to dress, how to entertain, how to make clever small talk or even how to play tennis. Jake's friends would feel sorry for him. And as the newness wore off, his feelings for her would deteriorate from love to embarrassment, to disgust, to contempt. In the end, he would hate her.

His hand tightened against her waist as he steered her toward the parking lot, where he'd left his rented Jeep. Snowflakes swirled around them, tumbling out of the black sky in tiny diamond chips that glittered under the street lamps. Their boots crunched diamonds as they walked through the windblown drifts.

Kelly swallowed hard, fighting back tears. *Oh, Jake, if you only knew how much this hurt...if you only knew how much I love you...*

She slowed her steps, clinging to each fleeting heartbeat of their time together. Minutes from now he would be gone. And this time, she knew, he would not be back. Jake had let down his pride once. It wasn't in him to do it again.

"Hang on a sec." He reached awkwardly around her, brushed the snow from the door handle and unlocked the Jeep's half-frozen door. Ice groaned and popped as the door swung open.

She was climbing into the front seat when he seized her waist and spun her to him in the lee of the door. His arms caught her close, trapping her against his chest. His mouth...oh, sweet heaven, his mouth...

Wisdom went up in smoke as Kelly caught fire in his embrace. Her frantic hands melted the snow in his hair as she pulled his head down, bringing his lips tighter, harder against her own. Her body sought his through the impossible thickness of sweaters and parkas. She whimpered wildly, frantic for his love as his arms crushed her close. She could feel the whole world shaking as Jake kissed her. The walls of sense and reason, so carefully built, were crumbling in the heat of desire.

"Kelly," he rasped against her ear. "If you're going to stop me, you damned well better do it now—"

"No..." Her answer came in broken sobs. "No, Jake, I'm not going to stop you—I can't. I couldn't stop you if I wanted to...and I don't."

He caught her bare hand and moved it beneath his coat, to where he jutted like a rock beneath his woolen trousers. "Then I want to make love to you, Kelly," he grated, pressing her fingers to his hot, hard need. "I *need* to make love to you—so badly that I'm ready to do damned near anything to get you in my bed. Do you understand?"

Dizzy with longing, Kelly nodded against his coat. From somewhere inside her brain, like a muffled shout, came the protest that she'd be sorry later, that she needed to study, that she'd already gone too far for her own good. But it was no use. The heat of Jake's body seared her hand, its warmth so compelling that she moaned out loud. Her own response pulsed in her secret depths, wild and savage in its urgency.

Somehow Kelly found her voice. "Please," she whispered. "Please, Jake, let's go—now."

They lay in the warm darkness, legs and bodies tangled in damp, delicious exhaustion. Jake kept still, afraid to shatter the spell of what had happened between them. He had gambled his pride, his integrity—everything that was important to his manhood. It remained to be seen whether he had won.

Kelly stirred against him, the sweet, bare curve of her buttocks nestling deeper against his groin. At least he knew she loved him—Kelly was too honest to give herself without love. But was it enough? He would soon know.

"I still need to study," she purred, kissing the side of his arm where it lay across her breasts. "Too bad I didn't bring my books with me. That way I could stay right here the rest of the night...."

"Marry me, Kelly," he said.

She stiffened against him. "What about school?"

"You could finish out the term here and then come to Seattle," he said, plunging ahead. "There's a fine university there, with a beautiful campus. You shouldn't have any trouble transferring your credits."

"And afterward?"

The bitter note in her voice disheartened Jake, but it was now or never, he told himself. "I could give you a wonderful life," he persisted. "We could buy a new home—any home you wanted. We could give parties for our friends—"

"*Your* friends."

He ignored the jab. "We could travel anywhere in the world. And if you wanted, you could even teach. Seattle has some excellent schools—all the latest technology and resources. Of course, you wouldn't have to work at all, unless you wanted to."

"I see." She had drawn away from him, into an unhappy little ball. "Naturally, if I got bored, I could always do charity work . . . like Ann."

"Kelly—"

She sat up, jerking the sheet across her bare breasts. "Don't you see how hopeless this is, Jake? I love you, but that's not enough. It's not *me* you want. It's a replacement for Ann! You want a woman who'll be everything she was— beautiful, elegant, socially accomplished—"

"Kelly, you're not being fair." Jake tried to speak calmly, but he could feel the cold blackness moving in on him again, and he realized he was going to lose her.

"Jake, I know you mean well," she said. "The life you're describing would be a dream for most women. But *look* at me! I'm Kelly Ryan. I fly airplanes and fix engines and go to school. I get nervous in crowds, I hate parties, and my idea of dress-up is something nice from the L.L. Bean catalog. My past includes an out-of-wedlock baby and a nervous breakdown—"

"Damn it, Kelly, I love you!" He reached out to pull her close again, but she shook her head vehemently.

"Let me finish, once and for all. I'm not Ann. I can't step into her place and finish out the missing chapters of her life. So please don't ask me to, Jake. Go home to Seattle and find someone who's more...suitable. I can't imagine you'll have any lack of qualified candidates."

The blackness was closing over Jake's head. "If you'd just listen—"

"No," she said more gently. "I love you, Jake, more than you'll ever know. But right now I'm doing both of us a favor. One day you'll look back and realize that—and you'll thank me."

Jake sank back onto the pillow with a groan as the fight went out of him. He'd done his best, but it wasn't enough. The lady had said no. It was over.

Kelly slipped out of bed and was fumbling for her clothes, dressing in the faint neon glow that flickered on and off through the curtains. Jake knew he should do the same. She had exams to study for, and he would need to drive her back to campus. But right now, the sense of loss was so deep that he could not will himself to move.

"It's been Ann all along, hasn't it?" he said, struggling to understand. "All these crazy, evasive games of yours— you were afraid I'd compare you to her, and that, in my mind, you wouldn't measure up."

She paused in the act of pulling her sweater down over her bra. "Not that I wouldn't measure up," she said softly, "only that you would compare."

Jake forced himself to sit up and ease his legs over the side of the bed. "There's no basis for comparison," he said. "I loved Ann. She was a wonderful, intelligent, warm, tender woman. You'd have liked her—everyone did. But she's not *you,* Kelly. You have your own beauty, your own strengths. It wouldn't make sense to compare you to Ann."

Kelly gave him a sad little smile. "Not here, maybe. But Seattle would be different. I'd be stepping into her element, into her shoes. It would be like . . . like putting your lovely Ann at the controls of a Beaver and expecting her to do barrel rolls in a high wind."

He sighed. "Can you do barrel rolls?"

"Uh-huh. And I'm not too bad at crash landings, either." She snatched up a loose sock and tossed it into his lap.

"Now get your clothes on—unless, of course, you want to drive me back to the dorm naked and be attacked by thirty-five screaming coeds."

"I love you, Kelly," he said.

She paused at the foot of the bed, one hand dangling her unlaced boot. "I love you, too, Jake," she whispered over the tears in her voice. "And as Humphrey Bogart would say, I guess 'We'll always have Paris.'"

"If you ever change your mind—"

"I won't. It just wouldn't work, Jake. We both know it."

"Then I guess there's not much more to say." Jake bent to gather up his clothes. He would be all right, he told himself. There were plenty of women in Seattle, and sooner or later, a relationship would fall into place. But right now he felt as if he'd just been gut-punched by Mike Tyson. He would be hurting for a long time to come.

The devil of it was, he didn't understand. Oh, he knew what Kelly was saying. She was insecure and afraid of being compared to Ann. But that was rubbish. He loved *her*. He needed her in a way that had nothing to do with the loss of Ann. And he was ready to do anything to make her happy.

So why couldn't she at least give him a chance? That was the hell of it—the thing that was driving him crazy. Kelly said she loved him, and he knew she meant it. But she was closing the door. She wasn't even willing to try.

Jake pulled on his boots and jerked his sweater down over his ears. "Come on," he growled. "Let's get going."

They drove back to the campus without talking. Kelly sat rigidly on the seat of the Jeep, fighting tears. It would have been better if they'd quarreled, she thought. At least anger might have cleared the air. As it was, the silence between them was black with questions, unasked and unanswered.

She stole a glance at Jake's tense profile. She'd tried to make him understand, but it hadn't been enough. He was hurt and angry, and there was nothing more she could say.

Oh, Jake, don't you know what I would do for you? If I could be like Ann, if I could take her place and make you happy, don't you think I would?

Snow drove against the windshield, so dry and fine that it rustled like silk. Jake turned on the wipers. The heater roared inside the cab of the Jeep.

If I could believe it was me you wanted, maybe we could work this out. But all you want is to make me into someone I'm not, and can never be. You want to take away my wings, Jake, and I've only just found them.

He pulled the vehicle into the dormitory parking lot and found an empty spot. His gloved hand reached down to switch off the ignition, but Kelly stopped him with a touch on his sleeve. "I'll just get out and go in alone. Less gossip that way."

He turned to look at her, his eyes black hollows in the ghostly light. "Take care, Kelly," he muttered.

"Yeah . . . you, too." She was drowning in her own emotions. Her fingers unclasped her seat belt and groped for the door handle. She knew she had to get out of the Jeep before she fell apart.

"If you ever need anything—" he was saying.

"Uh-huh. I appreciate that." The door swung open so abruptly that she tumbled out into the storm. Her boot soles grazed bare ice. Her feet splayed wildly. Only her frantic fingers, clutching at the seat, kept her from sprawling in a snowdrift.

"Are you all right?" Jake's hand reached out to her from the shadows of the cab. Kelly pretended not to see it.

"I'm...fine. Nothing like a dignified exit," she joked, her eyes stinging. At least her acrobatics would dispel any notions Jake had of her replacing the swanlike Ann.

"Well, goodbye then, Kelly." Again that leather-gloved hand, reaching toward her across the passenger seat. This time she could not ignore it. She fumbled for the fingers through a blur of tears and gave them a hearty squeeze.

"Stay well, Jake," she whispered. Then, tearing her hand away, she turned and plunged through the snow toward the porch. Behind her, the engine roared as Jake geared down to pull away.

Don't look back. You won't be able to stand it if you look back.

Tires spun on the ice, then dug in as the Jeep shot out of the parking lot. The sound faded as Kelly reached the steps. When she finally turned around, half-blinded by snow and tears, all she could see was the twin red blur of taillights, vanishing into the night.

Chapter Fourteen

Kelly spent most of Thanksgiving break curled in the empty dorm lounge, reading *Rebecca*. Outside, the weather was dead white, windy and so cold that a too-deep breath of air could frost the lungs.

As Kelly stared out across the deserted campus, she found herself wishing she'd given in to temptation and caught a flight home. Thoughts of the cheerful log house, the crackling fire, visits from neighbors and the mouth-watering smells that wafted from her grandma's kitchen were enough to make her ache with homesickness. But no, she swiftly reminded herself, she had vowed to stick it out here until Christmas. She couldn't weaken now.

Nearly six weeks had passed since she'd said goodbye to Jake in the parking lot. She'd hoped that time would ease the hurt. It hadn't. It was still Jake's voice that stirred her sleepy brain every morning. It was Jake's smile, Jake's eyes, that drifted with her into slumber every night. More than once, Kelly had cried herself to sleep.

That was why, on impulse, she'd wandered to the library and checked out Daphne DuMaurier's classic novel. Restless, burned out with studying, and at odds with herself, she'd hoped the book might be cathartic. The story of the awkward, nameless young bride, struggling against the memory of her husband's dazzling first wife, Rebecca, touched an all-too-familiar chord in her.

But it hadn't worked. She was nearly finished with the book now, and the premise that Rebecca had turned out to be the "wife from hell," and that her husband had not only hated her, but had actually killed the wretched woman, glittered like brass in the light of Kelly's experience.

She needed a different version of the book, Kelly told herself, closing the cover with a sigh. In her book, Rebecca would turn out to have been as perfect as she appeared, as sweet and kind as she was beautiful. And the husband would adore her forever, while his poor, mousy little second wife simply faded into the wallpaper and vanished.

Now, *that* was reality.

Flinging the book onto the far end of the couch, Kelly stood up and paced restlessly to the window. Her breath clouded the glass as she leaned against the frame. Her eyes softened as she gazed into the swirl of falling snow.

Was it enough? she asked herself. Was her dream of being a teacher worth giving up the love of a man like Jake Drummond? Once she'd thought she knew the answer. Now, faced with the loneliness of this place, on this long, dreary weekend, she was no longer sure.

Had she sent Jake away because of the dream? Or was the dream a smoke screen, an excuse to protect her from the risk she dreaded so much?

In her mind, she had gone on and on about Ann Drummond, and her own fear of comparison. Was Ann another smoke screen? Another excuse? Another reason to run away from what she feared—and wanted—most of all?

This was reality, Kelly told herself. Jake had loved his wife. He had cared for her, protected her, and when she had died, a part of him had died with her.

And *this,* too, was reality. Jake had loved once. He was capable of loving again. More than capable. He was ready, even eager, to give his heart. He had offered her a lifetime of shared love, and she had turned him down because she was afraid—afraid, not so much of being hurt, as of being *happy*.

What a fool she was.

Kelly gazed out at the falling snow, her illusions shattering in the face of the truth. *Come back to me, Jake,* her heart whispered. But she knew that Jake couldn't hear. And even if he could, he wouldn't listen anymore.

It was too late.

Jake pulled the BMW out of the parking lot and headed up Union Street, in the direction of his new apartment. He'd planned to spend the afternoon updating figures on the SEA-MAR contract, a project that was taking more and more of his time. By midmorning, however, a high wind had begun to sweep away the cover of damp, gray clouds. By lunchtime, a rare blue sky had emerged from the fog. The dazzling fourteen-thousand-foot cone of Mount Rainier towered in full view above the city, and sun-hungry Seattle declared an unofficial holiday. Nobody wanted to stay indoors. Not even Jake.

The streets swarmed with people, hatless in their unbuttoned raincoats, eyes blinking happily at the sky. At Fifth and Union, a pretty, dark-haired girl in a plaid wool shirt paused to check out a window of the Eddie Bauer store.

Kelly...

But it wasn't Kelly, Jake realized as the girl turned aside. It was only his imagination running amok, as it had countless times before. When was he going to get it through his head that it was over? Kelly had walked away, leaving more bruises on his male ego than he'd ever suffered in his life. Nobody but a complete idiot would ever think of going back for more of the same.

But, incredibly, he had done just that. He'd lain awake nights, racking his brain for a way to make things work. If he could get her to Seattle on some pretext, get her to see how much she could like it here....

But what was the use? Kelly was in his system like a drug, and there was just one antidote. All he needed to do was find it.

Maybe he already had.

The new woman in his life was Brenda. She was an easygoing Alabama blonde, and Jake enjoyed her company. But he was taking it slowly this time, especially the physical part. Kelly's memory was still painfully close—too close for him to jump in over his head with someone new.

Wrenching Kelly's image from his mind, he picked up his car phone and punched in Brenda's number. Brenda was a free-lance decorator who worked out of her own home. Her schedule was flexible, and she didn't seem to mind last-minute arrangements. Since it was such a beautiful day, maybe she'd be open to spending some time with him.

"Jake, honey!" Brenda responded enthusiastically to his greeting. "Mercy sakes, have you looked out the window! The mountain's out! It's gorgeous!"

"I know. In fact, I'm in my car right now. I was hoping you'd be up for tennis and lunch at the club."

Her laughter bubbled over the line. "Jake, I wish I could. But I'm baby-sitting. My brother and his wife are in town, and I offered to watch their two youngsters for the day. I was planning to take the little nippers to the zoo." There was a pause on the line. "Say, why don't you come with us? You were telling me you hadn't spent much time around kids. Here's your chance."

"Uh...okay." Jake wasn't all that fond of zoos, but there was no gracious way out. "I can change and be there by one-thirty. How does that sound?"

"Fine. You're a great sport, honey. See you." She smacked him a little phone kiss as he hung up. Brenda was a good woman, Jake told himself as he geared down the car at the next light. She was warm and honest and giving, and she knew how to laugh. Maybe he ought to make more of an effort to get involved.

But no, it was still too soon. His mind was still seeing Kelly everywhere, still hearing her voice. He was still waking up in the night, rock-hard, sweat-soaked and aching from the memory of her love. It wouldn't be fair to Brenda or any other woman to push a relationship before he was ready. And he knew he wouldn't be ready again for a long, long time.

Even the zoo animals were enjoying the sun. One bear, a huge Alaskan brown, lay belly-up on a rock, eyes closed, basking like an overgrown puppy. Jake remembered the bear he'd seen from the cabin porch on Admiralty Island. He remembered how majestic it had appeared, how wild and free. No, this wasn't the same.

Brenda slipped an arm around his waist. "See, I told you this afternoon was going to be fun," she said. "You're a good sport, Jake. In fact, I think you'll make a great father someday. The kids have really taken to you."

"Uh-huh." Brenda's young niece and nephew were leaning on the fence pointing and laughing at the bear. They really weren't bad kids. In fact they'd behaved decently all
afternoon. But as for their "taking" to him, Jake sensed
that Brenda was nudging him a little too warmly.

"Come on, honey." She linked her arm through his,
pulling him along after the two youngsters. "Another half
hour and they should be wound-down enough to go home.
Really, Jake, you've been wonderful with them. Maybe it's
time you thought about settling down again, and raising a
few kids of your own."

"There's plenty of time for that," Jake hedged, stumbling over a crack in the pavement. The hell of it was, he *had*
thought about having children one day. But whenever he
tried to imagine it, the children he pictured always had Kelly's Coca-Cola eyes and crisp, dark curls.

"Hey, look! Eagles!" Brenda's nephew seized Jake's wrist
and tugged him toward a high, wire-domed cage. Inside,
three bald eagles perched on a massive, gnarled stump that
was streaked white with droppings.

Two of the eagles were mature birds, with majestic,
snowy heads. The third was younger, dark all over, like the
fledgling Jake remembered seeing with Kelly atop the bluff.

But these eagles, Jake realized, were making no effort to
fly. They knew the boundaries of their cage, knew, by now,
that flight would only send them crashing into the cruel
mesh. These birds had nothing to do but sit, hour after
hour, glaring at the crowds with fierce yellow eyes.

Even their food—rabbits, judging from the remains—was
tossed lifeless into the cage. There was no hunt, no chal-
lenge, no danger. The eagles were cared for devotedly by
their human captors. Nothing was lacking.

Except freedom.

"Jake, honey, what's got into you?" Brenda tugged at his arm. "I declare, you've done nothing but stare at that cage for the past five minutes!"

Jake did not reply. He stood thunderstruck as the swirling pieces settled into place. He saw Kelly in Seattle, deprived of her usefulness, her livelihood, her very identity. He saw her pampered and bored, struggling to please him, striving to become someone she was not.

How could he have asked her to do it? How could he have expected her to say yes?

"Jake, are you all right?" Brenda's voice had taken on a strident edge that buzzed like a wasp on the fringe of his awareness.

Kelly.

Maybe there was still a way to have her. Maybe it wasn't too late after all.

"Really, Jake, there's no need to be rude. If you're tired, just say so, and we'll leave."

Jake dragged himself back to reality. "I—no, I'm sorry, Brenda, it's fine. We'll take all the time you want."

"Well, everybody's getting tired, I guess." Brenda took his arm, possessively this time, as if she were claiming a wayward child. "Come on. We can see the other animals on our way out and then maybe get some corn dogs."

Jake's mind churned with plans as he walked through the rest of the zoo. He would need to talk with Shamus and Roger first thing in the morning. His partners would be surprised, to say the least. But when he pointed out how important the SEA-MAR contract was, and how much of his time it was demanding, his idea ought to make perfect sense, even to them.

As for the rest . . . but he couldn't get too far ahead of himself with Kelly. For her, promises wouldn't be enough. She'd had promises the first time she'd fallen in love. This time it was solid realities she needed—things she could see and grasp and understand....

Jake suddenly realized he was walking too fast, dragging the protesting Brenda along behind him. Muttering an apology, he slowed his pace to a stroll. For the next half hour, he even tried to make pleasant conversation. But it was no use. His mind kept leaping ahead, making plans, weighing the odds.

If he wanted Kelly to trust him, he would need to have everything in place before he spoke with her. That meant...yes, by Christmas. That was when she'd be coming home again. That gave him only a few weeks to make the arrangements.

What he was planning could turn out to be the biggest gamble of his life. He would be putting everything on the block—his career, his property, his whole carefully laid-out future. But then some things, Jake reminded himself, were worth the risk.

A lifetime with Kelly was one of them.

Christmas tree lights—the old-fashioned kind with silver-star reflectors—glowed in the winter darkness. Outside the snug log house, sleet and hail clawed at the windowpanes. Inside, however, everything was warm and cheerful, just the way a Christmas morning ought to be.

Bundled into her white terry robe, Kelly curled on the hearth, sipping hot chocolate and warming herself by the fire. She had always loved Christmas. To her it was a magical time, a time of joyful innocence when, for just a short while, she was allowed to become a little girl again.

She sat very still and waited for the feeling to come. From the kitchen, she could hear her grandparents making cinnamon toast. In a few minutes they would come into the living room and the three of them would open their gifts, as they had every Christmas for as long as Kelly could remember. But it wasn't the gifts that made the magic. It was the anticipation, and even more, the sense of love and security that radiated into every corner of the house.

She closed her eyes, filling her senses with the warm crackle of the fire and the sweet scent of spruce. Any second now it would begin, that tingly, childlike feeling she loved so much. She held her breath....

Nothing.

Kelly opened her eyes. Oh, she knew what was wrong. It wasn't the house or the tree or the gifts. And it certainly wasn't her grandparents. The problem was *herself*. It was the awareness that if she'd handled things differently, Jake might be here with her right now, the two of them bundled in their robes, cuddled close together, wrapped in the magic of the morning.

But Jake *wasn't* here, she reminded herself. He didn't belong here, any more than she belonged in Seattle. She had made her choice, and it was time she learned to live with the consequences.

Restless, she uncoiled her legs and prowled across the room to the window, where she stood stiff-spined, glaring out at the storm. What would Jake be doing this morning? she caught herself wondering. Would he be alone? Or had he already found somebody else?

Stop it, Kelly Ryan! she lashed herself. *Whatever happens, you're not going to let Jake or any other man ruin your Christmas!*

Feeling worse, if anything, Kelly turned away from the window and walked slowly back toward the tree. She had come south only yesterday, on an Alaska Airlines flight from Fairbanks to Juneau, and had taken the ferry to Angoon, where her grandfather had met her in the motor skiff for the ride home. She would have come sooner, but a bad

case of flu had kept her in the dorm until the last possible
minute. Even today, the dregs of the illness lingered in her
system. She felt drained and exhausted, her mood a match
for the storm that howled around the house like a sullen,
gray wolf.

But this wouldn't do, she reminded herself. It was
Christmas morning, the happiest of times, and she had no
wish to spoil the day for her grandparents. Forcing her face
into a smile, Kelly strode resolutely toward the kitchen.
Maybe her grandparents could use some help, or at least
some company. In any case, the sooner she focused on
making other people happy, the sooner she would stop wal-
lowing in her own misery.

She had just come into the kitchen when she heard the
crackle of the old radio in her grandpa's office. A Christmas greeting from one of their neighbors, Kelly surmised.
She stepped aside as Frank hurried past her, then moved to
the doorway to listen.

But this was no Christmas message. The woman's voice
that filtered through the static was frantic and tearful.

"Frank... Harlan... didn't get back... over."

"What?" Frank was shouting into the microphone. "Is
that you, Peggy? You say Harlan's down? Over."

Kelly felt a sick weight in the pit of her stomach. She knew
who was calling now. Harlan and Peggy Fitzroy lived thirty
miles up the channel. Harlan was a charter pilot, like Kelly.
The Fitzroys had five young children and another on the
way.

And today was Christmas.

"I don't know...." Peggy Fitzroy's anguished voice
crackled in and out of the static. *"...flew... ruptured
appendix to Juneau last night... haven't heard...
storm... over."*

"Now, Peggy, girl, did you call Juneau?" Frank thundered. "Do you know if he made it that far? Over."

"...*couldn't get through...storm...Harlan always calls me*..." Peggy's voice blurred and faded. Kelly thought of Harlan Fitzroy, a big, affable man who was always willing to help people. She thought of Harlan's children, the oldest scarcely nine, the little one waiting to be born.

"Grandpa, tell Peggy I'm going up to look for him," she said.

"No!" Kelly's grandmother had come up from behind. Her hand gripped Kelly's arm fiercely. "You've been sick, Kelly. And it's storming. There are others who can go—"

Kelly shook her head. "Grandma, it's Christmas. That poor family's worried sick. And you know that if it was me who'd gone down, Harlan Fitzroy would be the first one in the air."

"But you won't be here when—" Doris broke off the sentence. "Frank, tell her—"

Kelly's grandpa glanced up from the sputtering radio. "No, she's right, Doris. This is an emergency. Everybody's got to do what they can." His eyes darted to Kelly, and she glimpsed the pride in them. "There's plenty of gas in the shed, honey. After I find out more from Peggy and rouse some other folk, I'll help you haul the Beaver out. By then, we should be getting some daylight."

"I'll...find you some warm clothes," Doris offered, biting back her objections. "It'll be cold up there, and you've still got that blasted flu in your lungs. I don't want you catching your death..." She bustled off down the hall, too agitated to stand still another second.

Kelly gave her grandfather a quick embrace. Then she ran back to her room and began tugging on her double-layered thermals. Flying would be murderous in this weather. The worst of it was, if she wanted to find Harlan Fitzroy, she couldn't stay above the storm. She would need to hug the mountains and skim the channels. There would be no margin for any kind of mistake. Even with perfect flying, a single wind gust could topple her into the water or fling the fragile Beaver against a ridgetop.

But this was no time to think about the danger. A pilot was lost. A good man. A neighbor, a husband, a father. And she had no decent choice except to do what she could.

Thrusting her own troubles to the back of her mind, Kelly flung on the rest of her clothes, snatched up her boots and raced back down the hallway toward the kitchen.

It was early afternoon by the time Jake reached the island. Rather than risk a plane in the storm, he had used the company's heavy motor launch, piloting the big boat himself through the six-foot waves in the channel. The trip had taken twice as long as he'd expected. By the time he'd rounded the point and passed into the calmer waters of the inlet, he was battling exhaustion.

All the same, nothing could have kept him away. This was the day he had been planning for weeks—his moment of truth with Kelly. Everything was in place. Doris and Frank were expecting him. They had promised not to tell her he was coming.

Dizzy with anticipation, he slowed the engine. He had tried to convince himself that everything would work out. But what if he'd taken too much for granted? What if Kelly wasn't interested? What if she'd met someone else at school and fallen in love? Despite the wind-driven sleet, Jake realized he was sweating beneath his heavy wool peacoat.

As he glided up to the dock, the first thing he noticed was that the Beaver was missing from its storage shed. For the first instant, he was puzzled. Then a band of cold fear tightened around his chest. No one but Kelly would be flying that plane, and the idea that she'd go up in a storm like this was enough to...

His thoughts dissolved as he saw a figure running down the walkway in the storm. His heart leapt, then fell into place with a thud as he realized it was Doris. By the time she'd reached the dock, Jake had secured the boat and was scrambling up the ladder. His breath stopped as he saw her pale, strained face.

"Doris, what the devil—?"

She was windblown, shaking and out of breath. "One of our neighbors—a pilot—he went down last night. Kelly and some others have been out searching all day. Frank's trying to keep up radio contact, but in this storm—"

"She's flying in this?" Jake glanced helplessly at the sky as Doris nodded.

"Come on!" Sick with fear, he grabbed her arm and the two of them staggered up the walkway, clinging for support against the powerful wind gusts. He remembered the storm that had brought himself and Kelly down last August. This one, he calculated, was far worse.

They lurched across the porch and flung themselves into the living room. From off the kitchen, they could hear Frank shouting into the microphone of his antiquated radio set.

"*What?* What's that again? My God, Harlan, is that you? Over."

Doris raced for the kitchen with Jake behind her. The deep male voice that crackled through the static was barely audible.

"*...damned storm blew...off course...crashed in Petersburg. Found a doc...appendix...banged my head...the guy's okay and so am I...over.*"

"Harlan, listen!" Frank bellowed. "Peggy's been frantic! We've got three pilots out looking for you! Over."

"*. . . Peg knows . . . finally got through to her. She said . . . call you. But get those planes down, Frank . . . get 'em the hell down now . . . storm's a killer . . . over.*"

"Roger, Harlan. Glad you're okay. Out."

Jake's knees had gone watery. He sagged against the wall, weak with relief. Everything would be all right now, he told himself. The missing pilot was safe. Kelly and the others could turn around and fly home.

Frank was calling the three pilots, telling them the crisis was over, telling them to land and get out of the storm. Jake heard the first man respond, then the second. He held his breath and waited for Kelly.

Nothing.

"Kelly, did you hear me?" Frank was shouting into the microphone. "Harlan's fine, honey. You can come on home now. Over."

For the space of an agonized breath nothing came through the receiver but static and silence. Then, ever so faintly, Jake heard Kelly's voice.

"*Grandpa, I think I'm lost . . . nothing but white up here, in all directions. I know I'm over the island, but I can't see anything. I can't tell where the mountains are . . . over.*"

She sounded terrified, like a frightened little girl, Jake thought, and suddenly he was wild with fear for her. Forgetting manners and propriety, he lurched through the doorway, into Frank's office.

"Kelly, what's your altitude? Over!" Frank was yelling into the microphone.

"*Thirteen hundred feet.*" Kelly's voice swam eerily through the static. "*I know—I've got to climb. I've got to get above the mountains before . . . over.*"

"*Climb*, honey!" Frank bellowed. "Do it *now!* Don't stop till you've cleared five thousand! You can get your bearings later! Over!"

"The wind..." Jake could feel the fear, the agonizing struggle in her voice. *"Grandpa, the wind, it's—"*

The transmission stopped.

"Kelly!" Frank's hand whitened on the handle of the microphone. His face had gone gray. "Come in, Kelly!"

Nothing. Nothing but the faint buzz of static and sound of the storm outside, howling around the eaves. That and a strangled, broken cry from Doris.

"Come in, Kelly!" The old man was pleading into the microphone. His whole body had begun to shake. "Kelly—"

Suddenly Jake's control snapped. This couldn't happen, he told himself. He couldn't lose her now.

"Kelly!" He had snatched the microphone from Frank's hand. "Kelly, listen to me!" he shouted. "This is Jake! I'm here! I'm waiting for you! Just take it easy and come on in— you're going to be fine!"

Empty words, he realized. He did not know if she could hear him. He did not even know whether she was still alive. But he couldn't let her go. He had to go on talking. He had to tell her everything.

"I love you, Kelly! I want a life with you, and I've done all I can to make that possible.... I live in Juneau now. My company's opened a branch office there, to handle the SEA-MAR business.... Kelly, I'm here, whether you'll have me or not. But right now, all I want is for you to be safe... for you to come back to me...come back to all the people who love you."

Frank had slumped in the chair with his head in his hands. Doris had disappeared into the living room. Jake clutched the microphone and willed himself to believe that Kelly was still out there somewhere, that she was all right.

"Just come back, love," he whispered. "I know you can do it. You're the stubbornest lady I've ever met, and one of the bravest. Just check your instruments, get your bearings and come on home. That's all I'm asking...."

Jake kept on talking as the minutes ticked by in slow agony. He was no longer conscious of the words—did not know, even, whether they were making any sense. He only knew that he mustn't stop, that he mustn't give up and let her go.

"There's a whole lifetime out there waiting for us, Kelly. A home. Children. Working for your dreams and mine... Just come back and share it with me, love. Just come back...."

"Frank! Jake!" Doris's shout from the living room galvanized both men to action. They charged through the kitchen to find her standing in the open front doorway, her hands cupped to her ears. "Listen!" she hissed.

They moved out onto the covered porch, straining to hear above the pelting rain. Seconds passed before Jake's ears caught the faint but unmistakable drone of an airplane engine.

"It's a Beaver, all right!" Frank rasped. "I'd know that engine sound anywhere!"

"It's not just any Beaver," Doris whispered. "It's Kelly."

"How can you be sure?" Jake spoke cautiously, scarcely daring to believe.

"How many hours do you think I've spent standing on this very porch, listening for that very plane? I know what I'm hearing, Jake. It's Kelly."

"There she is!" Frank whooped as a dark speck materialized through the clouds. "Come on, girl! Come on home!"

Jake was running then, scrambling down the walkway, slipping on the rain-soaked boards. The plane was unmistakable now. It was gliding downward, floats skimming the choppy water of the inlet. Kelly. Alive. Safe.

Jake reached the dock and suddenly stopped cold. This was the woman who had eluded him, evaded him and sent him away twice, he reminded himself. What if he was making a fool of himself? What if Kelly just plain didn't want to see him?

He hung back long enough for Frank and Doris to catch up. Then, in a torment of uncertainty, he trailed them out onto the dock. He would stand back and let Kelly greet her grandparents, he resolved. Soon enough, her eyes would find him, and when he saw her face, he would know.

In the next moment, the Beaver was taxiing in to the dock. The engine sputtered and stopped as Kelly cut the throttle. Frank and Doris were there to secure the lines. Jake stood a dozen paces back, holding his breath as the door opened.

There she was. He filled his eyes with her as she swung out of the plane. Kelly, swathed to the chin in Frank's old sheepskin flight jacket, her hair wind-whipped, her freckles standing out against a milk-pale face that was bare of makeup.

She was magnificent.

Jake's heart stood still as he watched her. She stepped away from the plane, slightly unsteady on her feet, and turned toward her grandparents. Had she seen him? Had she heard the things he'd told her? He waited in an agony of suspense.

Kelly returned Doris's tearful embrace, then seized Frank's hands. "Grandpa, you've got to replace that old radio! It went completely dead on me! I couldn't get a—"

She glanced up, and suddenly her eyes met Jake's. Her lips parted. Then, with a little cry she was running to him, sprinting up the dock to fling herself into his arms.

Jake caught her close and held her to his heart. She hadn't heard a damned thing he'd said, he realized. All that time, all those words—he'd been talking to a dead radio. But it was all right. He could tell her again now. He would have a whole lifetime to tell her.

And Kelly would have a lifetime to listen.

Epilogue

Kelly passed out the fat manila packets to the three wide-eyed children. "Here are your new math units," she said. "Now, try to have all the problems done when your new teacher comes in September. Can you promise to do that for me?"

"Yes, Mrs. Drummond!" The youngsters chorused, crowding around the table where she sat. Their small hands tore at the flaps on the envelopes, eagerly fishing out the booklets inside. Kelly glanced across the tiny two-room cabin, to where their mother was carving a haunch of moose on a makeshift counter. Scenting the meat, a big malamute dog had thrust its head in through the open front door.

"Do you think your children understand, Mrs. Jackson?" Kelly asked her. "Will they be able to do the problems on their own?"

The woman grinned, her dark eyes almost disappearing in her pretty moon face. "Oh, I will help them," she said.

"I listened to all your lessons. I remember everything you said. And when their father comes back from hunting, he will help them, too."

"Not too much help," Kelly cautioned. "Give them a chance to think, to figure the problems out for themselves. That's how they learn."

"Here, Mrs. Drummond." The youngest of the children, a lively five-year-old girl, had dashed outside and returned with a fistful of wild daisies. "Take these with you when you go. Then you won't forget us."

Kelly's eyes misted as she accepted the flowers. "Oh, I could never forget you, Mariette! I could never forget any of you!" She spread her arms and gathered the children close in a heartfelt farewell hug.

The daisies lay on the passenger seat as Kelly revved the new Cessna 185 across the tiny backcountry lake and rose in a tree-skimming ascent. In the two years since she'd started teaching, she'd become an expert at pinpoint take-offs and landings. Jake worried about her, she knew. But even with the risk, he'd cared for her too deeply to stop her from doing what she loved.

When his work allowed time, Jake flew with her. Together, they'd seen some glorious country and enjoyed some great adventures. This week, however, Jake had stayed behind in Juneau for some meetings. Kelly had missed him—missed him terribly. Now, as the plane glided above the snow-crested peaks, she ached with anticipation. She imagined the sight of him standing at the terminal gate. She imagined his arms crushing her close, the heaven of his welcoming kiss. She imagined, later, the warm darkness of their bedroom and the sweetness of their lovemaking.

A smile flickered across Kelly's face. Tonight she would tell Jake her secret—in seven months he would be a father. She laughed to herself, imagining his reaction. He would be surprised. He would be delighted. And he would be relieved when she told him she planned to stop flying after the first trimester. She'd be able to teach in Juneau on a substitute basis until the baby came. After that... But that decision could wait. There was always room in her life for new plans, new dreams.

For now—yes, she quivered as the familiar tingle stole over her, and she knew it was Jake, waiting for her, wishing her home. She'd experienced the feeling for the first time that Christmas, in the storm over Admiralty Island, when her radio had died. Lost and terrified, Kelly had been on the verge of panic when she'd heard—but no, she hadn't really *heard* anything. It was as if Jake's voice had come from inside her own head. It was as if she had known he was somewhere below, pleading with her to come to him. Pulling herself together, she had flown toward his call, and dropped out of the clouds above the inlet, miraculously safe.

She could not explain what had happened. But every time since, when she flew alone, it was as if she felt Jake beside her. She could feel his love. She could feel his calling her home. Now, very soon she would be home to stay.

The lights of Juneau were emerging through the summer twilight. As Kelly eased the Cessna into a long glide, she thought of Jake, waiting for her. She thought of the new life their love had begun. Her heart soared.

* * * * *

Get Ready to be Swept Away by
Silhouette's Spring Collection

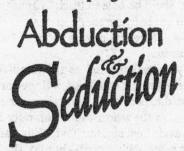

Abduction & Seduction

These passion-filled stories explore both the dangerous
desires of men and the seductive powers of women.
Written by three of our most celebrated authors, they are
sure to capture your hearts.

Diana Palmer
Brings us a spin-off of her Long, Tall Texans series

Joan Johnston
Crafts a beguiling Western romance

Rebecca Brandewyne
New York Times bestselling author
makes a smashing contemporary debut

Available in March at your favorite retail outlet.

Take 4 bestselling love stories FREE

Plus get a FREE surprise gift!

Silhouette

SPECIAL EDITION™

WHAT EVER HAPPENED TO...?

Have you been wondering when much-loved characters will finally get their own stories? Well, have we got a lineup for you! Silhouette Special Edition is proud to present a *Spin-off Spectacular!* Be sure to catch these exciting titles from some of your favorite authors:

HUSBAND: SOME ASSEMBLY REQUIRED (SE #931 January) Shawna Saunders has finally found Mr. Right in the dashing Murphy Pendleton, last seen in Marie Ferrarella's BABY IN THE MIDDLE (SE #892).

SAME TIME, NEXT YEAR (SE #937 February) In this tie-in to Debbie Macomber's popular series THOSE MANNING MEN and THOSE MANNING SISTERS, a yearly reunion between friends suddenly has them in the marrying mood!

A FAMILY HOME (SE #938 February) Adam Cutler discovers the best reason for staying home is the love he's found with sweet-natured and sexy Lainey Bates in *Celeste Hamilton's* follow-up to WHICH WAY IS HOME? (SE #897).

JAKE'S MOUNTAIN (SE #945 March) Jake Harris never met anyone as stubborn—or as alluring—as Dr. Maggie Matthews in *Christine Flynn's* latest, a spin-off to WHEN MORNING COMES (SE #922).

Don't miss these wonderful titles, only for our readers—only from Silhouette Special Edition!

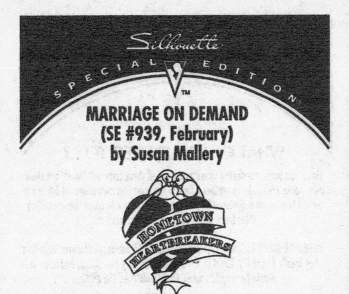

Silhouette

SPECIAL EDITION™

SILHOUETTE SPECIAL EDITION BOOKS ARE MOVING!

Your favorite Silhouette Special Edition books have been available at your local retail store in the last two weeks of every month. Special Edition is moving!

Starting with February 1995 publications, Silhouette Special Edition books will be available two weeks earlier at your local retailer.

Look for all Special Edition titles in the first two weeks of every month, and happy reading!

SILHOUETTE BOOKS—WHERE PASSION LIVES!

Silhouette

SPECIAL EDITION™

The new year brings readers a powerful new trilogy—

This Time Forever

by Andrea Edwards

In January, don't miss A RING AND A PROMISE (SE #932).

Just one look at feisty Chicago caterer Kate Mallory made rancher Jake MacNeill forget all about Montana. Could his lonesome-cowboy soul rest as love overcomes unfulfilled promises of the past?

THIS TIME, FOREVER—sometimes a love is so strong, nothing can stand in its way...not even time.

Look for the next installment, A ROSE AND A WEDDING VOW (SE #944), in March 1995. Read along as two *old* friends learn that love is worth taking a chance.

AEMINI-1